Huia Short

Huia Short Stories

4

Contemporary Māori Fiction

First published in 2001 by Huia Publishers,
39 Pipitea Street, PO Box 17-335,
Wellington, Aotearoa, New Zealand.

ISBN 1-877266-82-5

Cover artwork: Reuben Paterson, The Wharenui that Dad Built

National Library of New Zealand Cataloguing-in-Publication Data
Huia short stories. 4, Contemporary Māori fiction.
ISBN 1-877266-82-5 (pbk.)
1. Short stories, New Zealand. 2. Short stories, Maori. I. Huia Publishers.
II. Contemporary Māori fiction.
NZ823.0108—dc 21

Contents

Mushrooms

Te Awhina Arahanga

I'm eighteen.

It is Sunday.

I work the shift between the settling frost and the afternoon thaw.

I have arrived early.

I wait outside.

I wait with my workmates, my comrades-in-arms.

We are the Bloody Māoris, the Coconuts, the Chinks and the Bald Heads, our differences temporarily camouflaged under a shroud of woollen hats, hooded jackets, swannies, gloves and scarves. We shuffle feet and clap hands. Above our heads a whirl of frozen breaths twists and twirls. At our feet the grass wilts with frozen dew. The stones and earth are frozen together like peanuts and chocolate in a Whittaker's Peanut Slab.

It's bloody cold.

My body is aching.

My ear lobes have become engorged. They hang from my head like two legs of frozen mutton. The warm orange wax usually found accumulating in the inner ear has turned to concrete. Black ice is forming. My eardrum is beating a deafening beat.

My nose is tender and moist. Fine hairline cracks have surfaced amongst the redness between my nose and top lip. Each little cut throbs and stings. Hūpē drips from the passages above and acts as acid, stinging and stinging.

My lips are cold and inflamed. The saliva licked from my tongue adds nothing but further discomfort.

My eyes have turned into frozen puddles of ice. Splintered slivers shattered by stones and well-worn tee-bar sandals.

Along my arms and hunched shoulders a whispered chill goes exploring. I want to hug myself, but I can't bear to bring my hands out from their safe warm sanctuary. My chubby fingers and swollen hands sit crunched and clinched in their pocketed space.

It's bloody cold.

It's so bloody cold. Feet stamp. Hands don't clap. Feet stamp. Hands fiddle dee dee.

Half an hour ago I was asleep. I lay in a shared bed, my niece, Mihi, tucked into my puku, her brother, Paora, along my back. We lay like little mussels fighting for space on a rock along Sumner Beach. I didn't want to move and destroy the tight huddle we'd created. I wanted to hide from the world. Next door I could hear the beginnings of the day, my sister Tuakana moving about.

Tuakana is eighteen years my senior. She has three children, a husband and a home – a combination cherished. During the week she works at the local poultry processing factory. For up to twelve hours a day she electrocutes, guts and bags chickens. I've seen her walk around the factory in her white overalls, white gumboots and white hat. She's a Zena warrior dressed as an angel.

During the weekends I get sent to her home. I have heard them say it's about time. I was guilty of taking the road less walked – I'd decided to pussy around at school and become a seventh former. My family were in shock. Yeah, it's fine for me to continue at school, they said, but what's that going to get me? Everyone knows someone who knows someone who has a friend whose son or daughter went to university, and where did that get him or her? Sweeping the streets!

I'd become an embarrassment to the family. When my sister said that she had a job for me in the weekends I felt obliged to say yes. I could finally prove my worth. I too could be a Zena. But I really didn't have a choice. The decision had already been made. Made by the family.

Within seconds Tuakana had entered my room. My eyes remained closed. I'd tried to open them, but they kept falling shut.

She spoke. 'Come on Baby. Baby. Baby – it's time to wake up.'

A voice inside screamed, for god's sake eyes, open up. I was shoved from behind. Paora wanted me out. His mum had pulled back his side of the blankets. Once again the choice was made for me. My eyes may have struggled, but they opened. I was wide awake.

Like I'd imagined my sister had done only minutes before, I pulled my legs from under the weight of the bed linen. I pushed the grey woollen blankets, flannelette sheet and faded red candlewick bed-spread to one side. Kissed Paora's cheek along the way. It was an apology for the disturbance I caused. Mihi yawned and searched for a cuddle, but I'd already scampered to my pile of waiting clothes. In my mind I promised to niece that I'd buy a fluffy woollen rug for her bedroom floor with my next pay. I hated the feeling of cold welcoming me each time I placed a foot to the ground. I cursed Housing Corporation for not carpeting my sister's house.

The cold air began to eat at my flesh. I fought with my clothes and soon I transformed into a windmill. My arms and legs acted as sails, faded track pants, socks and jersey fought to stay on board. My bladder cried for attention. I had to mimi. Quickly I rushed from bedroom to wharepaku. I tore down pants and undies. Planted my cheeks on the cold porcelain. I sat and waited. It took me a while. The toilet was built between two bedrooms. The walls were as thin as tissue. A fart is audible from the house next door. If I wasn't careful, my early morning deposit would echo through the whole neighbourhood. I tried the old trick of flushing the loo at the same time as peeing. It worked. Well I thought it did. I cursed my inadequacies.

'Baby your kai is on the table.'

I stumbled to the kitchen where Tuakana had stacked the fire and set the table. She'd cooked porridge, buttered toast, made a pot of tea and placed the knitted cosy on its hot head. She'd rolled another cigarette and was waiting for me to sit down so she could light the end and pour the tea. She reminded me that I hadn't brushed my hair. I ran my fingers over the knots and tucked the loose strands in behind my ears. 'I'll do it later,' I said. She shook her head.

I was expected to consume food at turbo speed. Tuakana was on my back. I sliced butter and dolloped it into the bowl of too-hot porridge. I'm not keen on sugar so I sparingly sprinkled a full dessert spoon over the top. I watched the crystals melt and once they were clear I lavishly poured the cream. With a spoon in one hand and a piece of toast in the other I began the consumption. Strangers to our table are amused at our porridge ritual. I liked to think of it as an art. Dip, dunk and slurp.

I was just mopping the ends of the crème when a car chugged up the drive. A horn beeped.

They'd arrived.

Tuakana reminded me that I still hadn't brushed my hair nor had I washed. I assured her that I'd be fine. I tucked a curl behind my ear, but another bounced back. I flicked the biggest piece of sleep from the corner of my eye, but another remained. I'm not passing the Zena test this morning, I thought.

The car was full of big Samoan smiles. Big smiles by big lips. Big black lips. Each pair of lips smooched a juicy morning kiss. They excited me with their tenderness and passion. They confused me with their sadness and hurt. I wondered what those lips have done. I wondered what those lips have said. Those beautiful lips.

'You alright Babe?'

We drove along the road. The Holden automatically changed gear from second to third. Rumble, rumble. There was a hole in the muffler.

Throughout the night tiny mushrooms had sprouted from their beds of straw and shit. They fought toward the man-made light. Gasping for air. Gasping for life. In a few minutes' time, workers like me will rip them from their friends and family. We will slaughter and murder. Dissect and dismember. We will strip them of life, sort them into sizes and throw them onto the sorting trays. It's a powerful feeling.

They tell me that I'm quiet and placid, but give me a knife and a mushroom, and the mushroom gets it.

When people ask what I do during my weekends, I usually say I look for goodness amongst the shit. It confuses the hell out of them. The truth is I scramble around a mushroom factory cutting mushrooms for the early morning market. The location for this career training and social outing is a corrugated shed. From the outside it looks like a big shearing shed, but once you take a sniff, you soon realise that it's no ordinary sweatshop. The inside reminds me of an old war movie. It's a scene from inside a barracks, where the beds run in two rows along the walls. The mushroom garrison is exactly the same. Along the walls mushrooms lie in their beds. Each bed measures four single mattresses on a wharenui floor. The beds go ten levels high. The contents of the bunks include rotting straw and decaying animal faeces, but blanketed over the compost is a quilt of white button mushrooms. They look innocent and pure.

At the beginning of each shift we are taken to our allocated areas. We are told by Mr Boss Boy what size mushrooms we are to cut. The size is ranked by the bigness of the head or the head of the bigness. A size six is the kingpin. It's the classic, the most wanted fungus. To complete our task we are given a knife, some gloves and a aluminium ladder. The ladder is to help you reach the dizzy heights of the mushroom beds.

My ladder is never innocent. It is never pure. Every shift I have been allocated the ladder from hell. My ladder always has a broken leg or a wobbly base or a faulty mount or all of the above. It never stays still. I'll be at the highest possible position. I'm like a kererū, fat and full of miro. A kererū balancing on a kōwhai limb, the branch wobbling and trembling. All of a sudden the ladder gives way. The branch snaps. As delicate and majestic as a falling kererū, I crash onto the mushroom beds. There I'll be, stranded on the top shelf, tray fallen to the floor, knife embedded in my thumb and the ladder gleaming at me from somewhere down below. I guarantee that every worker in the whole damn factory will just happen to be walking past at that very damn time. Everyone will see; my friends with the black lips, my friends with the pink lips, my friends with the thin lips and my friends with the swollen lips. Everyone will say Babe. The lips will say Babe.

It's been twenty years since I last climbed a ladder. It's been twenty years since I last fell from grace. Fell from grace in a mushroom shed, crashed big-time. I was beaten and bruised. I spent the rest of that shift recovering in the Holden, under the weight of the black-lips jackets. I lay there and tried to work out how I was going to tell my sister that I was useless. That I, her youngest sister, would never be a Zena. That I, her youngest sister, didn't care if my hair was not brushed or that sleep remained in my eyes. I prayed to God. I prayed to Buddha. I prayed to lost ancestors and stars and planets. I prayed for divine intervention.

I think I prayed too much. On my way home my father died.

As Dad lay in his coffin, as the coffin lay in the wharenui, I decided I would never work in a factory again. In the middle of the night, when everyone had finally fallen asleep, I whispered in his ear. I told him I was sorry. I told him I couldn't be a Tuakana. I apologised for being lazy. I apologised for taking the road less travelled. I told him that I didn't want to carry another bleeding ladder. I didn't want to pick another size-six button mushroom. I was not going to spend another frosty morning waiting outside the factory gates.

We buried my father on a Friday. I didn't go back to work on Saturday. Nor did I go on Sunday. I never went back.

Tuakana lost her battle and let me stray.

I finished my year at school and went on to university. In between studies and lectures I watched the moon cross the night sky. I watched trees grow. I watched the sea crash and foam. The only mushrooms I ever saw I either ate or smoked and to my family's bewilderment I never did get that job sweeping the streets.

It's been twenty years since I last climbed a ladder. It's been twenty years since I fell. Tonight I sit with my new comrades. A strictly orthodox mix of well-to-do Kiwi Europeans and me, the complementary Māori. We are thirty-somethings. Or would like to be. We are fucking yuppies. Or would like to be.

Tuesday night's café is decorated with a combination of Asian decor and New Zealand memorabilia. Thai gods with long fingers and stiletto nails beckon you from dark nooks and crannies. The waiter flits around the Formica tables and matching chairs. He passes us a laminated menu, wine list, and a smile.

He's gay.

He's Māori.

He gives me the look. It's a greeting, a raised eyebrow. Colleagues see it, but don't understand its importance. I return his gesture with my eyebrow elevation. My forehead moves upward while the whole head subtly jolts forward. The whole procedure is completed in .25 of a second, it's fast and it's silent. I've passed the test. He recognises me as one of his own. I am a black babe. He'll now give me an extra scoop of rice. If the boss isn't looking he might even give me a bit off the bill. We'll cover the financial discrepancy by discussing whakapapa as he rings up the totals.

The conversation at my table is focused on art and foibles of nature. Everyone is drinking well-chosen wine. I've decided to stay sober and drink the complementary water instead. Usually I'm keen to join in. I love the banter and the comedy of errors created by the conversation and the wine, but it's been a long day. I'm finding it hard to keep up with everyone. I just want to go home.

I just want to go home?

When I finally make it back to my abode, where I can finally wade in the shag-pile carpet and Turkish rugs, where I can finally mimi in the strategically placed wharepaku, I'm going to be alone. I'm going to sleep in my king-sized bed. Alone. I'll wake in the morning. Alone. I'll eat my museli at the kitchen bench. Alone. I'll drive to work alone.

Alone.

My new relative and waiter arrives with our meals. He gives them to the appropriate people. I ask him to return with a glass and more wine. I've decided to partake.

In front of me sits a huge bowl of rice. On the plate containing the main lies a collection of size-six mushrooms, lamb and Thai greens. I can't help but notice that each slice has been delicately cut and flavoured. I leave my chopsticks to one side. I pick a mushroom up and let it hang between my chubby thumb and pointer finger. The smell is divine. I can feel the warm texture; I can feel a past life. I place it between my lips and gently suck it backward to my salivating tongue. A Tuesday-night friend passes me his glass and I sip a delicate red. I close my eyes and I see a ladder fall. In the distance I hear someone call out Babe. Babe.

Rangitoto

Kerrie Blackmoore AhKiau

At the top of my list of things to do is this word, Rangitoto. This list was compiled months ago. Taking action takes longer than I had thought it would. But I finally do it. I have the most wonderful company: my friend Liz. Missing the original departure time by three minutes, we race full tit to Devonport to try and catch the ferry on the other side. Missing that one too is all part of the fun. Hunger suggests it's a good time for a lunch break on the pier.

We stop at Takapuna when we see a sale sign in a store window. 'Look – we are saving money,' smiles Liz as we open our purses. Racing back to Auckland in time for the last afternoon ferry.

Standing on the top of the *Quickcat* I feel as giddy as a schoolgirl. Clear sky and fresh salty air. Giggling with excitement and anticipation. Wind thrashing my hair backward. Nipples erect. So when we arrive on the other side of the harbour we can say that 'we are very surprised, and happy, to see you'. I can't help but laugh. The force of the air makes my mouth dry. I don't want to stop laughing. So I don't.

For almost twenty years the island has been for me a constant. If ever I feel lost, confused or just plain fucked off, I will spend minutes in her gaze, maybe hours, and always seem to leave with something. Hope mostly. Looking at her from a busy shoreline. Perhaps at Mission Bay Cafe, Bastion Point among the roses, or maybe parked up at Bucklands Beach, Kohimarama, or Okahu Bay.

'For goodness sake, it is just a mountain. Why do you call it a she, it's an it?' His hollow, empty eyes stare at me.

Coming out of Devonport around the bend she graces my view. A lonely sentinel in the Waitemata Harbour. She is beautiful in a rugged and neglected way.

I read once that she was purchased in 1844 for a coat and a hat, fifteen blankets, one bridle, one shirt, one vest, a pair of boots, a pair of trousers, and ten spades. I find that extremely cheeky. Her value is far greater than that.

I too have sold myself cheap. Been bought for a few tokens, trinkets, promises whispered from drunken lips.

She once provided a perfect vantage point for observing the approach of war canoes. Rising two hundred and sixty meters in height.

Beneath the basaltic stone and ash is a freshwater lake. Symbolic really. Barren on top – could lead one to assume that she is waterless – yet beneath springs a well of fresh water, or perhaps a well of fresh hope. Remaining untapped because of the heavy traffic flow in the harbour.

So often I have sat and stared at her without really seeing her.

So often I have taken my fill of her image and then just passed her by on other days. But today I take the time to walk her paths.

They are rough, steep, hot, and barren in places. Then a few metres further on it becomes shaded and cool; lush too. The journey up is not as I had been warned. 'It's real steep and the ground is unstable. Take plenty of water and wear good shoes.'

The hard road is one I have travelled all my life. I find her paths rugged, but familiar. Her incline is steep, but I am accomplished at climbing mountains. This half-breed has been climbing them since she was born.

I stand at the crest of the crater. Such depth. I feel so tiny. This is where Rangitoto was born from. Wounds heal leaving scars. And life goes on.

It is saturated with plants of all kinds. Kohurangi, mist of the skies. Rewarewa, māpau and māhoe. The vibrant pohutukawa shouts its colour to the heavens. Mānuka and mingimingi share the rock with the mangroves.

At the summit I fill my lungs and heart with a sense of accomplishment and a hint of pride. For so long I have wanted to do this. Longed to be here. Why has it taken me so long?

From here I see the city of Tamaki-makau-rau spreading its fingers, reaching for a better view. I see from high up here that I am responsible for my outlook. Here I see things that I dream to do. Other places I want to be. I fill my eyes. The view from here encourages me to try more, to do more, and to be more.

I see Auckland from Rangi's view. To my eyes it looks so distant and so plain. Like I am looking at the dull past, a time I should move forward from. I equate it to this saying: 'I may not be where I need to be, but thank God I am not where I used to be.'

Liz and I sit with our backs to Auckland, sharing hopes and hiccups. Looking seaward past Motutapu Island while the blue free ocean embraces the sky and dances for us. Sways, tantalising me with dreams of many wonderful days to come.

I can still close my eyes and see. The watery highway is flooded with vessels of all shapes and sizes. Three sails, one sail, motors and paddles. Fishermen and buoys, and waving hands from passing boats. The young and beautifuls, some old and tireds, visitors and discoverers, people with limbs and without. Lovers and loners. Friends and relatives smile for snapshots that catch a second in the day.

The white cliff faces of Musick Point. Browns Island, so green. Motutapu Island, with its seemingly smooth freshly mowed grounds. Looks like Tiger Woods should be over there playing eighteen holes. Mission Bay looks ordinary.

The star of the day was that beautiful, circular volcanic rock illuminating the harbour.

I am so glad to have had Liz there. We talked of the past year. The things we are grateful for, the simple things. Healed old wounds and I fell, again, in love with our friendship.

Men will come and go from our lives – this seems so evident – but what we share is something more precious.

Rangitoto: Her name has been interpreted differently, as red or bloody sky. Her name is actually an abbreviation. Rangi-i-totongaa-Tama-Te-Kapua – the bleeding of Tama Te Kapua, after the chief of the *Arawa* canoe who engaged in a fierce battle at Oruawharua in 1350. She was also a parrot reserve for the Māori chief Te Peretu in pre-European times. He also kept lizards. Some have said that those spirits guard the island. Once a lookout point and burial site too.

Inmates from Mt Eden Prison had been put to work on the island for ten years. She has hosted an abortion clinic as well.

She was once the red light in the night sky that drew her people safely to the land from across the waters.

She is that for me. I have gained guidance from my relative sitting in the harbour. She has shared her wisdom of no words to a lost generation in me. I have been guided by her shadow.

Gone is her flowing lava and declarations of majesty, but she continues her lonely reign. Continues to be whatever I need her to be. My solitary beacon of hope.

Rock of burnt black scoria, island of dust: she is beautiful in her ruggedness.

I like to think that I am like her: rugged and powerful, waiting for the right time. And when she blows, look out!

Rangitoto ... SHE is still standing.

Not Against Thieves

Lindsay Charman-Love

Marion felt the car hit the speed bump. There was a crunch as the suspension thumped against the body and the vehicle lurched into the car park, skidding in the gravel. Byron turned the headlights out. They could see an orange light on the wharf across the harbour. There was a full moon coming up and it stirred in the water with the current on its way out to sea.

'Wow, look at that,' said Marion.

'What?'

'The orange wharf light and the orange moonlight – they look like lost planets.'

'Lost planets?'

Byron glanced up from the stereo, wound the window down. He went back to pushing buttons.

Marion lit a cigarette and watched him before she said, 'It's not going to work.' Byron heard fish splash, a riffle in the tide.

'It's up to us to make it work,' he said.

'It's too complicated,' Marion said. Her fingernails clicked on a CD case; dull silver clinked at her wrists.

The lights went out on the stereo.

No music; fish, bangles, splashing planets.

Byron moved in the wide vinyl seat, leaned across to the glove box. Tattoos ran down his arm and merged at his fingers like kelp does with rocks. There was a soft click, a soft bulb glowed. He reached inside.

'What are you doing?' Marion asked. She looked at the shape of his hand; saw blood in the backhand veins and clean sweep of nails.

'You'll see.'

She watched his hand wrap around a screwdriver. It slivered in the glows, a thin stiletto.

'You wont solve anything with that.'

'Fix it or fuck it, I say.'

The screwdriver turned in the soft car light and the orange planet light from the water. Byron dived beneath the dashboard and disappeared.

She heard him scrabbling about.

'Fuck it, fuck it, fuck it.'

'What's up?' Marion asked.

'The screws – they're Phillips.'

Marion puffed on her cigarette. 'Who's Phillip?' she asked.

Byron pulled his head up quickly, whacking the glove box on the way, a small sliver of skin cut from above his eye.

'Shit! Are you all right? I was just asking –'

'A stupid bloody question that's what. They're Phillips head screws, this is a flat-bladed screwdriver. It doesn't fucking fit.'

Marion gave him a moment.

'I was just trying to be funny,' she said. 'My old man used to say that. He thought it was hilarious.'

Byron glared at the CD player. He made slow stabbing silhouettes.

'I can't say I do,' he said quietly.

Marion took the screwdriver. Her silver bangles clinked, turned to gold as the lights hovered and the glove box closed.

'Why can't we just get a service manual?' she asked.

Byron took a moment to answer. Looked out the window.

'If we went in and asked for a manual they'd be very interested in the likes of us having this sort of CD player. We don't exactly look the type.'

Marion looked at him.

'We could say we won Lotto.'

'We wouldn't be in an old Falcon,' he answered.

'I guess not.' She smiled and said, 'You shouldn't have pinched such a flash CD player should you?'

Byron looked at her. He reached up to the cut on his forehead.

'It seemed like a good idea at the time....'

'Come here, let me see that,' she said.

She reached across. A drop of blood settled in the corner of his eye. Marion licked her lips, leaned forward, tongued it away. Byron made a half-hearted effort to escape then changed his mind. He lay back along the car seat and pulled Marion onto him. He slid his hands up inside her skirt.

'Jesus,' he said, 'haven't you got any undies on? All I can feel is skin.'

'Lucky aren't you. I've got a G-string on. Everybody wears them these days.'

He fondled around.

'Lucky I don't. I couldn't keep my business in one of these things,' he said.

'You can hardly keep it in a pair of jeans,' she said, wriggling about.

'Why do they call it a G-string? It should be a B-string, or a –'

'Shut up and take your T-shirt off.'

In the lights, by the sea, the tide turned and pied stilts whistled in the night. Marion watched the smoke from a joint drift from the windows of the car.

'I was thinking about going back out to the Heads,' said Byron. 'There's been a few tourists around lately. Bound to be something we can get in to.'

'Yeah – we could use some cigarettes, maybe Marlboros, some clothes....'

'Bottle of bourbon....'

'That was choice last time eh? We got so much stuff. I couldn't believe it.'

'Serves them right. All packed up nicely in a campervan. And I hate the way they drive. So fucking slow....'

He started the car, tapped the fuel gauge.

'Have we got enough to get out to the Heads?' Marion asked.

'Yeah, just.'

'Let's go out there eh? We can sleep in the car. I'll keep you warm....'

'One day I'm going to put so much gas in this thing, it'll never run out,' he said.

In the morning they hid the car a couple of kilometres away and walked into the scrub. Byron picked a path amongst the pig fern and flax, through mānuka and foliage where they wouldn't leave tracks. A fantail followed them through the kānuka, and bees hovered at the small white blooms. They stopped where they could watch the visitors gaze at the sweeping view – the Hokianga, the fat body of water that bends its way between the Waima and Warawara mountains – the lurid sand dunes writhing in a swirl of textures and the deep blue tide, challenging the surf at the bar.

'There's a sign down there,' said Marion. 'It says the harbour is guarded by taniwha.'

'Not against thieves it's not,' Byron said. 'Look, here comes our first customer.'

A big white campervan, a Maui, lumbered to a halt. Byron watched the loud tourists trundle off down the short walk where they videoed each other and gawked and waved at the fishermen on the rocks below. Marion slipped through the shrubbery and checked the vehicle out.

There was no alarm light and through the curtain gaps she could see duty-free plastic bags. She was trying to look for more when she heard the whistle that told her the tourists were coming back. She hid in the scrub nearby.

'We just gotta do that coastal walk Chuck.' Marion heard an American accent. 'It says in the book that we can go for miles and there's absolutely nothing but nature. We sure could use some exercise. What do you say?'

'Why not honey, might help me sleep tonight. What about you guys?'

'Do you think our stuff will be OK here?' a woman asked.

'Sure – it's not LA. Look at this place – it's so beautiful

and it's broad daylight. Nobody's gonna touch our stuff.'

Marion heard them pack food and towels and talk about time there and back and where to stash a purse. She heard bottles clinking, being removed for the seaward amble; talk of sun-cream, insect-cream, hand-cream and beer.

She listened to their footfalls crunching in the gravel. She gave them about ten minutes then made a soft whistle like a bird, only different. From further up the hill Byron watched until the foreigners ran out onto the beach and headed off around the curve of the coast. He whistled back then sneaked through the undergrowth to the campervan where Marion was flicking the beading out of a rubber window surround.

'All clear?' she asked.

'Yeah. They've gone along the beach.'

'They took food and stuff. Sounded like one of them left a purse.'

Byron checked again for alarms and then lifted the whole pane of glass out so if another car arrived it wouldn't look like trouble with chips and glitter on the ground. He hoisted Marion through the window and she let him through the door.

'They've got a lot of stuff eh? Look at all the bags.'

Marion dragged one on to a bench seat. Byron sat beside her and pulled open the door of the fridge.

'We can have a feed – look at this,' he said. 'Cold piss, chicken, ham, cheese, even fucking chocolate.'

'Don't leave that in there,' Marion said.

'I don't intend to leave any of it,' Byron replied.

'All these clothes too, look they're brand new. These Levis should fit me....'

A cupboard door opened out a mirror. Marion held up the jeans like she was shopping in a mall and then browsed through blouses and skirts. She found a jacket, turned around.

'Look at this, Byron. It'd fit you. It's a real one.'

He looked across as she ran her hand over the embroidery on the back.

Marion looked at the label.

'LA Dodgers eh. Made in the USA,' she said

'Where did she say the purse was?'

'Under the mattress, on the top bunk, I think.'

Byron stood up and swept his arm beneath the bed to find a bulging pocketbook. He showed Marion a gallery of faces, jottings in a hurried hand.

'Look at this,' he said.

Neatly folded in a small purse, he showed her new notes and a rack of foreign plastics. He had a quick look then dropped them on the seat beside Marion.

'There's a couple of hundred there but the rest of it's funny money,' he said, looking for more.

Marion picked them up, examined them.

'Byron,' she said, 'these US notes are hundred-dollar bills. They're worth heaps.'

'Give me a look,' he said.

He reached out took the notes from Marion, thumbed through them.

'Rich Yanks eh? I wonder what else they've got?'

He began loading a bag with booty, bottles of liquor, Marion's new jeans.

'Check this out.'

She opened a woman's toilet bag. It was filled with flat plastic packs of pills. Some she recognised, contraceptives and Sea Legs, but a smorgasbord of others she'd never seen.

'Diazepam – that's Valiums isn't it?'

'Yeah – they're Vees eh. That's that shit your old lady takes. Helps her cope with your lot.'

'What's Ro-hyp-nol? It says, "Take one only when retiring".'

'Sleepers, I guess. They'll be alright with a few drinks.'

He was ratting around, going through all the pockets.

'We've even got sounds, check these out –'

He held up a pair of Discmans from the map holder.

'Choice eh? That solves one problem. I wonder what sort of music they've got?'

A few hours later, fuzzy with sedatives and replete with food and liquor, they rolled away south. Marion was singing 'Born to Run' at the top of her voice and Byron was listening to Elvis. As they drove along Marion reached down and picked up a CD.

'John Denver,' she said. She held it up in front of Byron, but he shook his head. She flipped it out the window and it spun like a luminous frisbee, flashing and sparkling as they cruised along the willowed river flats into Waiponga.

Sunlight seemed to flow through the valley like a melting prism. Coloured trees rippled in the overhangs and small wooden houses eddied in the shines.

'I feel pretty out of it,' Byron said. 'I could use a drink.'

'Me too. Must be the Vees.' Marion turned her head and pointed. 'Look at that,' she said.

A black vintage car was parked near a white iron shed with a gas pump. A grey dog stood like a rock in the middle of the road.

'Check him out,' Byron said as they slowed down. 'He's only got three legs.'

When they stopped Byron leaned out the window.

'King of the road, eh boy? Me too. Mind if we get some gas?'

The dog sniffed and wagged his tail. When the car moved to the pump he skipped over and cocked his missing leg against the wheel. A man in overalls, wet from the waist down, came out of the shed.

'What would ya like?' he asked.

'Fill it up. And the water. What happened to the dog?' Byron slurred.

'Tried to stop the mower from running over a stick. Where's your petrol cap?'

'Somebody pinched it eh. Bastards.'

'I've got a box full of caps in there if you want to have a rat around.'

'Nah. She's right. I'm gonna get rid of it soon,' Byron said.

He fumbled in his pockets, dropped and recovered a credit card, a Diners, waved money in the air.

'Right up eh? Right to the top. You got a toilet?'

'Yeah – round the back. First on the left.'

Byron stumbled over the windscreen-cleaning bucket and almost walked into the corner of the building. Marion got out of the car and fumbled towards the door of the garage.

'I'll just get a drink,' she said. 'You got a fridge?'

'In the corner. There's a few other –'

She didn't hear him. A rooster outside crowed.

It was dark inside the shed and there were several fridges. In the first she saw a jar of whitebait, gelatinous in the chill. An onion bag heaved beside it and she jumped back, slamming the door. What the hell was that? She carefully opened the door again and peeked inside. There were eels writhing in the onion bag. The whitebait flickered like dying glow-worms.

From the corner of her eye Marion saw something slide past a rack of ancient hubcaps and around a retired California license plate. As she turned, it dropped behind a bench and slithered past a shadow board. A furry snake?

She looked away at long spider threads and gleams of light scattering through the dusted windows. A stag's head hanging on the wall stared glassy-eyed at Marion. She whirled when a caged bird rang like a phone. 'C'mon,' she said to herself. 'You're getting jumpy.' As she opened a second fridge the small hairy animal scrabbled across the floor and stood up on its hind legs to peer inside. The furry snake? What was it? A ferret? Marion fled for the entrance. Outside she stared at the man in overalls.

'Grab a bag of oranges if you like,' he said, pointing near the door. 'You can have them.'

Marion looked around, expecting to see them moving about like everything else in the place. She pointed at a large mesh bag.

'All these you mean?'

'Yeah. I've got plenty.'

'Thanks,' she said.

As she put them in the car she asked, 'Where's he gone?'

'Ah – the toilet I think – round the back.'

At that moment there was a loud shout and a torrent of abuse from the rear of the building.

'Shit,' the man said, 'the ram's got him.'

The dog took off round the corner, dust and gravel flying. The man in overalls abandoned the fuel hose, ran for the rear of the building. Marion arrived a few moments later to see the dog tackle the sheep and the man in overalls go for the dog with a stick. Byron was behind an orange tree, trying to do up his fly.

'The fucking thing,' he said. 'It knocked me over.'

'His chain can't reach the toilet,' the man in overalls said. 'I thought that's what you asked for.'

He wrestled with the ram by the horns and the dog by the collar as they strained for a second assault. Byron limped away and headed back around the front. He went to the fuel hose and had it running down the wheel arches before he stuffed the rag in and soaked up the overflowing petrol. The man in overalls returned to watch him weaving around with the fuel hose, trying to get it back in the pump. A cigarette fumed at his lips.

When he'd finished Byron opened the car door and slumped into the driver's seat.

'Have you paid him yet?' Marion asked.

'Paid him? I should sue him. That bloody sheep hurt – and I got stabbed by that fucking tree.'

Marion laughed.

'Thanks a lot,' he said. 'Did you get a drink?'

'Nah. There's eels in the fridge. And I think it was a ferret guarding the other one. It did a little haka when I opened the fridge door.'

'This guy's weird. We should do a runner. Teach him a lesson.'

'No, we better not. He'd remember me. He gave me a bag of oranges.'

'That's what got me out the back,' said Byron. 'I thought I'd pinch a few while I was having a leak. That fucking ram knocked me arse over tit just after I put a couple in my pocket.'

Marion grinned. 'He'd have trouble forgetting you too, jumping round in your Dodgers jacket with your fly undone. He probably thought you were trying to screw his sheep.'

This time they both laughed and the man in overalls watched. The dog came up to the door.

'Look, he's sent in the bailiff,' said Byron. 'You pay him. You've got heaps.'

They both laughed again. Marion got out and gave the man some notes.

'Keep the change, eh,' she said.

The man looked down and back.

'That's a lot of change, Miss,' he said.

She smiled.

'Lot of oranges. Cheers.'

She waved as she walked away.

As they drove out, a duty-free cigarette butt flew from the driver's window. It arced up into the air and bounced on the boot of the car before it hit the rag in the fuel tank with a shower of orange sparks.

The Day You Died

Gerry Te Kapa Coates

I remember the day you died. It was on the news – you were that well known. I should have been told by someone close to you, or the tribe. But that's the way it works when you live in the city. There's no formal bush telegraph, no telephone tree. It depends on who is there and who talks to whom.

The news item was usual Pākehā brevity for Māori issues. Died at a tangi, suddenly. Well-respected elder of the tribe, involved in the fisheries settlement, member of the Waitangi Tribunal. It didn't sound like you at all.

You were always a Johnny Cash sort of guy. Telling jokes in the wharekai about police cars going 'darkie, darkie' as they raced to the scene of a crime that inevitably involved Māori crims. You were the one who could get up and do a mihi, obviously well rehearsed, but then lapse into diffidence, and slink to the back row of the marquee.

And the carvings – they didn't mention them. The whalebone I still wear round my neck – the kau whanake, or strong swimmer. The tuna being pulled through life by the cord. Or the manaia, intricately copied from a wood carving from long ago, that you turned into bone. I willingly became one of your bone people, disparaged by the cynics as Māori lovers, or neo-primitives wanting a return to the days when cannibalism ruled.

We're a strange lot, our tribe. When we lose someone, when a tōtara falls, we don't stop and think if this is someone who should be honoured in a special way. No, we tend to have a tangi for those around. The others will hear about it. Well I heard about it, and being at the back of beyond, there was no way I could afford the plane fare and rental car it would have taken.

Mum knew you too, when you were young. Almost married you I think. Maybe that's why you always had a soft spot for her kids, her kids with a Pākehā. Not a major slot for us, but the nod, the time spent when we were in your home town. Taking us out to the special places. Don't write it down, you would say. That's not the Māori way. See that kōhatu over there, that's an ahu – a sacred place. That patch of bush where the tui gather. There's a special energy there – the old people would take their sick people there and they would be cured. Maybe we should build a marae there one day, Hori. You and me.

We almost got that far. One weekend I shoved the bush saw in the wagon, and headed up to spend the weekend with you. We slaved our guts out clearing the bracken and blackberry away from the big pohutukawa. Five hundred years old, you said, and we needed to clear away the rubbish to save it from fire danger. We cut up a few wasp nests too, and that slowed the process down. Then I didn't see you again for a while, and next time I'm back the place is overgrown again, and you onto another project.

That was you all over. Have the ideas, spend a while doing it, and then have the next idea and move on. Like women. You were a one-woman man – one at a time. But Miriama was the constant. She let you follow your heart and head. Never hauled you back or to account. Your wayward nature took you to marae all through the rohe, and a few other arms as well. I never heard of other kids, but I'm sure there are some, probably getting to be my age now.

You were a bit of a charmer, even I could see that.

'Once you get your tongue down her throat boy, she's sure to be yours!'

What kind of advice was that for someone almost young enough to have been your son?

Now you've gone – beyond the veil. I wonder what it's like, to be here one minute and gone the next. I talked to those who had been with you at the time. There was nothing untoward. You just stood up to move towards the tūpāpaku and fell, silently, to the floor. You were never revived, never said final words, went immediately behind the veil to join your old friend.

I guess it's like being born really. We hover here, in the known, as a baby hovers in the womb, with everything about to happen unknown. Does the baby know it is to be born, and when, any more than we know we are to die, and how?

Having missed the tangi I still wanted to go back home as quick as I could. I needed to talk to people – find out what happened. Clear my mind, assuage my guilt at not having seen Uncle Bob for the last year. There is always the next hui, until there are no more times for some.

As I walked in the door, Makarete said, 'Where were you at Bob's tangihanga?'

'I sent an email,' I said. 'I didn't hear until too late. Tēnā koe, Makarete. Tell me what happened.'

'You go and see Miriama,' was all she said. 'She can tell you everything. She was totally wiped out by the suddenness of it all, but she'll be glad you've come.'

The house was the same as ever. Small, dark, the verandah on the front, stained glass either side of the door, painted wood tongue-and-groove kitchen, where Miriama was sitting over a cup of tea. 'E tama, why did it have to happen so soon? Why to Bob and not me, eh?' she said as we hugged and kissed each other, and the tears flowed.

She told me the details – time, place, who was there, how they'd tried everything, but it was too late. Two tangi together were too much for everybody, even though they were different hapū.

'Uncle left you his tiki, e tama. Least, he didn't exactly "leave" anything, but I know you were the only one he wanted to have anything that had his mana in it.' She handed me the worn pounamu, and it glistened in the sun pouring into the kitchen. 'Better get it blessed by the minita. He was wearing it when the mate came for him.'

As I took it in my hand the pāua eyes seemed to accuse me of treachery. Of only being here for what I could get.

Later, I could see the gap he was leaving in the hapū. It was as though by being behind everybody, suddenly the props had been taken away from the scenery, and everybody could see they were just playing at running a rūnanga. Time would allow others to come through, but right now it was a mess. Everyone was afraid to step in and take charge. Me too.

When I got back to Akarana, the tiki was burning a hole in my pocket. I finally felt brave enough to put it on. I remembered how the water had felt as the priest blessed it, like when we were leaving an urupā. The little automatic ritual that might – or might not – work its miracle. I knew that I'd often felt bad when I'd forgotten, or there'd been no water.

The tiki felt cool on my chest as I caught the shuttle from the airport back home where I knew Mum would want to hear about my trip. Another kitchen, this time with the smell of fresh-baked gems to greet me.

'Auē, who's there?' Mum said, startled at seeing me come through the door. 'I had a strange feeling it was Bob. He's here, I know he is. His kēhua has followed you here. He wants to say e noho rā, on his way to Te Rerenga Wairua, e tama.'

Part of me doesn't believe the literal idea of a spirit making the journey north. But maybe there was something going on. Just then I felt the tiki drop into my shorts. The cord had broken.

'Miriama said Bob wanted me to have his tiki,' I said. I pulled out my shirt and removed the translucent figure from its undignified place.

'He was always letting people take it for outings,' she said. '"Take it on a tramp round the lake," he'd say. "It needs to go back there again." That's a very old hei tiki, Hori. You take good care of it for him. It's an honour for you, and for us.'

Later, back at my flat, getting ready for work the next day, I noticed the kau whanake tohu I'd had for years was in two pieces, snapped cleanly along the grain of the whalebone.

'Keep it moist with a bit of baby oil now and again,' Bob had said when he put it round my neck. 'No need to take it off, if you don't want to.'

I remembered him saying about other things when they got lost or broken, 'Oh, well, boy – you can't need it any more.'

Maybe I didn't need it now. I was turning twenty-nine next month. I would make some resolutions to go back home more often. Maybe even offer to serve on the Rūnanga Komiti. There would be lots of work to do – carving was one thing, and the new marae had raised everybody's morale. But there was a long haul coming up with claim-settlement negotiations in the wind. Maybe I'd even move back home to the iwi-office township. Get involved.

I could hear Bob chuckling in my head.

'Good on you, boy. You're already thinking my way. Plenty of time for Akarana later. No hurry eh, but awhi the tribe, tama, haere mai ki tō tūrangawaewae.'

The tiki burned on my chest. Old tauparapara sang in my mind, and Bob headed off somewhere, maybe to the Cape. Maybe he would be around for a while though. I'd better get cracking and show him I had what it takes.

Is anybody ever really grown up? From whānau to mate is what it takes, but almost halfway there or so I felt very unprepared, very green. I remember the day you died. I'd felt that way then – that something had crept up on me unannounced. Now I had the feeling I was being pushed in directions I didn't really understand, that would tax my idea of being grown up. I remember the day you died. Very well.

Pickled Pork

Caroline Adair Down

There had been some wicked kai that day and Miro's puku was feeling a little delicate. To put it more succinctly – he was farting like a beast.

'Ooo-oohh!' Lyla screwed her nose up. 'Man that stinks! You should be called Pirau instead of Miro.'

Miro poked his tongue out. Neither of them knew it right then, but the best was yet to come. Earlier that day Miro had gone over to Aunty Kappa's to mind baby and feed the animals while Aunty Kappa went into town. She'd be gone till four she said, so at lunchtime he was to eat whatever he could find in the cupboard – but only bread and tinned stuff, and no leaving messes around when he'd finished.

Miro's choices of tinned stuff came down to creamed corn or baked beans. Beetroot and asparagus spears were both boring and he was pretty sure he wasn't game to try Jellimeat. He'd sampled his cat Loopy's coveted Aspic in Oil once at home, and that was quite enough thank you very much. Apart from making him ill, Loopy had treated him with utter contempt – ignoring him completely for a full two weeks.

So, come lunchtime, a feed of baked beans it was – and *what* a feed. Miro was so hungry he cleaned up the whole tin and four pieces of toast. Boy, it was good.

After lunch, when he'd fed all the animals, he happily wiled away the afternoon talking to the ducks over the fence. Baby slept without a sound the whole time. It was moments like these when Miro felt really grown-up.

Around four o'clock, as promised, Aunty Kappa came home with the biggest leg of pork Miro had ever seen. She set about brewing the most evil smelling boil-up in the world. It had cabbage, pūhā, silverbeet and thick-sliced carrots with pointy spiked roots poking out the sides. There were also potatoes and kūmara, all washed and chopped.

In amongst this dense bed of vegetables the large and somewhat elderly pork bone reclined, its sinewy pale meat flailing in tendrils as the heating water softened and loosened it.

By dinnertime Miro was starving again and downed three enormous helpings of boil-up before Uncle Matt dropped him back at home. Now he sat colouring at the kitchen table with Lyla, dreamily picturing the spectacular scene of the boil-up in the pot.

All the while he let out successions of small puttering farts that made his puku feel weird. He guessed it was better out than in, as Uncle Matt always said, and carried on drawing.

He drew a magnificent picture of a head of cabbage and some pūhā, and he chose a green marker that smelt like lime to colour it in with. When he finished he noticed that Lyla had shifted herself a safe distance away from him to the other end of the table. She was busy colouring and paid no attention to him and his putting nono.

After a while everything was getting too quiet for Miro so he decided to do some stirring.

'Had a nice boil-up at Aunty's, Ly,' he said.

Lyla immediately stopped colouring and looked up fearfully.

'What was in it?'

'Oh … a bit of everything,' he replied, inspecting his fingernails and deliberately avoiding her gaze.

Without a word Lyla put the lid on her purple felt pen that smelt like grapes, and calmly set it down next to her drawing. She was older and bigger than Miro … sometimes she was scary. Miro realised he'd pushed her too far. She glared at him with flashing eyes.

'Did you have pork Miro?'

He had to think quickly. Leaning over he grabbed an old copy of *Woman's Day* that was lying between them on the table. He wasted no time feigning the urgent thumbing-through thing he'd seen Aunty Kappa do when Uncle Matt was trying to get a rise out of her. He never looked up. He kept on until Lyla quit glaring and resumed her colouring. There was a large orange marker smelling of mandarins in her hand now. She hummed softly to herself.

Eventually Miro peeped up from behind the magazine ... boy, that was close.

When he lowered his gaze again he was disturbed to notice that the page he had the magazine open to featured a particularly unflattering photo of a whiskey-nosed Rachel Hunter, sprawling, legs akimbo, on the back seat of a white limo somewhere in London. A huge feather boa was thrown haphazardly about her shoulders and her tight hot pink spandex dress was hauled up around the very tops of her thighs. The caption read *Rachel Hunter shows her Glenfield roots.*

It was apparently a page of celebrity knicker-flashing shots. There were stars getting awkwardly in and out of cars, stars leaving nightclubs and tripping inelegantly over, stars playing tennis wearing next to nothing – all that sort of stuff. Miro was freaked out and chucked the magazine on the ground.

He was so horrified he let go an unexpected tirade of semi-automatic flatulence that had Lyla leaping to her feet, mandarin-flavoured pen jammed beneath her nostrils.

Miro felt really sick. He knew his puku hadn't been quite right today, but heaven help him now. He sprinted at top speed to the wharepaku just as an enormous load of vomit whirled from his mouth. Then another. And then another.

His gut lurched and his eyes streamed. He could see dancing images of stringy pork boiling in black water; flat carrot slices had spikes the size of tree branches. A thousand baked-bean soldiers gathered earnestly along the outer rim of the massive iron pot, and on the leader's command they all leapt into the pulsing water, tomato-sauce blood draining from their tiny white oval bodies.

The carnage was horrible and Miro was in living hell.

He pulled his head up momentarily to suck in some air, but instead of seeing the forgiving angelic whiteness of the toilet, there stood a huge hideous apparition of Rachel Hunter – her blotchy drunken face and rolling eyes leering from the cistern. Her hot pink spandexed crotch glowed like the sacred heart. Her arms, feather-boa entwined, reached out with palms turned upward to Miro.

'Hi Miro,' she cooed, offering him her wrists. 'Won't you have a smell of my new perfume?'

Miro was so scared he did as she asked and leaned forward towards one wrist. He took a really big sniff and immediately fell back, all ready to puke again.

'I hope you like it,' she said, leaning closer to him with her swollen red nose, her voice lowered to a malicious whisper. 'It's my new line. Rachel's Eau de Sanguine Pork.'

Miro collapsed and the world seemed to open up and fall away beneath him.

When he came round he was laying flat on his back on the toilet floor. Rachel Hunter was gone and it was Lyla who crouched before him now. She was waving the mandarin pen shakily around his nose, accidentally drawing panicky orange smudges on him.

'It's pork!' she was yelling half in fear, half in anger. She was shaking him hard and practically shoving the pen into his nose.

'It's *pork*, Miro. Mum told you not to eat bloody pork 'cause it gives you the shits and makes you mental!'

He watched her groggily, but couldn't speak. She kept on irritably.

'We told you Miro, we *told* you – you're not s'posed to eat pork.'

Miro closed his eyes again, relieved that the nightmare was over. He felt comforted that it was just Lyla yelling at him now and not Rachel Hunter flashing him.

He groaned, his puku was sore. Something smelt like oranges. He turned his cheek to the cool of the lino floor and started to sleep.

Pōrangi Tangiweto

Caroline Adair Down

Aunty Pani reckons the sky's going to turn red and burn everyone. She comes for visits Friday lunchtime and chain-smokes inside until she leaves at ten to five. I always know when she's been here. She brings Bub with her – sometimes even Mooks comes if he's on the wag from school.

Me and Lucy get hidings if we say anything mean about Aunty Pani. She's a bit loopy, 's all. Once Mum overheard Lucy say that Aunty Pani was loony-bin fodder, and that one night while Lucy was staying there, Aunty Pani got up and wandered around the garden naked while she sang 'Haere Mai' over and over to the chooks.

Lucy was acting her story out to us in the lounge and my other sister Mouse laughed so much she blew snot everywhere and some landed up in Mooks's hair. Bub just sat there sucking his fingers and dribbling all over the place.

Lucy was in full flight when Mum came roaring in with the short extension lead and belted her a good one round her back. She screamed and lost her balance, falling right on top of Bub, who toppled sideways and whacked his head on the corner of the coffee table. As he fell his fingers jabbed right down his throat and then there was blood everywhere instead of just dribble.

When Mouse saw it she screamed too and then pretty much everyone was bawling. Except for Mum. She told us we deserved what we got because we were so rude about Aunty Pani. It wasn't Aunty Pani's fault she had to live on medicine and that Mooks had to do all the housework and stuff for her. Mooks reckons Aunty Pani won't ever be able to do these things herself because she's pōrangi now for sure.

Then there was the other time when me and Lucy and Mouse took Bub to the playground at the motor camp. He sat in the sandpit howling because he got a bit of sand in his eye, and the more he rubbed it the worse it got and the louder he bawled. Well, Lucy couldn't stand it. She dropped her spade and dug up a huge handful of sand, running for Bub and yelling at him.

'Shut up! Shut up you pōrangi tangiweto.'

Then she threw all the sand into his face, going, 'There! That'll give ya something to cry about.'

Bub screamed even louder, so that all the starlings and blackbirds flew out of the pines around the sandpit. They flew for their lives from the pōrangi tangiweto taniwha that made such a horrible noise. Bub's face was all screwed up and stuck down with sand and snot. There was a big snot bubble hanging out of his left nostril and Lucy looked at him like he was dog tūtae or something, but then she rummaged through her pants pocket and found a really hardened-up old hanky and she chucked that at Bub. Then she just stomped back to her half-pie sandcastle and kept piling on mounds of sand with little angry slaps.

We all stared at Lucy but we said nothing. She just carried on with her sandcastle. Mouse felt sorry for Bub so she picked him up and tried to wipe his face with the hard hanky. It just scraped raw marks on him that made things even worse. Mouse cuddled him and started toward the road. She gave Lucy a menacing glare on the way and said she was going to tell Mum on her. Lucy just made a face and said she didn't care, but I know – I saw that look she had. Mum would get wild and Lucy would be in for it for sure.

Sometimes at night before lights out we're allowed to have the big purple egg-shaped candle going, to get us off to sleep. Then Mum blows it out for us. But when I lay on my side and stare at it I can see the pool of hot runny wax inside the candle and it all looks like the Pink and White Terraces because it's the purple running down – and the colour goes really light until it's pink and white. And there are hollows and caves with lots of rounded hanging bits.

That's what I thought of when we all got sent over to Aunty Pani's for our hiding later on. First Mum gave us all one – and like I thought, Lucy got the worst. Mum took her out the back for hers. Me and Mouse just got a few smacks for being there when it all happened. But Lucy got the primo one.

When we got to Aunty Pani's we all knew the drill. We had to knock on the door and wait until someone answered. Then we had to tell whoever answered why we were there – and then we had to very politely ask them if they could please give us a hiding for it. We always hoped it wasn't going to be Sam – Aunty Pani's boyfriend – because he was big and mean, and boy he could wallop like Mum probably wishes she could in her dreams.

But no. This time it was Aunty Pani. We told her why we were there and she waved us all inside. We waited silently in the lounge while she thumped back down the hallway. No one moved except for Lucy who was sobbing and holding her arms all like a cradle.

I felt mad at her and told her to shut up because it was her own fault and it was all because of her that we were getting a big hiding and – by the way – who was the pōrangi tangiweto *now*?

Aunty Pani came back into the lounge with Sam's weight-lifting belt. We shivered – Mouse was crying now. Aunty Pani peered briefly through the Terylenes, the belt dangling from her shoulder. Usually Mum would be listening out two doors away for the noise so she could be satisfied we were being dished out a decent hiding.

When Aunty Pani turned away from the window she was grinning. She gathered us all around and whispered her instruction to make all the noises like we were being whacked. Then she crossed to one of the big leather chairs in the far corner and set to, thrashing it with the belt.

Thwa-a-a-ak

'Aaaiiieeee!'

Thwak-thwak-thwa-a-a-k

'Oooweeee!'

We could've howled for Aotearoa, we were that good.

Mouse, Lucy and me kept those yells and screams coming as Aunty Pani made a fine show of it, whipping the nono off that chair. Mouse woo-wooed like a puppy – real sobby. Lucy was so good that I told her later she should live in Hollywood when she grew up and be a movie star because she was a born actor. She even cried real tears *on cue*.

When we left Aunty Pani's the sun was sinking low and the sky had gone all red. Right behind our house, two doors away, the fire closest to the surface of the sun blasted out and made our house look like it was going up in flames. Mouse caught up with me and grabbed my hand. She smiled up shyly, big orange lights reflecting in her eyes. I smiled back at her, squeezing her tiny fingers, and we giggled all the way home.

Logie and Marama

Caroline Adair Down

Logie stared at the TV. Blue white light flickered about the room, calming his busy nerves. He glanced at the window. With the blinds down he supposed some light could be seen through the narrow slits between each slat.

Logie didn't like the moon. It made his heart beat too fast, his breath pull too quickly. The fuller it became each night, the nervier he was.

His black eyes shifted quickly towards the window. Check the slats ... all that leaked through was the slow indian ink night. He sighed, wiping damp hands together.

No. Logie didn't like the moon. But he did like TV. All was well on TV. He hugged a rough brown cushion as he watched another one of those cheesy cop shows. The violence was OK – it was contained. Inside the TV.

He felt very safe.

It was best when the crim was arrested and marched to the pigpen, triumphant in his defiance – one finger jabbing upwards before the inevitable clamping of cuffs and gruff assertions from the slightly plonker-ish arresting officer.

'Awroit sunshine – yee-aaaw nicked! Yaw coming wiv us.'

Logie chortled. Cut to the usual courtroom follow through. The same old shit.

Some aging (but still most definitely very fuckable) chick barrister with a loud red mouth and tightly suited-up bod, fighting against the crusty male star of the show.

She was the defence. He was the prosecution. Logie knew what would happen. The crim would go to jail – though not without a hell of a scrap – and he'd go down in classic style. The bitch would fry (that'd fucking teach her for being such a smartarsey cocktease), and the star would ride off looking for his next villain.

Logie liked the thought of that outcome. He hugged his cushion tighter and felt very safe indeed.

When Marama sails across the evening sky she rises like a water nymph, bursting through the darkened night air. Her hair is stars and her eyes pure silver light. She shakes her head twelve times a year to loosen stars like flailing rain. The stars fall away and tumble forever through universes and eternities. As Marama rises to begin her long swim across the sky she mourns for the children she will never bear. Then she slides gently to earth, and her long fingers slip between gaps in curtains or slits in slats, looking for the children she will never bear.

And when Marama cries she disappears.

Grandma Nestor had scared Logie. She'd taught him that to stare through bare glass at Marama's full-blown beauty would send him insane. She had warned him about the nature of Marama's wanderings. If you were seduced by her sad beauty she would lift you from your bed and sit you right up there in heaven. Up there – like putting a glass ornament up on a high shelf.

She was lonely and selfish, Grandma Nestor had said. She wanted to possess everything. Turn the hastening sea into folds of flowing silk. Make lovers' eyes darker each night until passion became jealousy. And when she found you she would touch your skin so softly that you would turn weak at the heart with love for her.

Never could a heart be strong enough to hold a love so complete. On no account should you ever let her skin touch yours. Your heart will falter and break at once into thousands of blood-red stars. Surely then you will be dead....

The red-mouth bitch was doing her thing. Logie watched mesmerised. She stood before the jury, pointing to the crim. Her face was pulled to an angle of mock empathy. She then turned back to the bench; tears attractively moistening her cosmetically fattened lashes. The crim smirked and pulled his beanie further down over his eyes. He leaned back and folded his arms, tilting his chin up as he did so. This movement allowed him to stare comfortably downwards and survey the action while remaining staunch and intimidating. Logie smiled, pleased with the crim. Man, he had it right under control. Got the bitch working her magic for him – all he had to do was sit back and enjoy the ride.

Logie chuckled and stuck the cushion on his head, trying for the same lean and tilt. Perfecting the downward gaze was a piece of cake.

That was, until the moonlight stabbed his eyes. Cool relentless knives ... slowly slicing between the slats ... searing white stripes onto the floor like a brand.

The garish TV glare paled as Marama fed her streams of light into the room and smoothly hoisted her way inside.

Logie stood and stared in horror while two woman's legs, each about three metres long, stepped effortlessly through the slits between slats. Her toes were sharp and pointed with sliding mercury toenails. She folded her body like a ribbon, dropping and doubling up naked upon Logie's floor. Logie could not move as she began to shake out her glowing white hair. There was oceans of it, sodden with stars and minerals from the heavens. There was a peculiar smell like the sulphur Logie had burnt in science at school. And it was raining – like drizzle – but there was no water. Only stars. Everywhere there were more and more stars.

Stars fell into Logie's eyes, blinding him.

Marama embraced him in the form of Grandma Nestor. Her arms flowed about him, covering him as he shook with fear. Large silver stars cut his eyes like spurs – or wheels with tiny teeth.

Tears of blood wetted his entire face. Marama kissed the tears and wrapped him tighter. He could feel barbed-wire sharpness wherever the stars touched his body.

Never let her skin touch yours.

He was in terrible pain.

Grandma Nestor floated in and out of Marama's form. Her cracked old face in Logie's mind was not fully there. Every now and then he glimpsed her expression of terror. His eyes blinded, cut and bleeding, could not block out the powerful vision of Marama.

She beckoned to him. He could still hear the bitch lawyer spewing forth on TV. Marama's voice was the roar of a southerly gale as it is released to skim the caps of the Kaikoura Range. The roar pitched higher to a howl and hurtled like a rocket through the gullies and alleys of the lower North Island.

She reached for him with one long hand, mercury dripping and regrouping from her fingertips.

Never let her skin touch yours.

He tumbled over onto the floor, thrashing about in the luminous shadow of slits between slats. The brown cushion bounced hard against the TV and hit the far wall. As Marama's hands came nearer, two drops of mercury fell – one onto each of Logie's shoulders – freezing and lifting him up into the night.

Below him there was a tight close-up of the crim. The camera pulled back and the crim tilted his chin to the bitch lawyer. She smiled slyly with her red mouth.

He raised his eyebrows once more to her.

'Cher,' was all he said.

The Gate

David Down

Tania said, 'Thanks Dad,' as he put her coffee down on the worn Formica table in front of her and then settled his large frame down in a matching chrome-legged chair. He spread his arms out on the table around his cup of tea and laced his fingers together.

'I wish you would talk to him. It doesn't matter what you say –'

'There's nothing to say, Dad.'

'Just find something to talk about. Tell him about what the kids have been doing at school. Does he know Tyson won the junior school art competition? Does he know that you're taking Jade to swimming lessons? Tell him about your new job. Ask him about his. For goodness sake, talk about the bloody weather. It doesn't matter what. Just talk to him.'

Tania turned and called into the hallway, 'Tyson! Jade! I hope you've got everything ready. Your father will be here soon.'

'I remember when your mother and I had a bad spell once.'

'You and Mum? I thought you guys were like some match made in heaven or something.'

'Mostly, yeah we were. But there was this one time, just before you were born, when we had this bad spell of, I don't know, drifting apart I suppose. It really hurt me. Hurt us both.'

'What did you do?'

'We did nothing. It was Aunty Mae and Aunty Whena who did the doing. They came around one night. They told Mum to go and see her dad for a while so they could have a "chat" to me. I didn't know that they knew that there anything was wrong between me and Mum. Geez, I hardly knew myself. They sat down in here in this kitchen, May in that chair and Whena in that one –'

'We did offer you our dining suite Dad.'

'I know, and they say "Right boy. It's time to talk a bit of sense into you." I thought, geez I'm for it. And I was right. They gave me a bloody good dressing down, they did. Told me they knew we were unhappy. Told me all the things I was doing wrong. Too much pub. Too much rugby. Too much beer. Not enough Mum.'

Jade came into the kitchen crying, 'I can't find my *Lion King* colouring book.'

Tania looked into her coffee cup. 'It's under Granddad's video cabinet.'

As Jade scampered away Tyson called out, 'She's such a baby. Dad's just gonna buy her a new one anyway. She knows he will.'

'So what happened after that?' said Tania.

'Well it didn't get through all that quick, so of course the next night I was down the pub again and then Mae and Whena came around to have a chat with Mum. Same story. They gave her a good dressing down too. Too much looking after the neighbours' kids. Too much washing. Too much cleaning. Not enough Dad.'

'Like they're ever going to be my problems.'

'And then they came around one night and talked to us both together. Heh heh. It was funny even to us when we looked back later. But, oh my goodness, we did not realise the harm that can be done by ignoring even the little things. Like talking.'

'Well it's like I said, there's really not much to talk about at the moment is there.'

He looked at the bruise on her cheek. 'By geez, that took me by surprise, that. Never thought he was capable. And I know how much he loved you and how good he was to you.'

Tania said nothing. She looked guiltily into her coffee cup and shrugged. He gently turned her face towards him and said, 'You know Tania, we all make mistakes. We all do things we wish we hadn't.'

She turned her eyes away and looked out the kitchen window and into the street. 'And there you go. You don't talk and you don't talk and still you don't talk. So do something now. When he gets here, go out with the kids. Stand at the gate. You don't have to go through it. You don't have to touch him. You don't have to look at him. But say something. Say anything.'

She finished her coffee. Outside, a near-new Hyundai station wagon stole silently up the drive and stopped in front of the gate. She put her empty coffee cup down and looked at her father.

'Like what? What do you what me to say?'

He nodded his head toward the car. 'There you go. He's got a new car. Ask him about it.'

Jade danced excitedly into the kitchen. 'Dad's here! Dad's here!' Then she danced into the hallway to put her shoes on.

Tyson trudged in after Jade carrying both her bag and his. He hugged his granddad and then Tania. She squeezed him and then stood up. She felt her knees shake a little. This going out to the gate business was unexpected. The speaking would be unexpected. It would be unexpected for him too. She looked at her father and shrugged helplessly.

He said very quietly, 'Anything. Say anything.' Then he called out to Jade, 'Hey! How about a goodbye kiss from my little fairy?'

Jade skipped back in. Quickly she pecked him on the cheek and said goodbye. Then she skipped out again and opened the front door. 'Wow!' they heard her say, 'Dad's got a new car. I bet it's got a CD player in it.'

Tania's son just stood there with his arm around her waist. He rolled his eyes. 'Whoopee,' he said.

Tania ruffled his hair. 'Go on mate,' she said. He began to walk out and she started to follow. He stopped at the kitchen door and turned to face her. Looking at her in surprise he asked, 'Are you coming out to the gate?'

'Yes.'

'Why?'

She looked back at her father. He just shrugged. She said to Tyson, 'I have to tell your father something.'

'You want to tell him you're still angry at him for hitting you?'

Her stomach muscles tightened and a tear threatened. 'No mate, no. Let's just go out to the gate OK?'

He went out and Tania followed. Jade was at the gate. As Tania came off the front porch, the driver's door opened. A tall man stepped out. He looked with mild surprise at Tania. Jade jumped up and down, her dark curls bouncing. Tania and Tyson stopped at the gate and Tyson unlatched it. With a familiar creaking it swung open towards the car. It was caught and held open. Jade hugged her father tightly. 'You've got a new car Dad. Wow! It's so cool!' He smiled and went to the car to open a rear door for her. She stamped her foot. 'I want to sit in the front.'

He said no, it was Tyson's turn.

Tyson hugged Tania again, burying his face in her chest while she looked out at a house across the street. In the living-room window of the house a curtain was quickly dropped, prying eyes guilty at having been detected. Then he was patiently holding the gate open again, waiting for Tyson. Tyson had his eyes, large and dark. Jade had his build, slim, athletic. They both had his broad face and his skin colour. He looked down as he picked at a bit of moss growing in a crack in the concrete with the toe of his shoe. Tyson let go of Tania and said, 'See ya Mum.' He turned to his father and said, 'Hey Dad,' and then went to the car and dropped the two bags into the rear passenger seat next to Jade, who was still sulking. Then he got into the front passenger seat, shut his door and buckled himself in.

Tania looked down the street and noticed a couple of wheelie bins had been blown over onto the road by the wind. The gate was still being held open. He waited for her to say something. She looked at the clouds over the distant hills and desperately wondered if she should get the washing in, it looked like it might rain.

Then he closed the gate and got back into his car, backed out and drove away. Tania turned around. She was about to walk back inside when she heard the gate creaking. The latch hadn't fallen into place properly and the gate was swinging open again. She caught it and gently swung it shut. The latch dropped into place with a metallic click.

Inside the house, Tania's father got up and put the jug on for another cup of tea.

The Paper Boy

David Down

Mr King was waiting for his paper by his front gate just after five. It was his daily ritual, a nice cup of tea in front of the afternoon telly in his cosy little kitchen (he didn't actually watch the telly, it was just a little company), then down the hall to the front door, out the front door and a stroll to the front gate, picking at weeds here and there, checking the roses, and then waiting at the gate for his paper. It was a Wednesday, so he was clutching the little check card in one hand and Adrian's paper money in the other. He lifted the lid of his letter box and took a few ads out. Stedman's Pharmacy and Lotto monthly specials, Ching's Four Square coupon book, a flyer from the local MP. Mr King made a grunting noise in the back of his throat. Politicians. Pah.

He looked up Soldiers Road. Where was Adrian? Maybe he'd been held up after school. Then he heard the familiar rattle of the paper basket on Adrian's bicycle. There he was, coming round the corner. He looked down at the check slip. Adrian's name was at the top: A. van der Leus. The youngest boy of Pieter van der Leus, the vintner at the end of Kawhara Road. The vineyard itself was barely twenty years old, but had already produced, according to the local papers, some very good wine. Mr King admired anyone who was able to break in a bit of land and make it work for them, whether it was for growing kūmara or grapes. It took a lot of hard work. He knew van der Leus by sight. Tall, straight, with bright blue eyes and blonde hair. Worker's hands and muscles. The son, Adrian, was a dead ringer for him, although Mr King knew that the condition of his hands had been granted him by his cricket bat and bike handlebars more so than by handling woody vines and secateurs.

He watched Adrian's slow progress down the street. Wednesdays always took Adrian a long time, collecting his money and delivering. Eventually he reached Mr King.

'Hello Adrian,' said Mr King, 'you're a bit late today.'

'Yeah,' Adrian replied, taking his money and signing his card. 'We had a late cricket practice and then my oma arrived from Napier, so I started a bit late.'

Mr King frowned. 'Your what?'

'My oma: my grandmother.'

'Oh I see, well you better get going then eh?'

'Yeah, see you tomorrow Mr King, bye!' And he was off.

Adrian pedalled away, eager to finish his round. He always enjoyed his oma staying. She brought toys for him, and delicious biscuits and cakes that she made herself. Mum and Dad always took a little time off work, backed off on the stress levels a bit and enjoyed family for a little while. They would have a huge dinner and then sit back in the living room and try the cakes and biscuits Oma had brought. Then she would talk to Adrian and his older brother Martin about the war and life in the Netherlands when she was a little girl. They would look at their parents' photo albums full of pictures of old houses with thatched roofs, fields of tulips, and rows and rows of windmills. Adrian was fascinated by all this. There was nothing to compare it with in New Zealand, although his father had often talked about building a pretend windmill out near the entrance to the property one day. Then he and Martin would go to bed and listen to the grown-ups drinking wine and playing Rummikub until midnight.

So today was one of those days when he would rather not have to worry about his paper run. But normally he loved it. Martin had stopped doing it when Adrian was ten. He had spoken to Mr Smith, the man who distributed the papers, and Mr Smith had agreed that Adrian could take his place. It had meant that Adrian had to cut his cricket practice a little short, but he found that the round kept him fit, and he enjoyed meeting some of the people along the way.

Especially Mr King.

The first time he had done his round he had come around the

corner in Soldiers Road and seen the old man standing there waiting. He was quite a tall man, with a very large chest and stomach. His skin was dark brown and had a leathery shine in the afternoon sun. His broad and open face was a cartographer's delight of deeply etched wrinkles and lines, all symmetry and human grace. Adrian looked up every now and then, watching the old man picking at weeds, looking around his front yard. Finally he reached the letter box.

'Hello young fella,' the old man had said.

'Hello,' Adrian replied, pulling a newspaper from his basket.

'Where's young Martin?' the old man asked him.

'My brother gave me his paper round, I'm doing it now. I'm Adrian.'

'Hello Adrian, I'm Mr King. So are you my new paper boy?'

'Yeah.'

'Oh good.' The old man took his paper, said 'Thank you, thank you,' and turned away and started to walk down his path to the front door. Adrian watched him for a little while and then pedalled off to the next house.

The next day the old man had been waiting there again. 'Good afternoon Adrian,' he said.

'Hello,' Adrian replied.

'How are you today?' Mr King asked him.

'Fine thank you.'

Mr King noticed a cricket bat poking out of Adrian's saddle bag. 'Been to cricket practice?'

'Yeah, I have to leave a little early to start my round.'

'Oh, that's good, you keep it up. I used to play cricket you know.' Mr King smiled and took his paper and went inside.

Adrian delivered his paper, rain or shine, and Mr King was always waiting for him, rain or shine. Every day Mr King asked Adrian something about school or sport. Soon enough, Mr King was able to ask Adrian how his maths test went, how well he bowled on Saturday and if he liked his new class. He occasionally asked about Adrian's father, and whether the wine was doing well, but mostly he showed interest only in Adrian. Adrian enjoyed his five-minute chats to Mr King.

One day he pedalled up to the gate. Mr King was waiting. He held up his arms and said to Adrian, 'Notice anything?'

Adrian frowned. 'No.'

Mr King put his hand to his mouth.

'Oh, you're not smoking!' Adrian said.

Mr King smiled broadly, all gums and lips. 'No, gave up yesterday.' He leaned forward a little. 'It's not easy. Don't you go starting, young fella.'

Adrian hadn't. He said, 'No I won't.'

'Who are you playing on Saturday?'

'Waikere Primary.'

'Well good luck young fella, you show them who's boss eh?'

'Yup, see ya.' Adrian found after a while that he tended to save some of the minor events of the day to tell Mr King rather than his parents. Just the unimportant little things: his victory playing lunchtime bullrush; a dollar he'd found on the footpath outside school. They gradually became more important things though, as Adrian's confidences in Mr King grew. He was a little worried about his English test tomorrow; he'd had a fight with his best friend Andrew; he'd worked himself into number three in the batting order. Mr King always had time to listen and usually had some helpful or encouraging word.

Adrian learnt over time that Mr King had a very large family. A few times he'd pulled up to Mr King's letter box and there were a whole lot of cars in the driveway. Mostly big new ones, vans and four-wheel drives. Lots of talking and laughing coming from inside. Sometimes people would be sitting on the little porch at the front of the house. Even though he had lots of family visiting, Mr King would still come outside to say hello to Adrian and get his paper.

One day Adrian pulled up to Mr King's letter box and Mr King was waiting with something small, wrapped in a paper towel, in his hand. 'Hello young Adrian,' Mr King smiled. 'Here, this is a little something I saved for you.' He took Adrian's hand and put the something in it.

Adrian lifted a corner of the paper towel. It was a piece of chocolate birthday cake. 'Is it your birthday?'

'It was on Saturday,' Mr King beamed. 'Now I'm eighty-five.'

Adrian gasped. 'Eighty-five? You're even older than Oma.' Then he realised what he'd said and added a little sheepishly, 'I mean, you know....'

Mr King laughed. 'I'm very old, it's true, but look at me.' He stood up straight, pulled in his stomach and puffed out his chest. Made a fist and punched himself with it. 'Tarzan!'

Adrian giggled. Mr King could be quite funny sometimes. 'Happy birthday for Saturday,' he said, 'and thanks for the birthday cake.'

'Now don't you go eating that until you've finished your paper round, young Adrian,' Mr King said, 'or you won't finish it at all.'

Adrian smiled at him. 'Thanks Mr King, see you tomorrow,' and he pedalled off.

Mr King gave Adrian a little block of chocolate on each Christmas Eve, always Cadbury Caramello, and a card with a two-dollar note in it on his birthdays. Wished him good luck for his away games, wished him good luck for his fourth form end-of-year exams. He got to know Adrian pretty well as the years went by, and although he didn't know it, was aware of some things that Adrian's parents weren't. The first time Adrian kissed a girl, the fact that Adrian had ambitions of furthering his cricket beyond just playing for his school team, the fact that Adrian's heart was as far from making wine as he himself was from drinking it in preference to a cold beer on a hot day. He sometimes thought to himself that the lad was growing up and would soon be growing out of his paper run. He knew the day would come when some other young boy or girl would come pedalling around the corner into Soldiers Road, and he knew he would miss Adrian very much when it happened.

One day Adrian stopped and told Mr King that he might be a bit late tomorrow. 'I've got my first school cert exam in the afternoon,' he explained.

'School cert eh?' Mr King replied. 'You're growing up aren't you? You'll be too old for a paper run soon won't you.'

Adrian looked at him in surprise as if it were something he had not thought of. 'I s'pose, yeah, I'll keep doing it till Christmas though,' he added, thinking Mr King looked a little sad. 'See ya tomorrow.'

Adrian pedalled off thoughtfully. No more paper run? That meant he probably wouldn't see Mr King again. Well perhaps he could just drop in and see him? But then that would seem a bit strange really. Because in all the years that Adrian had been delivering Mr King's paper to him, he had never really learnt much about Mr King. He knew Mr King's front yard off by heart, the little path up to the front door, the roses that had grown with such care over the years, his white picket fence, the pot plants on the verandah. But he had no idea what might be on the other side.

He studied hard for his school cert exams. He visualised himself pedalling breathlessly up to Mr King's letter box with the exciting news – passes, all passes! This little motivational tool helped him to do that bit of extra study and stay focussed.

And on a day in early January his results arrived. He ran into the house. His father was out at the vines. His mother and brother Martin were there though, as was Oma, who was visiting for the holidays. He sat down at the kitchen table, shaking a little, as he nervously opened the envelope and shook out the papers inside. The little certificate itself fluttered to the floor. He bent down and snatched it and held it high up in front of his bulging eyes. 'Yes! Yes!' he yelled. 'Yes!'

'Yes what?' Martin asked.

'What?' asked his mother.

He almost sang the results in his delight. 'English 73, Mathematics 81, Social Studies 72, Science 82, Technology 84, Tech Drawing 89.' He put the certificate down and grinned at his family.

'Oh my good boy,' Oma said, patting his head, tears in her eyes. 'My clever boy!'

'I'll go and get Dad,' said Martin. But more than anyone, Adrian could not wait to tell Mr King.

And so that afternoon he was early to pick up his papers. He pedalled furiously from letter box to letter box. Up Kawhara Road, left into Elizabeth Street and then right into Hunters Crescent. Round Hunters Crescent and back into Elizabeth, then down Waitere Street and finally around the corner into Soldiers Road.

But Mr King was not there. He made his way down the road, number twenty-four, number twenty-six, number twenty-eight, looking up after each delivery expecting to see Mr King. Then finally Mr King's letter box, number thirty.

He got off his bike and propped it up on its stand. Stood there in dismay. Called out, 'Mr King.' The front door was open. That meant Mr King must be at home. He opened the letter box. There was mail there, and a couple of ads. The Warehouse, Stedman's Amcal Chemist. A Telecom bill, a letter addressed with a child's handwriting. He took them out and bunched them together with Mr King's paper. Then he opened the front gate and stepped into Mr King's front yard.

'Mr King?' He walked slowly up the path towards the front door. He could hear the TV going. He stood at the front door. Mr King's gumboots lay on the verandah next to the front door. He knocked on the door.

'Mr King?' He waited for the sound of a chair creaking and footsteps approaching. But all he heard was the TV. He pushed the door open. He looked down the hallway though the house to the back door. Hanging on a hook on the wall was Mr King's oilskin coat that he wore when his paper was delivered in the rain. Several doors sat ajar. There were pictures on the walls down both sides of the hall. Two Tiffany style lampshades hung from the ceiling. The floor changed from an old-fashioned looking carpet down the hall to bare floorboards at the far end, where Adrian guessed the kitchen must be.

'Mr King?' he called out. He could hear Oprah Winfrey on the TV. He stepped inside.

It took his eyes a little while to adjust to the light. On the left hand side of the hallway he noticed a long table with a glass case sitting on top of it. In the glass case was a model of a Māori canoe, a big model, over a meter long. He bent down and studied it. It was an extremely well detailed model, tiny bails sitting on little wooden seats, paddles laid out with tiny feathers on them, prow and stern intricate replicas of actual carved timber. Adrian marveled at the detail and the skill that created it.

'Happy Birthday Granddad!' the little ones sing in chorus. He beams at them.

'Oh my goodness, this is a big present isn't it eh?' He opens it slowly, teasingly, then with a dramatic flourish pulls the paper away. But even he is impressed. 'Ooh,' he says, 'gee kids, this is a beauty isn't it?' Later they help him place it carefully on a table in the hall.

Adrian looked up. Above the canoe was a row of old pictures of young men in boxing trunks, boots and gloves standing in various poses. One was a big white man with a fierce looking moustache and an angry expression on his face. But the rest were all the same young man, tall, muscular, dark skinned, shiny white teeth, hair greased back. Adrian stared in wonder. Mr King? Mr King had been a boxer? Wow. The photo of the white man had been written on. Adrian read, 'Next time, Llepowsky the Leopard will win.'

He checks in on Llepowsky after the fight. Llepowsky grins at him. 'My first time I lose, you bastard native, now come and have a drink with me!' Laughter.

'I will,' is the reply, 'but not in this stinking changing room! Get your best strides on Leo we'll have a couple down at the Met eh?'

Wow. Mr King had been a boxer. That was so cool. Adrian looked down the hall. There were so many more pictures. He walked on to the first door. It was the living room. 'Mr King?' Still no answer. He looked into the living room. There were many more pictures again in here

Above the fireplace was a family album-type gallery of photos, some of which Adrian thought looked very old. The centerpiece was a large wedding portrait. The photo was a little out of focus and had faded a bit to brown tones. A young man in army uniform stood looking solemnly at the camera. Perched on a stool next to him was a fairer-skinned woman in a long wedding dress with a veil pulled back from her black hair. At first Adrian thought she was very beautiful, and then two things occurred to him. Mr King had been in the army, and Mr King had been married. That wasn't so unusual, but Mr King had never mentioned either of these things and Adrian had not ever seen any sign of them. There had been the large numbers of visitors of course, but then why had he never put two and two together and wondered where was Mrs King? Underneath the photo was a framed official-looking document. Adrian read it. It was Mr and Mrs King's wedding certificate. Gee, he'd never seen his parents' wedding certificate, though they must have one. Yet Mr and Mrs King's was framed and hung on the wall. Adrian thought they must have been a very close and loving couple to hang their wedding certificate up.

'Arthur, what on earth do you want to hang that on the wall for?' she asks him, laughing.

'Because you're my lovely wife and I want everyone to know,' he laughs back, holding her firmly by her slender waist.

'Oh get away with you, you silly thing.' When she laughs, her eyes sparkle.

Adrian wondered if Mr King had learnt to box in the army. But then he thought that the photos in the hall had been a younger man. Perhaps he'd joined the army later. He looked at another photo, this one of a young boy standing outside a newly painted small wooden shop front. Above the shop a sign said W. R. King – Ohura General Store. In the photo the barefoot little boy was squinting at the camera. Resting on his shoulder was a long pole with strings of skinny fish hanging off of it. Eels, Adrian realised. Was that Mr King? He was only a little boy. Hardly eight years old even. Adrian shook his head in wonder. Why should he have not thought that Mr King was once a young boy himself?

'You did well boy,' the man under the camera hood says. 'Catch all those yourself?' The boy squints into the sun.

'Nah. Me and me cousin Bill caught 'em eh. Down at Wilsons Creek. Gonna smoke 'em for dinner.'

Adrian was now hopelessly absorbed in these pictures and had completely forgotten that he was here to look for Mr King. He turned around and looked at the wall facing away from the fireplace, the wall that was behind him when he came into the living room. This wall was almost completely covered in pictures. Pride of place was a large pencil sketch inside a very expensive and very old looking frame. Adrian could tell it was an original work. It showed a very old man with a pipe in his mouth sitting in front of the doorway of the meeting house on a Māori marae. He was looking downwards, contemplating an intricately carved walking stick. Adrian thought that it looked like a hasty yet extremely skillful field-type sketch made as a prelude to a studio painting. He was startled to read the signature at the bottom – C. F. Goldie. He shook his head. Surely not. But then he knew from his art studies that Goldie had travelled this part of the country and would've made a number of such sketches on any given day. So it would be real. But geez, he thought, what a piece of art to have hanging on the wall. Wow.

'What's that man doing?' the little boy asks.

'Shh. He's a very famous man. He's going to draw a picture of Koro.'

'Can I see it?'

'When he's finished son, when he's finished.'

To the left of the sketch (the 'Goldie' Adrian reminded himself) was a family portrait, but not Mr King's family. This was a cheap shopping mall-type portrait of a young couple, smiling, struggling to hold three obviously wriggling children.

'Dear Koro,' he reads, 'I hope you like this picture of me and Hemi and the kids. Don't you go hanging it next to your Goldie now will you....'

He thinks, no bugger it, that's exactly where I will hang it, that's my grandfather in that sketch and my grandchildren in this photo. They should be side by side.

Adrian began to think how strange it was to place something so cheap looking next to a work that must be worth a lot of money. Then he imagined Mr King hanging it on the wall and realised that Mr King wouldn't have cared whether it was cheap or not, nor would Mr King have bothered to clear a space around the Goldie simply because it was a Goldie. To Mr King, Adrian thought, these were all just pictures of his family, himself. His life encapsulated for all to see, and regardless of whether they were images made on Kodak Studio Pro or hand-stretched canvas as old as himself, they were all equally important.

Then Adrian realised he was still clutching Mr King's mail and newspaper, and still hadn't located Mr King. 'Mr King?' he called. He looked out of the living room, down the hall towards the kitchen. 'Mr King!' Adrian felt a quick wash of guilt at having spent so much time being nosey. He started down the hall towards the back door, which hung open. Walked briskly past the kitchen and then jerked back again.

Stood for a long time looking at the kitchen table.

The little TV on the mantelpiece was talking to itself. Mr King's last cup of tea was now cold. Mr King himself sat in his chair, slumped forward, clutching half a Cameo Creme in one hand and Adrian's check card and paper money in the other. Adrian blinked. He whispered, 'Mr King?' Cleared his throat. 'Mr King?' There was not a snore, not a twitch of the eyes to show any sign of life.

As quick as he was to accept the fact, it took Adrian a long time to take a step towards Mr King. He stood still for ages, somewhat ridiculously waiting for a sign that Mr King was actually dead. Realised the only way to get that sign would be to check his pulse. That meant touching him. Adrian shivered. He walked forward, around the table, until he was at a distance that he could reach out and touch Mr King's arm. He put his fingers out and gently pressed them into Mr King's upturned right wrist. Withdrew them immediately. His skin was cold and hard. He was dead, actually dead. Adrian ran his left hand through his hair. His lips began to tremble. Put his right hand on his back pocket. Felt a slip of paper there. Reached in and took out his school certificate. Held it in front of Mr King's dead unseeing eyes.

'I passed my school c, Mr King,' he whispered, and began to cry.

More of New Zealand On Air

David Down

Ramesh was new.

Because he was new he was subject to a high degree of intimidation. He was given a nickname which he did not like. He was pushed by hands he could not see, he was sniffed at for odours which he himself could not smell, he was scowled at for reasons he did not know.

And all this, at least at the beginning of his term, made him feel right at home.

And so most of the time he said absolutely nothing, as this was his most highly trained means of self-defence. When a hand shot out behind him, shoving him in the shoulder and causing him to stumble, Ramesh said nothing. When a nose went in the air sniffing at some phantom foreign dish, Ramesh said nothing. When he innocently took his dinner plate from the mess-hall bench and the man in front turned and glared at him for what he didn't know, still, Ramesh said nothing.

He really did feel very, very much at home.

Ramesh was New Zealand born, spoke flawless kiwi, drank Lion Red, and preferred Big Macs. He sometimes referred to himself as 'New Zealand owned and operated'. He was in for armed robbery and aggravated assault, having cocked up a hold-up at Doug McKenzie's Four Square Supermarket. The irony of which had not been lost on the Sunday paper cartoonists. Nor had it been lost on the other inmates. With a stony silence Ramesh endured the endless jibes about how he'd been on the wrong side of the counter, and how remarkable it was that he'd picked on the only Four Square in New Zealand not owned by someone who frequently enjoyed the spicier of culinary delights.

Comments that meant that sort of thing anyway.

Now, while the maintenance of his outward silence began to get on the nerves of those around him, the inward anger and frustration he felt as days went by began to weigh heavy on his own. More and more often Ramesh did nothing but sit at the window looking out beyond the bars and the high walls with their crown of barbed wire, talking in his head to himself, trying to reason his bitterness, and failing to do so. Eventually he reached a conclusion which was so logical he wondered why it had taken him so long to see it. Simply put, he was a New Zealander trapped in an Indian's body. And he stopped talking altogether.

The prison psychologist became quite concerned about him. His brothers stopped visiting him because of his seemingly complete lack of interest in them. Some of the prison staff became worried that he might be suffering some form of nervous breakdown. And his fellow inmates....

Well they got really, *really* fucked off with him.

'Oops! Sorry dummy!' 'Hey look. Punjab's here early, must be curry tonight.' 'Smell that? Punjab must be round the corner.' 'Chai wallah! Another cup of tea if you please.' 'Oops, sorry dummy. Didn't know you were there, my nose is blocked.' 'Say something you dumb Punjabi bastard.'

But Ramesh said nothing.

One evening he was wandering along corridors in silence when he decided to sit down and watch television. He wandered into the rec room. John Watson and Hemi Taratoa were playing snooker. Ramesh glanced at the scoreboard. It showed Taratoa leading. Watson would be pissed off, he was meant to be the snooker king. They both glared at Ramesh as he entered.

Ramesh said nothing.

Instead he went and sat down in the chair next to the magazine table in front of the TV. In the chair on the other side of this table sat the Australian Roger whatsiname, the one in for rape.

'Come to watch TV have you Punjab?' said Roger the Rapist.

'Well you're just in time, *Shortland Street*'s about to start.'

Watson snorted. 'Fucking *Shortland Street*.'

'Don't you like *Shortland Street*?' Roger asked. He leaned over and punched Ramesh on the shoulder. 'What about you Punjab? You watch *Shortland Street*? Eh? I bet you do. I bet you get off watching all the little nursies, don't ya.'

Ramesh said nothing.

Roger picked up the remote and turned on the TV. *Shortland Street* had just started. 'Is it you or is it me?' Roger sang happily in his annoying Australian twang.

Watson walked over to him and stood in front of him, holding his pool cue like a baseball bat. 'Fuck up rapist, I'm trying to play snooker.'

'Can't see the telly,' Roger protested meekly.

'Wanker,' Watson replied, and walked back to the pool table.

'You really like this shit?' Taratoa said.

'Fuck yeah,' Roger replied, 'though it's not been quite the same since that Rachel left....'

Taratoa thought about this. He had seen *Shortland Street* a few times. He said to Watson, 'Fuck yeah, she was hot, that one.'

'Mind you,' Roger continued, 'I wouldn't mind waking up in the morning and finding Nurse Caroline's uniform lying on the floor by me bed.'

Watson tapped Taratoa on the shoulder. Taratoa turned and grinned as Watson made a wanking motion on an imaginary two foot dick. A lot of inmates did this behind Roger's back. Watson leant over to play his next shot.

Roger leaned over and once again punched Ramesh on the shoulder. 'What about you, curry-breath? I bet you mind you wouldn't mind sticking your little Punjab sausage up Nurse Caroline, would ya?'

Ramesh said nothing.

'Go baby go baby go baby GO!' yelled Watson at the cue ball as it began to slow up directly behind the black ball. It lightly kissed the black and stopped. 'Woohoo!' Taratoa looked at the table in despair.

Watson asked Roger, 'What is it about this shit that you like so much rapist? Apart from the nurses?'

Roger thought for a while. Then he replied, 'I dunno, it's not real but it kinda is real you know? Like the people aren't real but the situations they find themselves in are sort of like real-life situations. And it's kinda fun to imagine what you would do yourself if something like that happened to you, you know?'

'You mean like you go to the bar for a drink and that Rachel's there and she says something like, "I'm a horny bitch on my lunch break, take me out back and fuck me?" ' Watson said.

Taratoa giggled.

'You don't have to be a wanker about it,' Roger said. 'You asked me what I like about it and I'm just telling you. It's like a little bit of New Zealand life that you can make up for yourself as it goes along and it's not real but it's kinda based on real, you know?'

Ramesh said, 'You must be fucking joking.'

There was a stunned silence.

Ramesh said, 'You watch this shit, this absolutely pathetic shit and you sit there and pretend that it's real? You piece of shit.'

'Fuck me,' Taratoa said. 'It talks....'

Watson put a hand on Taratoa's shoulder, 'Hang on, bro.' He turned to Ramesh. 'Why say that Punjab? What's about *Shortland Street* that makes you say that?'

Ramesh turned in his chair and replied, 'Because it's only TVNZ reality. It's not based on what happens in actual life. It's not based on demographic samples or average population or random picks of doctors in real hospitals. It's based on what the Salon Selective – Postie Plus – Tim Tam munching – *Woman's Weekly* reading mindless no brain *Shortland Street* viewers want reality to be! What the "I really need to have a smear test but I don't want some curry-munching Doctor Parbhu sticking his dirty brown fingers anywhere near me" Kiwi woman wants to see when they enter a hospital. Don't you understand that? That's not what they want to see on TV! That's their painful, embarrassing, humiliating, actual reality. This is their TV reality! This is the only place in this whole fucking country where you can go and get your tits checked for lumps by Doctor Ruggedly Handsome Ropata! Did you hear what I said? Doctor Ropata! Who the fuck is Doctor ROPATA!' His face began to get very red. His voice climbed in pitch. He marched to the telephone, ripped the phone book off the wall and marched back to stand in front of Roger and threw the phone book at Roger's head. 'Open the book at Registered Medical Practitioners and Medical Centres and see how many Dr de Silvas and Dr Budhias and Dr Singhs and Dr Kumarasinghams there are. See them! Count them!' He pointed furiously at the TV. 'Look at your piece of TVNZ shit! Look at it! When did you ever see a woman on *Shortland Street* spread her legs to be examined by Dr Goonewardene? When was the last time you went to hospital and got stitched up by Doctor ROPATA!' He turned and kicked the TV screen.

An ad came on with Mr and Mrs Kiwi travelling Europe and struggling to ask for a simple loaf of bread in six different languages. Ramesh turned back to face Roger. 'You want to know what reality is for an Indian on TVNZ? You what to see where we belong on TV? Here we are now! Look at us!' He began to prance around in circles flapping his arms up and down. 'Morning Bob, looks like rain! Morning Bob, looks like rain! Morning Bob, looks like rain! MORNING BOB, LOOKS LIKE FUCKING RAIN!' He pointed at the TV. Mr and Mrs Kiwi had arrived home to clean green New Zealand and, all but holding hands, were asking their local dairy owner for two loaves of Freya's. He leaned down and in perfect time with the dialogue on the ad he yelled into Roger's face, 'GIVE US A COUPLE OF LOAVES OF FUCKING FREYA'S, RAMESH, YOU DUMB CURRY-MUNCHING PUNJABI BASTARD DAIRY OWNER!'

Roger leaned back. He said nothing. Ramesh's face glowed.

Watson went to Ramesh and stood in front of him. 'Lose the attitude, Punjab, it's just the way it is.'

'Just the way it is! Just the way it is? This *is* the way it is you dumb Māori fuck!'

'Lose the attitude Punjab,' Watson said very lowly, 'and take that back, now.'

Ramesh put his face very close to Watson. Breathing hard and waggling his face from side to side he said, 'I'll tell you how it is, "Rangi"! I get to serve spearmint leaves to your ten fat, snotty, little bastard children while their fat, stoned, out-of-work father appears on nationwide TV as DOCTOR FUCKING ROPATA!'

There was silence. Watson pulled something out of his back pocket that flashed and shone under the lights.

In less than one minute it was all over. Two prison guards equal to Watson's size had each grabbed him by the arms and taken him away. He kicked and screamed. Punched and fought. A trail of red blood crept from Ramesh's stomach where he lay by the TV across the lino towards Roger's chair. Roger sat like a statue in his chair whispering over and over, 'Oh fuck, oh god, oh fuck.' Two medics tried to stop the flow. Working quickly. Working to save him.

Ramesh said nothing.

The following night Roger sat in his chair again, waiting for seven o'clock. He was a little early, but decided to turn on the TV anyway. He hated *The Simpsons* on Two and changed channels to instead catch the end of *One Network News*. April Ieremia was wrapping up the sports headlines. New Zealand had won the second one day international against Pakistan, the new cap van der Leus scoring his first test century in the process. Roger smiled. You show those paki bastards, dutchie, he thought smiling. April smiled too.

Roger wondered what April would look like stretched out on a satin-covered bed wearing nothing but a smile and a grass skirt. While he fantasised about this, Jim the circus clown Hickey lunged at the camera, and told him what the weather had been like that day. Wanker, thought Roger, I know what it was like today. I want to know what its going to be like tomorrow. A little yellow cartoon sun peeking out from behind brick walls and barbed wire, he mused poetically. The weather idiot closed up his presentation and wished viewers a 'good one'. The taut lines on his face gave away the difficulty he was having in restraining himself from performing an impromptu back flip with a half twist. The camera returned to blonde and bubbly Liz Gunn (she was wearing one of her trademark silk blouses that made Roger want to go up and stroke the TV) who thanked Jim for his stand-up weather routine. Then she in turn handed the camera back to youthful and handsome Simon Dallow (who was wearing his trademark boyish grin that made Roger wonder what he had waiting for him at home). Dallow dropped the boyish grin, made with a serious expression, and began to wrap up the news hour (twenty-one minutes of actual news if you excluded the ad breaks, recaps, and humorous news desk banter).

'Recapping the main headlines,' Dallow began, 'a police inquiry is underway tonight following last night's fatal stabbing of an inmate at Paremoremo Prison. Twenty-three year old Ramesh Peters was killed during a fight which broke out between himself and another inmate, John Watson. Peters had just started an eight-year sentence at Paremoremo for an armed hold-up and assault in April this year. Overseas, nineteen people are dead in Jakarta after riots....'

'Blah fucking blah,' Roger told Simon and switched to Two. Doctor Al smiled from inside the 'coming up next on Two' logo. He had his arms around Nurse Caroline.

Roger couldn't blame him for smiling, but didn't feel envious. It was, after all, just pretend.

Roger leaned over to the chair next to him and put his finger on a spot of blood that had been missed by the cleaning lady. He wiped it off with his finger and held it in the air, looking at it in wonder.

'Dumb fucking Punjab,' he muttered to himself, and wiped it off under his chair.

An ad from the Retirement Commissioner came on. Off camera, a voice asked, 'Now that you've read the pamphlet, do you think it's a good idea to put some thought into saving for your retirement?' A large overall-clad Māori stood outside an auto workshop, big beefy arms folded over a forty-four gallon drum body. He shifted awkwardly from one side to the other, considered the question, and gave his verdict.

'Oh, yeah.'

'And what's he?' Roger wanted to know. 'A fucking gynaecologist?' He slouched back for another night of medical drama.

When I Close My Eyes

Trish Fong

I painted purple tears the day my mother was buried. *Dark aubergine, like blood dripping from a sea-egg's spikes.* The painting kind of followed its own destiny, like the rose petals I had dropped into the hole in the ground; hot tears trailed down my cheeks before falling onto the paint palette. The colours mixed themselves. The picture drew itself.

The table in the corner of my room is where I think, create and breathe. On top it's organised chaos; pastel crayons and coloured pens sprout from chipped mugs, a tray of still-life objects (a handful of seed pods, a pāua shell), plastic takeaway containers stained with paint residue, brushes, paper, chalk – and the photo of my mother lying in a hammock eating a plum. Her smile is eternal; her eyes are shiny-black freshwater pearls.

Since my mother's death my father's eyes have tarnished, like two pieces of silver left in a display cabinet that nobody wants to look at. I try to avoid those lifeless eyes. They're like tunnel shafts; if I look in I might never see light on the other side.

He is out again tonight, there's always a reason not to come home now.

I have become quite handy in the kitchen, a matter of having to, really. I don't think Dad has ventured in here since....

He leaves the housekeeping money in an envelope by the phone now, not on the kitchen hutch like he used to. I guess there are too many memories here; pleasant memories spoiled by absence.

Watering the potted herbs lined up along the window sill is easy for me to remember, the scent of oregano and rosemary always lingered after my mother. I try to keep fresh flowers in the glass vase on the kitchen table, but they are never arranged 'just right' like

Mum's were. I read through her recipe book the other day, its corners creased and some of the pages dusted with traces of flour. I need to learn how to make a banana cake – Dad's favourite. It's his birthday soon, maybe he'll even eat some.

My dinner is a bowl of two-minute noodles. Afterwards, I retreat to my room and turn on the bedside lamp with the blue light bulb. Some people find their peace in drugs or a bottle; I find mine in colours.

I pull back the curtains and survey the twilight sky. I can lose myself in the moon for hours, watch it gracefully glide up and over an invisible arch, stare until I can see the shape of the pipe-smoking caterpillar from *Alice in Wonderland* stamped on the moon's face. Tonight the sky is without its moon. *Shadow black.*

I curl into my duvet and on low volume play my mother's favourite jazz CD, Dinah Washington. The sultry voice that reaches your soul and makes you float....

I am disturbed out of sleep by a V of light shining across the floor.

'Turn that off now!'

Drowsy, confused, my movements are too slow to stop my father from storming his way to the stereo and tearing the CD out of the player.

'No, Dad. Don't! Pleeease.'

I catch a glimpse of his eyes – *red shooting stars with orange flaming tails* – as he snaps the disc in two, then leaves my room shattered.

I never intended him to hear it. Never thought he'd bother to check in on me when he returned home. I get dressed and run from the house.

The park is deserted. During the day it's popular with the kids from school, a place to share a bottle of coke and eat hot vinegar-soaked chips from a hole torn in top of the paper. At thirteen I scratched my name deep into the dried bird shit and lichen on the wooden picnic table, just above 'KJ 4 MT' and 'Hunny King'. I wonder if it's still there.

Beyond the children's playground a bank slopes toward the creek, barely visible through the weeds and unpruned trees. A pipe the colour of dull bronze connects the banks like a metal stitch sewn into the grass. I'd like to be sitting astride that pipe now, leaning forward, letting my arms and body go limp until I drift off to sleep like a panther on a branch. But instead I am here. In a red box on top of the children's climbing tower peering out a small plastic view-dome. A tiny space that smells of wet nappies and earth. For now, my refuge. For now.

The criss-cross branch shadows have stretched halfway up the opposite bank since I arrived. The embankment trees are placid, their leaves drooped in a melt that was frozen before they touched the ground.

I breathe out, and manoeuvre my legs until I am kneeling. *Hmm. Slap a stamp on this box and post me to the Caribbean. Or Wellington would do. Anywhere.*

I place my palms face down against the floor and rest my knees on the tops of my hands like cushions. The aches return within minutes. I slide out and slip down into the tunnel, it's pretty roomy for kid-size. My spine curves with the blue plastic wall and I flex my feet against the opposite side. I plait my hair to pass the time, remembering my mother's touch....

'I had a bad dream, Mum.'

'Shh. It's alright.'

She strokes my hair and hums softly, her delicate palm caressing my troubles away.

My body is tensed, cold. I tuck my legs into my chest and stretch the sweatshirt over them to keep warm.

Outside, I hear the swing chains rattle, then another sound. *A mixture of green and blue.* It is music, a guitar, lightly strummed. And then I hear a male voice. He is singing to a melody that my spirit recognises even if my head does not.

One verse, one voice.

I bury my face in the sweatshirt, pressing into the hollow between my knees. The fabric is wet with tears by the time I realise the music has stopped and the musician is kneeling at the tunnel's mouth, the guitar balanced on his knee, his arm resting in its curve.

'Hey.'

I am not afraid; his voice is my assurance. I use a patch of sleeve to wipe my eyes and nose. I stare at the ribbed edge of my sleeve while my fingers tie knots in a stray piece of thread.

'You okay?'

'Yes,' I reply. 'Thanks.'

'Jeez, you had me worried for a minute. Usually when I see someone alone in a park at night crying it means something's wrong.'

My smile is on the inside, a small warm flash. He sits down just inside the entrance and begins to strum again, humming under his breath, as if to himself

The night air is chilling and I shudder in the dampness of my sweatshirt.

'Here, put this on.'

I accept his jacket. It is blue denim and takes a minute to mould from his shape to mine. The sheepskin lining has retained his warmth and smells faintly of the sea. From the corner of my eye, he is gazing up at the darkened sky, his face in profile.

'You look like someone I painted once,' I say.

'Musta been a good-lookin' fulla.'

My smile widens. 'Yeah, he was okay.'

'So, you paint, huh. Cool.'

I think of my table. My mother's photo.

'Do you live near here?' I ask.

He continues strumming, no set tune, just different chords.

'Nah. Just passing through.'

'Where are you from?'

'East Coast.'

His voice gives me goose bumps, warm ones, like the kind you get when you step into a spa pool. I cease with the questions, even though he doesn't seem to mind, and turn a little more to face him. Tied around the neck of his guitar is a green woven friendship bracelet and he is wearing a pounamu carving which in the dim light looks like a wave tip curled against his chest.

I rest my head against the tunnel wall and pull his jacket snugly around me, my eyelids falling shut. I am warm. Safe.

Discomfort wakes me and I shake bits of dirt and grit from my hair, the plaits now tangled and straying. He is still there, sleeping sitting up and holding onto his guitar.

Outside, the sky is turning pink. I gently place my palm against his arm and only when he stirs do I lift it.

I speak quietly. 'I'd better be going.'

'What's your name?'

'Teal.'

'Mine's Tane.'

'Thanks for your jacket, Tane.'

He doesn't take it back, but looks at me. Our eyes connect completely for the first time and neither can break the gaze. *A mirror lake.*

'Let me walk you home.'

He drapes the jacket over my shoulders and leads me out of the tunnel.

We stand at the garden gate, the house is hushed and through the glass front door I can see the hall light still on.

I brush the weeds growing between the concrete cracks in the path with my toe and again find the stray thread on my sleeve.

'I don't think I want to go in just yet.'

He nods. 'You wanna keep walking or sit a while?'

'Let's sit.'

Flakes of mint-green paint lift off the wooden porch steps with a little help from my fingernail. I fix my eyes on a clump of fern fronds stretching out between the gaps in the stairs, somehow continuing to grow and look beautiful despite being rooted in the darkest, most neglected spot of all.

He plucks the strings on his guitar, not hard twangs but gentle taps with his thumb, and I realise I could listen to him play music for the rest of my life. It's a strange feeling, like listening to the sound of whales or catching a glimpse of an aurora sky.

I tell him the reason I ran to the park. Tell him everything, about losing my mother and how I sometimes wish I could follow her. Tell him about the stupid mistake with the CD.

'You didn't mean for him to hear it.'

'I know. But it was their music. They danced to it, made love to it and –'

'And you needed to feel close to your mother. He'll understand that in time.'

'My father needs me now more than ever to –'

'What do *you* need?'

I snap the thread. My needs?

I need to be noticed I need to be cuddled and understood I need to be loved and listened to. I need someone to tell me everything's going to be okay.

Inside me, mortar chips begin to fall from the wall cemented around my heart.

'I need to hear my mother's voice. I've forgotten what she sounds like.'

He tilts his face to heaven, his eyes lost in the clouds and says, 'Close your eyes.'

I do as he says.

'Picture yourself alone with your mother. A time when you felt close to her.'

We are walking along the beach collecting shells in a basket. Our feet smart from the sand's heat, we move toward the water and paddle ankle-deep through the tide. The air is fresh, sea-scented....

'Do you see her?'

'Yes.'

'Clearly?'

'Yes.'

'Do you hear her?'

I pause, and listen.

The sun is warm on our backs, a flock of seagulls fight over a discarded bread crust. I am speaking about my hopes, my dreams. And then, over the sound of the waves splashing against our skin, over the breeze, over everything, I hear her.

'Paint from the heart, not the head. Paint what you feel, not what you think. Your horizon is endless, Teal. Trust me, a mother knows these things.'

The tears spill from beneath my eyelids. I remember the painting I did of the beach that day as soon as we got home.

After a moment I look to Tane. 'Thank you.'

He smiles, and nods.

'How did you learn to do that?'

He shrugs.

'Wait here.' I quietly enter the house and get something from my room. When I return, his guitar is resting against the stair rail and he is gazing up at the brightening clouds, the unwavering tilt of his eyes softened by the dawn.

I hand him a rolled-up piece of paper tied with a ribbon.

'It's one of my paintings. You can look at it later if you want.' *A thousand sundrops sparkling on tranquil green bay-water and a girl sitting on a rock.*

He tucks it into the pocket of his jacket, the left side, so it rests against his heart.

'Thanks.'

I know he will be leaving soon. I can't look up. My eyes focus on a lone ant zigzagging across the wooden floorboards. Tane unties the green friendship bracelet from the neck of his guitar and gestures to me. I hold out my hand and watch as he secures it around my wrist. When he looks up I see his eyes, earthy brown and shining. He reaches out, taking my hands in his, and the touch of his skin radiates a warmth that enters the coldest part of me.

'Someone once told me life is for the living. Reckon that's true.'

I rest my head on his chest.

'Where will you go now?' I ask.

'It's time I went home.'

'Will I see you again?'

'Well, if you're ever back east and you see a cool lookin' dude ridin' the waves at Makorori Point – chances are it'll be me. But I reckon if two people are destined to be together, they will be. Somehow.'

Before parting, he whispers into my hair, 'Kia kaha, Teal.'

I find my father alone at the kitchen table, his head buried in his arms. The floor creaks beneath my feet as he jerks his head around and pulls me onto his lap like he used to when I was a toddler. I feel his pain releasing with each heave of his chest and place my arms securely around his neck, clinging to each other until the tears subside.

I painted a mosaic the day my father told me everything would be okay. Greens, blues, reds and yellows, all my favourite colours bursting open like fireworks in the night sky.

The Prophecy

Trish Fong

I don't know what wakes me up first – the waves lapping cold against my calves, or nearly choking when I try to swallow with a sand-coated throat. I just lie there for a while blinking my eyes and trying to focus on the sky. The moon has moved several metres since I passed out and now it floats over the cliff-top pines. The sound of waves has turned irritating; it tears through me like a giant piece of Velcro ripping apart, together, apart, together....

Debris is strewn about me; crumpled beer cans, an almost-empty JDs bottle, my dak pouch. *Shit*! I jump up and retrieve the pouch just before a crashing wave slinks its way onto shore, darkening the sand around my feet. I glance around me then check my stash, give it a quick tuck into my leathers and collapse back onto the sand.

My head is hurtling toward the mother of all hangovers, and there goes my guitar floating out to sea. I stare a while at my imprint left in the sand, slowly disappearing with the incoming tide. Already the sharp heel marks of my boots are barely the size of eyebrows and a black sheet of water is reaching steadily towards the tiny hollow that pillowed my head.

It wasn't often my old man and me had a man-to-man talk. Or any kind of talk for that matter. But the one we had when I was eight wasn't to be forgotten.

I was shooting some hoops – well, putting a flat soccer ball through the crooked circle of number-eight wire stapled to the garage roof, when Dad leaned out the kitchen window and called me inside. It was a hot day and my shorts clung to my skin. I left the ball on the concrete and bounded up the front steps two at a time. Dad was sitting at the dining table. He must have just showered because his hair was damp; the scent of his aftershave stung the inside of my nose.

A plate of home-made biscuits and a glass of milk are on the table.

He motions me to sit down.

'How's the b-ball, boy?'

'Good.'

'Jay, I have something very important to tell you. But first finish your milk and biscuits.' I down the milk in non-stop swallows and pull the plate closer. The biscuits are a little light on the chocolate chips and a bit burnt on the bottom, but I smile and get stuck in.

Chewing, smiling, I think of the silver hard-covered notebook in my drawer. Nan gave it to me for Christmas and told me to write down special moments in it, so I could look back when I was older and remember what things were like when I was a kid. I was gonna give it to my cousin, she's always writing in her diary about boys and stuff, but I decided to keep it. I have been waiting for something important to happen to write about. I wonder if now is that moment?

Dad has lapsed into silence and seems lost in tracing the scratch marks on the table top with his thumb nail.

He often visits another world. Mum says it is a land of secrets and daydreams.

'Can I go there too?'

'No, son. It is your Dad's own private world.'

'Why does he look so sad when he's there?'

'Maybe because he can't share what he sees with us.'

'Oh.'

I push the plate with one remaining biscuit over to him.

He looks from the table to me and says, 'You will die by the time you're twenty-six.'

He could be reading the racing results from the paper. Same tone.

'W-what? When?'

'I told you. Before you're twenty-six.'

'B-but how?'

'I don't know. Could be any number of ways.'

He takes the last biscuit and puts it in his mouth, plucks a red apple from the bottom of the fruit bowl as the others tumble and bruise, then walks outside into the blazing sunlight.

I didn't write about our talk in my notebook.

That winter I got the flu. I thought I was going to die. I asked Dad if it was time, but he just shrugged his shoulders and sat on the edge of my bed trailing his finger along the tartan wool blanket.

I searched his eyes, deeply, looking for a hint or hidden clue. But I found nothing and started to feel dizzy, like looking over the edge of a steep cliff I closed my eyes and listened to him stand and leave my room in silence.

It was never mentioned again until my thirteenth birthday. After spending the day with my mates at the flicks and swimming down the waterhole, I got home to find Dad in the kitchen and 'Boogie Shoes' playing on the transistor.

'Hey Dad.' I open the fridge. 'Want some cake?'

'Your mother wanted to put candles on it, but she didn't have any.'

'It's cool. I don't need candles.'

Bopping to the music, I carry the cake and two glasses of juice to the table. 'How 'bout we celebrate me making it to halfway, eh Dad. Lucky thirteen and I haven't carked it yet.' I hold up my glass to toast.

His fists slam the table and the chair crashes to the floor as he stands towering over me. I spill juice on my new T-shirt.

'If I were you boy, I *wouldn't* be laughing.'

From then on I got it into my head that life for me was on a fast track. I had my first screw two months later, dropped out of school at fifteen and hitched the roads to see the world – well, Auckland. I needed money and took a job pumping gas. The graveyard shift suited me fine. My main customers were chicks, half-cut from partying at the night-clubs, buying hot dogs and cigarettes on their way home. Everything was sweet until the robbery; faced with a sawn-off shotgun, my heart pumping crazy, my only thought was, *So this is how it ends.*

But life continued.

I got involved with the underground dance scene and met Nicole. She was serving drinks behind the bar, black lace bra showing through a silver mesh top, her glossy hair piled high on her head. I couldn't resist. When we made love she wore her hair down, silky strands that reached her waist. I called her my gypsy sweetheart. We moved to an inner-city flat, waited tables by day and danced by night.

One summer morning we were lying on the car bonnet, smoking a joint, watching the dawn streak across the harbour.

'I'm four months pregnant.'

I looked at her stomach, hidden beneath purple velvet ruffles. I didn't know what to say; I was eighteen. It took me a while, then I thought, *Of course, this is meant to happen. I'm meant to experience this before my time is up.*

I figured it only fair to warn her of my father's prediction. Only it had become more than a prediction to me, it was set in concrete. And I was not prepared for her reaction.

She laughed.

'How can you believe such rubbish? That's the most crazy –'

I slammed her with my fists until she lay still on the asphalt. Everything still except the dark trail of her nose-mouth-blood and my pumping heart. I knew I had hurt the baby, I must have. When the police came the ambulance officers were still crouched over her.

Several times while I was inside Parry could have been the end. I didn't care. I taunted death, dared it to come and take me. Earned me the nickname Evil, after the daredevil Evel Knievel. A few stunts got my parole revoked and time extended. But I didn't care.

The only contact from Nicole was a letter saying we had a son and she was taking him overseas to live.

His name is Adam, he is 30% brain damaged.

I was released one week after my twenty-fourth birthday. I headed south, drifting from town to town, doing odd jobs in return for food and board.

Waiting for something to happen.

It is strange to me that I can't erase my father's words from my mind. I see myself rubbing out the words, like a pencilled mistake. But still the impression is left, existing unseen. I know his statement was crazy, that he couldn't possibly predict the future. But the impression remains.

So here I am, the eve of my twenty-sixth birthday, on a deserted East Coast beach with my name peed in the sand dunes and my guitar lost at sea.

I've imagined every type of scenario for my last day on earth and now I've reached this point I'm thinking, meteor shower, tidal wave, spontaneous combustion? May as well go out tanked. Waiting....

It is some time before my brain clears enough to realise it is past midnight. That the moon has completely disappeared and the horizon is brushed with blue-grey light. The tide is on the move out, one surge forward, three back. The sand is flat and perfect, unmarked, like the new pages of the silver notebook Nan gave me all those years ago. No imprints, no beer cans, no bottles. I stare over the indigo water, searching. With the first ray of dawn comes a vision: Nicole in her purple dress. She is holding our son by the hand, pointing to me and saying something.

I straighten my spine and try to smile, but they disappear in the sun's soft glow and I am left alone again.

I roll a fat joint and start to spark up, but the match drops from my hand as I hang my head between my knees and sob. Then wail. And I don't recognise my own voice.

Several minutes pass before the words emerge from my mind, gently releasing like small green shoots that only need a little light to appear.

I use my finger to write in the sand. *My name is Jay. Today is my 26th birthday and I am alive.*

Zeta Orionis

James George

I suppose it's – what do they call it? a statement of the obvious – to say prison makes your world smaller. But it's not that simple. Your world was small *before* you went into prison. You just leave yourself with nowhere else to go.

I was never much one for 'thinking outside the square' as the suits say. 'How it is is how it is is how it is ...' was my motto. I reckon I got surviving mixed up with living. Easy to do.

Some people even say prison is an education and you come out with more than you went in with. Unless they're talking about scars, nightmares maybe, then I'd say it's a bunch of crap. The only thing keeps you from dying of boredom is the fear maybe you won't live long enough to die of boredom. Stuff I could've done without learning.

I remember one day a priest (priest, vicar, whatever) came. He didn't much talk about God, just talked about us. He didn't know stuff-all about us, but he wanted to talk, so what the hell. Then a couple of minutes later someone turned on the radio and we drifted away to listen to the footy.

Later though, I thought about what he'd said. You get a lot of time to think, after you've counted every paint bubble and stain on the ceiling. But he set me thinking about what I had to do with God and what God had to do with me. And the answer was – nothing. I tried hard to be worried about it, but I couldn't.

'I don't reckon there is a god,' I said.

I figured he'd come up with all sorts of answers. Except for the one he did.

'Why?' he says.

Buggered if I could answer.

When I first got locked up, I told a couple of people Jacky ditched me because I went inside. That's the kind of stuff you tell yourself, but it's not true. She'd ditched me long before. Going inside just meant she didn't have to say it to my face. I'd at least spared her something. I reckon the kid was supposed to be some kind of last stand for us, a bridge, sort of. But I never crossed it. I was never one for building or crossing bridges.

I once read that New Zealand is slowly drifting north and in around thirty million years we'll be crossing the equator. Thirty million years, maybe I should mark the date on my calendar. And if it's true I'm planning to kick back on a hammock strung between a couple of coconut palms, sipping on one of them fancy cocktails with an umbrella in it.

There was an astronomy book I found in the library at Parry. Half the size of the table and mostly a bunch of maths stuff I couldn't figure. But there were them amazing photographs. Hell, I could never take photos of people without cutting half of them out, but these dudes get clear pictures of stuff thousands of light years away.

I sat there for hours, looking at the photos of new galaxies, solar systems being born. There were waves of pink dust, floating like sand in shallow water. And the stars like the tiny flecks of sun you see when you open your eyes beneath the waves. And most of all, the sculpture of the Horse's Head Nebula, astronomical number NGC 2024, in the quadrant of Zeta Orionis. I'd imagine myself drifting in the pink sky, rolling my body over like a swimmer taking a breath. Then turning onto my back, putting my hands behind my head. I'd wave, a tiny gesture no one was around to see. I'd smile. 'See ya around sometime, eh,' I'd say.

I thought about the ultrasound Jacky had done when we went to see the doc when she was five months gone. Before my sentencing, the last time. Squeezing the milky stuff over her then running the camera across her, like he was drawing the little one's shape on her skin. And there it came out on the TV screen. This tiny figure, delicate, almost transparent. Like a tiny horse, drifting in a field of stars.

'It's a little scary,' she said, 'seeing something alive inside you.' And it *was* scary. I hadn't thought about it until then. How you could be inside someone, part of you, you and not you. They gave us the photo. I wonder if she still has it.

The doc asked us if we wanted to know whether it was a boy or a girl. Jacky squeezed my hand and said, 'No, we don't want to know yet.'

I still don't know.

I ripped the page out of the book and put it up on the wall of my cell.

'What that?' the fellas used to say.

'The Horse's Head Nebula,' I'd say. 'Number NGC 2024. Quadrant of Zeta Orionis. And it's a part of me.'

The red giant, Antares, in the constellation of Scorpius, is two hundred times the diameter of the sun. Astronomical name Alpha Scorpii. You could fit the earth inside it a couple of million times. Everything; the continents, the ocean, the people, everything. What is it can create something so huge, and so far away no one will ever reach it. But it's dying, like those giant trees up north. Nothing bad, just the dying part you get after the living part. One day it will go supernova then the only thing left will be darkness. A black hole.

I wonder if he/she ever thinks of dad. I wonder if *you*, wherever you are, ever think of your father. Maybe even just once in a while. Or is whoever Jacky's living with 'Dad' now. Maybe you don't know anything else. People think when someone goes inside, freedom's the biggest thing they give up, but it isn't. Not even close.

So you'd be ten ... no, eleven years old now. Time enough to forget everything. But how can you forget what you never knew? And how long will I be able to remember.

What would I say anyway, if I did see you. What is there to say. I could start at the beginning, the happy times, then just skip everything else. Why not? Yep, my life, pages ripped out, the good times measured in minutes and the bad times measured in years.

You'd think in ten years I could've thought up a name for you. Even just a make-believe name. But there's this hole in me that just won't let me. As if I'm not supposed to. Astronomers have thought up names for eight thousand different stars and then some, but I can't think of one child's name.

So I reckon I'd just say:

Hiya, do you know who I am? No? It's OK. It's not important. Wow, look at you, all grown and everything. Got your own bunch of friends. A person needs friends, and family too. People to look after you. And more important – people for you to look after. That's what everyone needs. How's Mum … does she ever say anything about me? No, no need to answer. I don't want to know. I just want to see you and you know, just sit and talk for a while. Hey, don't go….

On Mars there's a volcano named Olympus Mons, three times the height of Mount Everest. Astronomers once thought the streams of colour visible in the telescope's eye were canals. One dude even took a stab at the population there. Came up with twenty million or some such. Twenty million what?

No it's OK, like I said, I just want to talk. Tell me the names of your friends. Nah, no heavy reason, I'm just interested, you know. What do you like doing? What's your favourite kai? What's the icky stuff you doooooon't like to eat. What do you like watching on TV? I'd just like to know. No big thing.

The canals on Mars turned out to be sandstorms.

If you don't mind, I'd kinda like to stick around a while, not real close, but you know, close enough just to be able to see you every day. Wouldn't even have to be every day. Just now and then. Nah, you wouldn't have to talk to me or anything, well, not unless you wanted to. And then it'd be sweet. Just you and me.

There's a space probe named *Voyager*, been sent out to the end of the solar system and beyond, to send back info. Only, you see there's no program in it which'll make it turn around and come home. It'll keep sending photos to Earth until it either goes out of range or just runs out of juice and dies.

No it's OK, I'm not a stranger. Not really. I just haven't been around for a while. Been away. But I'm here now and that's all that matters eh.... You know I could maybe walk you to school, no it's OK, I don't want to crowd you, just want to see – to be – a little piece of your life. Like I said, it's no big thing.

The *Voyager* space probe will never reach Zeta Orionis, never even come close. It's just too far away. But I can see it, now I'm out. Now I got more than just a piddly little window or a wire fence to look through. On a real clear night, I just have to wait for the right time and I can hold my hand up next to it. My tiny hand against something so big. I can see it, walk my fingers around it, do everything but touch it. And with my bare eyes the whole nebula is just a smudge.

No it's OK, I don't have to walk you to school. I understand. It's not cool, with your mates. No, really. It's OK. I'll just stand back here a bit and watch. I just wanted to....

I still have the photo from the book, all crumpled and flattened out and crumpled again. Stuck with Sellotape at the edge of the busted glass of a mirror. Antares, Aldebaran, Alpha Centaurus, Beta Persei, Cygnus.... I can think of a hundred more names, but not yours.

No, it's OK. Really. You have your own life. I understand. See ya around some time, eh....

Horse's Head Nebula, NGC 2024. Quadrant of Zeta Orionis.
The closest I'll ever come to knowing you.

Rainsong

James George

In my last year at high school, we went on this class trip to the aquarium. I'd been hassling Mrs Cleary the day before, so she got mad. 'Leonie,' she said, 'when are you going to learn you're not the only person in the world.'

I thought about it, about being the only person in the world, and I liked the idea. Just me, lying back in a huge bath filled with water that never goes cold. Nah, not water. Milk. Warm milk. Oh yeah and a million videos and CDs and no one to hassle me. Bliss.

That night I woke up to the sound of rain on my window. I lay listening for a while, then lifted my blankets off and moved out the door and down the hall, pausing at Mum and Dad's room. I didn't go in, just leaned my head against the door, one hand on the handle. I stood there for ages, listening to my breathing and theirs mingling with the rain. I thought about going in, but I didn't.

Then, out of the corner of my eye, I saw a face. Well, sort of. Like when you're looking at something and then close your eyes and there's just a ghost of the image, half formed. A sketch on the inside of your eyelids. And it was singing, not words, just a wave sound, like wind or water. Or it could have just been the rain. A rainsong.

At breakfast Dad and Mikey and me sat at the kitchen table while Mum bustled round. And I knew – I suppose for the first time – their faces weren't my face. My face had been drawn from somewhere else.

Oh, I knew I was adopted – sure – but what had it ever meant? Adopted. Mikey used to tease me about it, but so what? It was just a word. Like matchbox or elephant or Bulgaria. And I'd always known

I had another Mum and Dad somewhere, but your Mum and Dad are the people you can hear breathing at night, not someone who makes a fingerprint then leaves. But sitting at the table, among faces which weren't mine, and never had been, I realised adopted wasn't just a word. It was a someone. A me.

It rained all the way to the aquarium. I leaned back in the big, cushy bus seat and turned my face to watch the drops trickling down the window. I sat staring at my face in the glass. I scrunched up real close, so close our cheeks touched. Like, for a moment, we were sisters. And I began to sing, real soft, my breath steaming the glass. Circling both of us.

At the aquarium the sharks were beautiful but scary, and the penguins were cute, but there was this one tank that captured me. Some rocks, a plastic coral reef, and a sea horse, just hovering there. And the closer I got, the more he seemed to be looking at me. He began to drift, head nodding, as if there were music in the water.

'Hey there,' I said. 'Where do you come from?'

I blew onto the glass, misting it. He went on dancing, in my little halo of breath. I moved my hand down so he was almost in my palm.

'You and me have something in common,' I said. ''Cause I come from somewhere else too.'

And I think then I could hear his music. So I began to sing, sing him my rainsong.

In the night I had the dream again. There it was, looking down from the ceiling, and I suppose I knew then it was my own face. I got up and walked to my door and out into the hallway, and there it was leading me all the way. When I stopped at Mum and Dad's door the face kept on moving, moving away.

His name is Jackson and he has the softest voice. Delicate. Like something hidden away in a jewellery box. When I first saw him, he looked like just another rugby-hero type. All swagger. But his voice didn't fit. So I'd watch him – out of the corner of my eye of course – to see if it was his swagger or his voice which didn't fit, because they just didn't go together. I couldn't make up my mind. It wasn't much of a secret his dad was in jail and Jackson had been shuffled from home to home, but if any of that was in him somewhere, it wasn't in his voice, or his eyes.

I was sitting under a tree when he came wandering up, then stopped when he saw me. He raised his eyebrows and stood, so I shifted further into the shade and he sat down.

'The aquarium was cool, huh,' he said.

I nodded. 'Did you see the sea horse?'

'Yeah. I thought it looked sad.'

'Sad?'

'Yeah, you know. Like it didn't belong there, stuck in a little glass case.'

He picked up a leaf, cradled it in his fingers.

'Sorry,' he said, 'that sounded kinda dumb. But it just got me thinking.'

'It's not dumb. I thought the same thing.'

'Some stuff's just hard to understand,' he said. 'That's all.'

And he said it in his 'jewellery box' voice. I reached out, held my hand beneath his. He looked at me, smiled, and dropped the leaf into my palm.

When I was little Mum used to bath me and tell me all these wild and wonderful stories, which I was always the centre of. I'd be a princess in Arabia, or maybe Guinevere or even someone she made up. She'd soap my tummy and walk her fingers over my skin and tell me about all the things I'd do. All the handsome princes who would come searching for me. I'd lie back in the bath and giggle and she'd touch the tip of my nose with soap suds and I'd blow them away. Princes, hah. Looking for me. Princes with castles and servants and white horses and whole countries named after them.

'And whole rooms filled with ice cream?' I'd say, and she'd nod and say, 'Hokey Pokey.'

I guess I never thought that somewhere there was another mum who maybe wanted to tell me stories about princes and touch the end of my nose with soap suds.

The first time Jackson and I lay together there were no skyrockets going off and waves rolling into the shore, but there was a rightness about it. Like something missing had found a place to be. We were both scared, I suppose. Scared of ourselves, of what we were capable of. So I just listened to his voice, his breathing. Held it against me, inside me.

Afterward we laughed at our fumbling. Like we'd been two little kids trying to play the piano or something, maybe with boxing gloves! Hitting all the wrong keys. And I think I loved him for that more than the warmth and fullness of his body against me. That he could laugh about it, about himself. About how we both knew yesterday and today and tomorrow were not now the same and never would be again.

When I missed my time I got scared and made the appointment to see our doctor, on the quiet. She was cool about it. No heavy adult trip. She said I should just call her Jill. We did the test and then she took a plastic lunch box from beneath her desk and we went out behind her office to this little garden with benches and some shady trees and we sat.

'Can I tempt you?' she said, offering me one of her sandwiches.

'Nah. It's OK. I'm cool.'

'Salad and French dressing?'

'Nah. It's OK. What's on the other one?' I said.

'Peanut butter.'

'Peanut butter?'

'I like peanut butter.'

'Sprung!'

'What?'

'It's OK. Your secret's safe with me.'

She laughed and slipped her feet out of her shoes and sat with her bare toes on the grass, wiggling them in the sun. We talked for ages, about me, about the future.

Then she said 'six weeks' and I nodded and we talked some more. And amongst what she said I remember hearing the word 'adopted'. I looked up at her. Not really seeing her. Just hearing the word and looking up at the leaves and the sky. The pale smoke trail of a jet plane against the blue.

I wanted to tell Jackson first. I tried to think of the words. We were walking down by the stream and every couple of minutes I was going to say it but I couldn't.

He crouched next to the reeds above the water's edge.

'When I was little we used to fish down here,' he said. 'Dad used to bring me. Just me and him. He was OK back then.'

'I didn't know there were any fish in this river.'

'There were then. Don't know where they went.'

'You caught them all.'

He laughed.

'I wish,' he said. 'I never caught stuff-all.'

'Do you think much about your dad?'

He took a deep breath and let it out. Then he nodded.

'Sorry,' I said.

'It's OK. I can't change what is.'

'Maybe we can.'

He lifted a stone from the path, sent it skimming across the water. I stepped in front of him. He looked up. I tried to tell him, but the words wouldn't come. So I reached down and took his hands and lifted them up against me, under my T-shirt. Running them across my tummy, against my bare skin. Bringing them together and holding them to me. He raised his eyebrows and smiled. I held his hands tighter. His face was beginning to blur. I tried to blink him clear again. Then I saw through the tears that his eyes were huge.

'Really?' he said. 'Wow.'

I nodded and he moved close against me, touched his lips against my wetted cheek and we stood there, rocking. I could hear footsteps of people walking by, the sound of cicadas. The running water of the river. We just stood there for ages. Never letting go.

Jill came and sat with me when I told Mum and Dad. Dad picked up his tea cup and stared into it. He put it down then picked it up again and put it back down. I don't think he even took a sip. Then he got up and went out. Mum sat down on the couch and just said my name over and over, like I'd got lost somewhere and she was trying to find me. Then she looped her arm under mine and we sat, no one talking. Listening to Dad getting out his gardening tools, and his footsteps on the path.

Jill said there were some questions to think about and I heard the word 'adopted' again. I got up and went out to where Dad was lost among his roses. He sort of glanced sideways, but not at me. He reached out to drop some weeds into a pile on the grass. But when the weeds had fallen he left his hand there, just hanging. I walked up behind him and slid my fingers into his and they closed around me. He didn't say a word. Then with his other hand he lifted the hose and pulled the trigger and a spray came out over the roses and we just stood there, listening. I raised my index finger and wrote the word 'adopted' into the falling water. Invisible, unheard. Never to be spoken or written again. And I began to hum. Hum my rainsong.

Footprints

James George

Nana,

Auē. That's what you used to say. Remember? Whenever there was something you couldn't agree with, or just didn't understand. Maybe you'd just seen some stuff even if you wouldn't talk much about it. I reckon maybe I have now, too.

Kataraina

All the good little girls kept diaries. I didn't write much in mine, but I stuck things in it. We had this jar of paste, where the lid came with a sort of ice-block stick thingy attached to it. Smelt like seawater.

I used to cut pictures out of magazines – Dusty Springfield, Dionne Warwick, all cosy in my little book. Like those displays of butterflies you see in museums, just hanging there with pins through them.

Nana, I know you'll never get to read these words, but that doesn't matter. I heard that when you were a kid they whacked you with a cane just for speaking your own language, so you just decided never to learn to read theirs and that was that. Done. Your own personal utu.

I read somewhere that when Vikings died, their people would put their body in a little boat and set it on fire and push it out to sea. Back home, I used to imagine the house was a boat and the farm was ocean and if we wanted to we could just lift the anchor and sail away.

Home, sleeping with Matty. He would start off in his own bunk but end up in mine. Then when his dreams came he would start kicking out. Ten knees and elbows and twenty bloody feet.

'In the city, kids got rooms of their own,' I'd say to Mum, and she'd say, 'Look around you, nei. Does this look like the city to you, Miss high-and-mighty?'

And then; 'When you win the Golden Kiwi you can buy yourself a big house with a dozen bedrooms,' she'd say.

Yeah yeah.

I bet city girls didn't have to sleep with their little brothers.

We moved away from you, when I was still a little kid, after that bust-up you had with Mum. I never knew what the bust-up was about. I only saw you a few times after that, when Pop would take us up to you, without Mum knowing. Dion would moan and want to leave, and Matty would just stare. First time Pop took us up, I didn't even recognise you.

After Dion headed off for 'The Smoke' it was just me and Matty against the world. Pop made Matty a tree house. Tree house, hell, it was three feet off the ground. Pop wouldn't build it any higher 'cause they were afraid Matty'd fall out and hurt himself. And he'd go there and sit, staring out at the world like he was at a bus stop, but the bus never came. We'd have to drag him out for his kai or he'd starve.

There was the time me and him were lying on our tummies on the floor watching the old movie *The Sound of Music*. Julie Andrews comes running up that hill and starts singing away. So Matty jumps up and starts spinning around with his arms up, yelling his head off. I got up too, and there we were, both of us spinning like helicopter whatsits and shouting. Then Pop come in from the woodpile with that Dobermann voice of his and we shut up.

Nana, you reckoned when Matty was born, all of him never came out. The part of him that 'thinks' stayed behind in the place where babies are made. But you sensed him, more than any of us.

'That boy's not dumb,' you said. 'He's special, that's all.'

Dion would make a face, but only behind your back.

'Anyone make fun of this boy,' you said, 'they'll have to deal with my walking stick, nei.'

Eighty-five years old and still with that big 'move-mountains' voice. There's been times when I could've done with that voice.

I'd go swimming at the back of Charlie Mohi's place, where the rain had filled in the old quarry. Stretch out on the rocks and lie still like a leaf. I'd draw my knees up and sit staring at my reflection in the water, so still the image was perfect, painted almost. 'Hey,' I'd say, 'you ain't so bad. You could pass for OK looking.' Then some bird would land on the water and I'd shatter.

Sometimes I used to wait until everyone was asleep, then sneak out my window and go back in the dark. I'd lay on those rocks again, with an old cardie over me, or a blanket if it was real cold. Looking up at the moon, shining like a pearl. I'd imagine it was a spotlight, just for me. The rocks were a stage and the sound of the water was people clapping. I'd lie there, wrapped tight in the blanket. But inside I was dancing.

Then I'd go home to the yard polluted with cannibalised cars. Wading the creeks for watercress, sometimes eels. Pipis from the coast. I bet none of the models in the magazines had to dig in the sand for shells. I used to dream of the day the moon would vanish into the horizon and so would I.

I starved myself to stay slim, take my dinner back to my room, and hide it in my dresser draw until Matty came in to go to bed. I'd sit on the floor and watch him wolf down every last scrap. After I'd tucked him in he'd lie there in silence, his doll's fingers picking crumbs off the blankets. Those huge eyes, too big for his tiny face, staring at me.

When I told Dion, over the phone, about how I was going to be a famous model, he just laughed. 'They'll pay for your black ass to be in magazines?' he said. I don't reckon I ever saw him as my brother again.

The last time I saw you, I hitched up to your place. You were so frail then. I remember I didn't say much. We sat on your verandah and you looked out towards the hills and started to roll off a bunch of names of people I'd never heard of. You were telling me my history and I never knew it. I didn't want to know.

When I left there, I left you my diary.

The night I went, Matty was playing on the floor with his toy trucks. I wanted to hug him or something, but he'd just start kicking and clawing. Words were no use, he never did know what to do with words. I closed the window behind me. I looked back once and he was standing there, staring. He raised a hand. I raised mine too, to wave back. But he was just reaching for a moth on the glass.

In the city I got a job in a takeaway, had some photos done and put into a fancy portfolio which I lugged around the agencies. The first line-up I went to, turned out they just wanted hands, for a soap advert. But not mine. The guy took one look at me and said, 'You don't have the right face.'

'But you only want hands,' I said.

It was always the same routine. Blokes standing with their legs planted, scratching their chins like a butcher looking for the best cut. Wanting to poke at you. Hours waiting for line-ups, seconds taken to make the decision. Then the blonde got the job.

If the magazines didn't want my black ass, others would. And they'd pay. That's what Angel said, the first time I met her. Angel. Leaning into the shop doorway out of the rain, lighting her ciggy off mine. She stepped back against the glass and looked me over.

'Pay top dollar,' she said. 'If you're smart. The ones in the suits pay the best. The ones that don't roll their car windows down more than an inch to gawk at you. If they could screw you through that little bitty window opening they would. They wouldn't even have to touch you.'

She blew a smoke ring. 'Top dollar,' she said. I told her to get lost. She laughed.

'You will,' she said. 'I seen your kind a hundred times. Every bus from the sticks brings a couple more. But if you try and work this street I'll kick you all the way back to Te Nowhere.'

I got some work, in shopping malls. Bikini in the middle of winter. Sucking my tummy in until my muscles hurt and I had cramps. All that stuff I used to carry around in my handbag, like a soldier going to war. A bit of blusher, vanishing cream. Eye drops because the bloody lights stung. Eyeliner pencil, seven different lipsticks....

There was a guy (there was always a guy). 'You've got talent,' he'd say. 'You could be something.' They knew it off by heart. Polyester suit, strands of thinning hair plastered flat across an empty scalp. A couple of flashy rings or maybe a medallion. 'Come with me and you'll go places.' Places. Yeah, I went places.

A year making myself up, then four years making myself down. Way down. You could always say you were only doing the other stuff just to pay the bills, until the next modelling job came up. Or the 'big break', heehee. But 'next' can be a hell of a long word. Just four letters. I reckon one letter for every year I ended up waiting to be 'discovered'.

'What kind of massage do you want today?' I'd say. 'We got "The Gentleman's", "The Deluxe" and "The Super Deluxe".' Always the same question: 'How much for the Super Deluxe?' They'd never look at my face. I could have had a bag over my head. And they always wanted a shower afterwards, before they went home to the missus, the 2.4 kids and Lassie.

Once I even got out. Yep, got brave and packed it all in and took off with my savings to Oz. Gonna head up north, Queensland maybe, where the wild horses are. Become a sugarcane cowgirl.

I got as far as Kings Cross.

When the punters were on top of me, they'd let out one last grunt and then go all limp, like a rag squeezed out. I'd be staring at some speck on the ceiling, imagining I was in an ocean or a river somewhere. Maybe just the lake in the old quarry. You see, it wasn't me they dumped into. 'Me' didn't come into it. 'Me' still lived in my mangy old diary. Like Matty's inside self, 'me' stayed hidden. I'd locked the door long ago.

Did you ever catch that moth, Matty. Sometimes I think *our* boats were burned the day we were born.

Then Nana you sent me that box of stuff. Buggered if I know how you found me. Must've had one of the cuzzies look for me, I guess. There was a single sandal I'd left at your place when I was tiny. A dry old piece of a biscuit I'd bitten into when I first got teeth, which had these puny little teeth marks. A tiny, broken half-moon.

And that old diary.

I stuck the tiny sandal on the mantelpiece whatever dump I was staying in at the time and then forgot about it when I moved on. Wish I could remember what happened to the biscuit.

But I kept the diary.

What little writing there'd been had just faded away and the pictures were falling to bits. But there was a faint set of muddy footprints, from a cat I'd once had, back home. She'd just shown up on the doorstep one day. I'd fed her, loved her even. Not for long, but so what. I don't remember her walking across my page, just finding the paw marks and being pissed off. The rubber on the end of my pencil wouldn't get rid of them, just scratched the paper. Then one day she was gone, just like that. I don't even remember what I'd named her.

I wonder if Julie Andrews left footprints in the grass.

My daughter was taken from me thirty seconds after she was born. I wanted it that way. I didn't want to see my face in her. Didn't want to see some tiny mark that would stick in my memory and keep coming back to me. Some hint in her eyes. Anything. An elbow, a foot maybe. Anything that would say 'you and me'. I'd done right by her. I hadn't killed her. Flushed her down some sink and down into the sewer. No, she got to breathe. But I couldn't look at her, so I just rolled over and stared at the wall.

Then I saw this tray, a silver dish, all shiny with the theatre lights. Just sitting there on a table like some huge diamond. So I focused on that, tried to block out the sound of her voice by screaming inside. I guess I'd somewhere along the line I'd swapped dancing inside for screaming. But even with all of that, I heard a nurse say, 'It's a girl.' I nodded my head, focused on my diamond again. I'd done right by her. I gave her life. Maybe to most people that wouldn't be enough, but it was all I could give.

She got to breathe.

Nana, the last time I saw you, you told me about slaves, in the old days. About how you're not a slave because of what you are, but because of what you hold on to or let go. And how people can't take your heart, you can only give it away to them.

Then you laid them crumpled old hands over me.

'Wherever you go Kataraina,' you said, 'Don't you ever forget the road home. You promise me now.'

'I promise,' I said. A kid's promise.

I must've lost track of that last bit somewhere.

The grapevine tells me that Matty and even Dion went to your funeral. But I didn't. I didn't even know.

So the weirdest thing happened, I started writing in the diary again, on the blank pages I'd never got to. So:

Hey diary, it's me. I've found you again. Moth-eaten old thing you are. (The diary I mean – not me. Although, have you looked at yourself in the mirror lately, girl?)

So ... well ... here goes, just a buncha random thoughts, the thoughts I couldn't put down a million years ago when I closed you for the last time.

1) I think the cat's name was Truffles, or Ruffles, or Muffles, or....
2) You were wrong, Nana, about one thing; you can give your heart away.
3) Paste now comes in little plastic bottles with a soft rubber titty thing on the top.
4) I used to hate Julie Andrews.
5) The cat's name could have been Muffet. Or Buffet. Or Tuffet.

This morning before dawn I went to the beach and walked round on the sand. I lifted up my skirt and used it to scoop a couple of handfuls of sea water, then carried them up the sand and tipped them into my footprints, leaving a speckled pattern, like words on a page. I knelt, taking the wet sand onto my fingertip.

Sometimes I dream; I'm sitting cross-legged in front of you, holding one of your hands like it was treasure. Looking into your face, moving through the lines of it, the creases. Like the lines tattooed into your own Nana's skin. But not ink, just years. I reach out, run a finger down across them. You don't say a word. You just let me touch, feel, on and on. Like a little baby in a crib, feeling its own skin, feeling the air, the world, for the first time. You just sit there, letting my fingers find every inch of you. Every second of your life, carved into your skin, your pale grey hair. Painted into your grey eyes.

Then I stand and you stand with me, not old anymore, but any age, or no age at all. You slide your arms around me. I can't feel your hands, the end of your arms, there's just this hugeness to you. No corners, no edges.

Like the reflection of moon I used to watch, lying there in my blanket. Something I could slip into and float within.

I walked back into the sea until it was up to my waist. Lifted off my dress and tied it around my neck and walked on, letting the ocean find me, all of me. The bits that people paid for and the bits that no one wanted.

I looked at my face in the water, just glimpses. The sea was way too alive to leave my face still like it had been on that creek. I let myself sink, let the water find my nipples, my folds, my inside parts. And I thought of that cat and lifted a paw, began to lick off the taste of the sea. I stood washing myself, letting the sea wash over me.

6) *The punters with the best suits were the worst. It doesn't mean the punters with the worst suits were the best.*
7) *The cat's name was Huffy, no, Puffy. Muffy? No definitely not Muffy.*
8) *Some things can't be bought and sold like paste. I don't care what kind of bottle they come in.*
9) *I don't hate Julie Andrews any more.*
10) *Nana was right, actually. You can't give your heart away. You can lose it. Leave it someplace and forget where you put it.*

The cat's name doesn't matter. I think I'll just call her … me.

Hello Me. Nice to meet you. My name is Kataraina, and I'm coming home.

On a Wave

Wiremu Grace

The tide washed across the board's surface in front of her. She stretched as if waking from a long sleep, then turned her face to the sun, welcoming the relaxing warmth. Listening for the beat of a heart.

'I can do anything,' she quietly said to herself.

Moments later she jerked her head and gripped the board with white knuckles. Pushing forward she ducked through the wall, taking white foam in her mouth as if first communion, spitting salt.

Even from a distance, she could tell they were nervous.

'We did it when we were kids, it's not that hard!' she yelled over the hiss of waves on the shore. And now, facing the surging lumps of water that excited and frightened her, she felt a tide in herself, turning.

They'd met in the sun. Sun-browned arms in the sun-burned grass. Sweaty brown skin, melting in the summer's heat. A picture she owned inside, that couldn't be stolen or taken away. The golden times, when Midas touched the world.

Seeing the crest break before her she dug the bareness of her arms deep, grinding her teeth, heading parallel to the violent onslaught of energy. She was just able to negotiate her board into safe water, puffing. She sat upright looking directly into another clear face bearing down on her.

She succumbed to the power when there was no use in fighting. Turning over, and over, and over. Darkness, enveloping.

Drowning in turmoil. Blindness. Generations of blindness, passed down through the years, stalking his shadows.

And giving life only sped up the process he had playing in his mind.

How were they to know he was only borrowing what little he had?

Finally he turned away and took on his journey himself, following behind. A shadow of a shadow.

She kicked from the bottom, finally clearing the surface, her mouth agape, sucking air.

'Precious fucking life ... precious ... fucking ... life! Scars will heal, you'll hardly ever know. Time is the greatest healer.' She heaved.

Releasing her breath, she smoothed her silk black hair away from her face. Squinting stinging eyes to the sun.

They taught her. Nurtured her, brought her into the world as if she were the newborn. How could they possibly have known darkness when they hadn't lived? And she led them in hand as if the leader. Dress, school, home, people, friends and family, she showed them. And they pulled her, pushed her, shoved her, forcing the light in her eyes. Unable to turn away.

'Only me, it's only me!' she screamed. Head back, opening her mouth to the sky. And the seagull returned with a karanga of its own, wings tipped with ease, following the vast blue to where it meets the sea. As it has always done.

Painfully waiting, waiting to release the words, speaking only in darkness, the voice that hadn't spoken for so long. A beginning pain, deep in that place. Turning again. Turning.

The tide washed in its familiar voice. And again she lay, listening. Her heart beating life, warming in the sun. Still.

Clean sheets tucked with smoothed blankets. A familiar warmth, when Mum came with secure arms. She always liked to listen when Mum came. With an ending the way it's supposed to, how stories are supposed to end.

And the end became the beginning.

The swell broke the flat horizon like a brush of paint over a clear white page. She dipped her arms, confidently stroking. From the shore the kids pointed and yelled, deaf on her ears. Across the face she pulled, joining the pace of the thick surge of unbroken water.

Gathering momentum they met, her final strokes silently slipping behind. Standing, taking the steep drop down the wave, she focussed. Thrusting her hips, pulling the thick phallic shape into line. Precision entwining itself through threads of insecurity. Nostrils flared, arms spread, legs wide, teeth clenched, clutching quivering power. Passing countless reflections, still on the water. Salt-water tears merging with all that had ever been cried.

Could the sea extinguish the sun?

And they were there, clothes wet, dragging her to shore pulling her back and laying her down. Faces, questioning, loving. 'You did it! You did it Ma! You really did it!' they repeated over and over. Wiping the salty tears from her body. Straddling her, pulling the laugh from where they knew it would be.

Letting go now….

One Night

Aroha Harris

It was Friday night again. Puawai was at the kitchen bench, preparing the usual post-pub boil-up – kūmara the colour of sunshine, a whole pork backbone, watercress. And doughboys – the kind that caused her dad to boast, 'No one makes doughboys like my girl, just like the ones Mum used to make.' Meanwhile, Dad and her brother Kapi showered, soaping and rinsing away the dust and gum and monotony of a fifty-hour week at the sawmill. Dad poured an icy beer down his throat and said 'Aaaah. Didn't even touch the sides.' Kapi chose carefully between Levis. Levis blue? Levis black? By six o'clock, he and Dad were off, blatting down the road to Happy Hour at the Queen Mary Tavern.

Emery arrived, usually pronounced Em'ry, although his Mum and Nanny called him Emmy. Sometimes he called himself e'Mere, and said that the *Queen Mary* was named after him. If Emery and Puawai thought about it, they would probably see that they were best friends. Cousins, schoolmates, confidantes, they had designed fantasy weddings together, chosen music and readings for their funerals, and named their imaginary children. On Fridays, Emery took it upon himself to dress his 'Flower', which he could only do while lip-synching to Macy Gray:

I still light up like a candle burnin' when he calls me up.

He bemoaned the absence of glam in Puawai's wardrobe.

I still melt down like a candle burnin' every time we touch.

He threw his hands up at the over-abundance of jeans and sweatshirts.

Oh say what you will, he does me wrong and I should be gone.

Puawai yelled over the music that she had bought a new top. It was still in the bag.

I still – be loving you baby and it's much too much.

Emery was in the kitchen again. The shirt was good. Turquoise was a great colour for her, perfect for her skin tone. But she really should take him with her when she went shopping. 'You could be so much more adventurous, honey,' he said.

At seven, the two friends relaxed in front of *Shortland Street.* Emery provided commentary and storyline predictions. Afterwards he played Macy Gray again while Puawai showered and put the boil-up on hold. Around nine they walked to the pub at the top of the hill. Puawai's last obligation for the night would be to taxi home Dad and Kapi and an assortment of mates.

Emery and Puawai fell over their laughter and through the double doors, and there was Kapi, hassling the staff to turn up the jukebox. He relented when he saw his sister, and ordered her a gin and tonic – single in a tall glass, lots of ice – just like Emery had taught her. The one drink would last her all night. Dad was at his usual table, closest to the bar and facing the TV.

Then, in a gasp, the typical Friday night was transformed. 'It's Dane Rauhanga, Dane Rauhanga. Talking to Dad.'

Emery's eyes widened and he feigned a shriek. 'Get over there. Get introduced. I'll be there in a minute, just need to compose myself.' He headed to the bar.

Dad had already seen her and was waving her over. 'Here's my girl,' he said, greeting her with the outstretched hand that only a father can offer.

'Hey Dad.'

'This is Dane Rauhanga. I knew his father – used to be a regular here one time.'

Puawai said 'Kia ora,' and leaned across the corner of the table to receive the pending kiss and handshake. She imagined the kiss contained a trace of intimacy, a momentary pause on her lips. Kapi arrived with her drink. He nodded a gruff 'Kia ora bro' in Dane's general direction, and went back to the pool tables. Then Emery was there, lining up for his hongi. 'Dane Rauhanga, eh,' he beamed.

'That's me,' Dane said.

'It is indeed. Saw you yesterday, you gave that talk on te reo and public broadcasting.' Emery brought Dane up to speed. Explained that he and Puawai were both at tech. He was doing design. She was doing journalism. The Māori students had guest speakers twice a semester, and getting Dane in was their best score yet.

Puawai didn't mind Emery's undisciplined rush of information. It gave her a chance to view Dane Rauhanga. He was tall, and maybe older than she believed. His face chiselled by the hands of a master carver. Honed into assured lips and promising eyes. Proud. Brown. She inhaled him. She was just about to mentally attach his name to one of her fantasy weddings when he said he recognised her. Hadn't she asked the first question?

'Yeah,' she said, 'asked you about the new Māori-language ads.'

'Yesss,' Emery intervened. 'We do not like the Māori-boy-slash-Pākehā-girlfriend scenario.' He grimaced. 'Not a good look. Handsome young tāne like him should have a beautiful Māori gal by his side – or a stunning Māori queen.' He laughed.

Puawai agreed, and Dane was interested in what she thought – about the ads, the latest *Mana* magazine, theft of art, Māori politicians. In fact, Dane was interested in Puawai, period. He was happy to accompany her on conversations that visited the four winds and exhausted every current affair. They judged and assessed, laughed, flirted and critiqued. And, when Kapi and Dad were ready to leave, Emery insisted Dane follow them home. After all, half the locals did on Friday nights.

By that time, Dane had Puawai fully assessed. He liked the packaging. She had the blackest black hair he had ever seen. It poured down her back to her waist. She was great – curvy, fluid, very natural. And she was definitely bright. He liked that too. But he also sensed a more elusive quality just beneath her surface – a soft centre, a slight apprehension. Whatever it was, he would have to take the lead, because she was not the pursuing kind. Hell, she even limited her eye contact.

At the small impromptu party that followed, he took control of the guitar.

A few confident strums, and his honey-coated baritone unfurled across the room.

I ngā wā o mua....

Puawai responded, molten-voiced.

Ko au tō hoa pūmau....

His sound, bold and throaty, licked over and under hers – fiery, eternal.

Tū mokemoke koe....

And Puawai was alive, singing through her nerve-endings.

Maumahara noa ahau.

Their voices liquefied, fuelling the flames that had warmed their evening together. Before long, Puawai found herself walking hand in hand with Dane Rauhanga, still chatting and singing, back along the stilled and moon-struck road to the motel just beyond the pub. Later, in the quiet of his room, they made love – instinctively, like their harmonies – twirling, searching, searing, consuming. And she was alive again.

When she woke the next morning, she could hear him in the shower, doing Ray Charles. *I can't stop lo-ving you....* She sat up in the pillows, expectant, eyes closed. She could still smell him, feel his breathing on her neck, the soft kisses that lingered but barely touched. Mostly though, she could hear his ethereal whisperings. 'God, you're gorgeous.' Things she had never heard before. 'Your skin is so soft, so perfect.' Even her name sounded new, smoothed over by his attentions. 'Puawai.'

And then he was standing at the end of the bed – shaven, fully clothed, zipping up his toilet bag. 'Oh, you're awake, babe. Good, 'cause I'm outa here.'

That's when Puawai noticed his luggage ready at the door. 'Oh, I thought you said you were staying for a few days.'

'Well, in the district, not here exactly.' He sat next to her and kissed her long and possessively. 'God, you have no idea how beautiful you are, do you?' She didn't know what he meant. He ran his forefinger down her cheek, and got up to leave. 'The room's all paid for. Lie in. Read the paper.'

Halfway out the door he looked back. 'You should ring me when you've graduated. I'm always on the look out for new talent.' And then he was gone.

She sank back, submerging herself under the pillows, then under the blankets. 'Faarck! Faarck!' Her arms and legs flailed noisily until just the sheet clung weakly to her naked waist. It was still early. She washed, dressed, and went straight to Emery's. He answered his sleep-out door wearing crisp white cotton – figure-hugging boxer shorts with a matching singlet that flaunted his rigorously sculpted body. When he saw it was Puawai, he burst into Diana Ross, *touch me in the mor-or-ning....*

'Just shut up and let me in.'

'Okay. But only if you're here for the post-coital analysis.' He stepped aside and rubbed his hands together mischievously.

'Don't you ever stop, Emery?'

'Mm-mm. What's the matter then? His morning-after encore not up to scratch?'

'What?' Puawai was distracted, plumping up the pillows on his futon. 'Just make the coffee, Emmy. And by the way, if anybody asks, I slept here last night.' She took off her jeans and settled in under the duvet, sighing. She could see Emery fussing in the kitchenette – rinsing, arranging, toasting, slicing.

When he finished, he stood in the middle of the room, holding a bountiful tray and stamped an impatient foot. 'Oh Puu, you know that's my side of the bed.' She shuffled over. He grinned, and slipped under the duvet, positioning the tray carefully between them. The coffee was always good at Emery's. And there were toasted muffins, daubed with sticky blackcurrant jam and cut into quarters. Fresh strawberries and grapes, halved. Chilled watermelon chopped into rough cubes. 'Now, tell me everything.'

'Nothing to tell really.'

'Oh yes there is. Like, is he more magnificent with clothes on or clothes off?'

She cupped her hands around her coffee. 'I s'pose magnificent is a good word for him.'

'Well say it like you mean it girl.'

'Whadd'ya mean?'

'Puawai. What's going on here? It's not even eight o'clock. Now I know that's not significantly early, but it is Saturday, we were up late and, shouldn't you still be in bed with your handsome suitor?'

'Suitor? Shouldn't suitors stick around a bit longer than twelve hours? Oh I don't know. I guess I'm just no good at one-night stands.'

'Ah! This is gonna be one of those *serious* girlfriend talks. But I can see what the problem is.'

'What problem?'

'Puawai, my flower, are you pissed off because it's just a one-nighter?'

'I don't know. I don't really think so. I just ... don't understand it.'

'What's to understand? You have sex. You leave satisfied. Everybody's happy.'

'Yeah, but, can't you have coffee together first? A short, friendly conversation? I mean, you don't have to just sneak out while the other person's sleeping.'

'Is that what happened?'

'Well, not exactly. But he has gone already.'

'And?'

'And nothing.'

'So you're shitty because?'

'I don't know. It's just. He was so nice to me last night.'

'Nice? Well, that's one word for it.'

'Oh, you know. You saw what he was like. He talked. He was interested in me. And this morning. Well, he didn't seem so interested anymore. The flattery was all there. But he didn't ask if I was okay, you know, if I wanted to eat, if I'd be all right getting home. Nothing.'

'Maybe he thought you were a big girl. An adult.'

'Yeah. I know. But I just felt uncomfortable, used or something. Last night he was so careful with me. And this morning.... He called me babe! And it was like he couldn't wait to get outa there.'

'Well what were you expecting? Roses? Him on bended knee? You're forgetting that I know you Puawai. If you thought it had the slightest chance of going anywhere, you would never have slept with him in the first place. You wouldn't have wanted to spoil the image.'

'But I like him Emery. He's –'

'Yeah, yeah. We all know what they're like. They're a type, aren't they, men like Dane Rauhanga. That's why we love them so much. And if you were honest, you'd admit that you knew what you were getting before you lay down with him. Anyway, you should be pleased, that's quite a prestigious headboard to put your notch in.'

'God, you're vicious some times.'

'Whaddya mean?'

'Your tongue. It's a wonder you've never cut yourself with it.'

'Oh honey, I don't mean to be heartless or trivial or whatever. But ... yeah ... get over yourself. You fell into bed with your hormones. You let your brain disengage for a moment. I think it's great. And, for you, it's totally wild. You know I think you're fabulous. And he's fabulous – at least to look at, and talk to. You had some fun together, and now life resumes.'

Puawai groaned. 'I know you're right somewhere along the line. But –'

'One day you'll see it for what it is, a titivating – no – *scandalous* interlude in our otherwise ordinary lives. The folks at the Queen Mary will be loving it, they'll speculate on it for weeks.'

'Don't remind me. And remember, I slept here.'

'Oooh. And we can do exclusives with *Woman's Day*. "My Night of Passion with Senior Public Broadcaster." "He Left Me Naked in Cheap Motel." '

'Ha ha,' Puawai said dryly. 'Hey, you know what he said?'

'Is it gonna be rude?'

'He said, "Give me a ring after you graduate. I'm always on the look out for *new talent*." '

They rolled their eyes at each other and laughed. 'That is rude. Good headline though: "He Promised Rewards for My Fresh New

Talents." ' They laughed some more. Puawai put their tray on the floor, and clicked a remote. Macy Gray came on softly.

Get up, get up and do somethin'

She slid further down the bed. 'I need more sleep.'

Don't let the days of your life pass you by.

She turned on her side, and life repositioned itself in its usual groove.

'Emery,' she said.

'Mmm.'

'If I'm still single ten years from now....'

'Mmm.'

'Will you marry me?'

'Of course I will, honey. But I'll choose the dresses.'

'Okay.' She closed her eyes, and smiled.

Media Studies

K. T. Harrison

Down the road from our house, there's a Chinese knocking shop. I heard Simon, my mother's boyfriend, say it to her once. There's the dairy, the hairdressers and next to that, the Chinese takeaways. They run the knocking shop because it's next door to them and because they're Chinese. Above the door in big red letters they've written the name.

It's a dojo.

My brother used to go to one when we all lived in Auckland. He did martial arts. When I grow up I want to be like my brother and do martial arts too. He calls me bro! But he's not my real brother, my Nan said. He's only my half-brother. My mother is his mother, but we have different fathers. His father lives in a place called Paree, that's really Paris Texas. My sister goes there to buy her clothes. My father is dead. My brother used to let me practice with him sometimes. He showed me some blocks and how to always keep my guard up. I can't wait to see him again. I'll tell him about the dojo. He said that you don't just walk in and have a jack around. So mostly I just sit on the brick wall opposite it and I watch the people going in and coming out. And one day, I know I'm gonna be allowed to go in there.

Every time I go up for chinese, I bow to the man at the takeaways because he's the sensei and that's what you do. My brother told me. But I don't think I'm doing it properly because he never bows back. And I wonder if people look shorter and fatter to Chinese people because of their eyes. So the next time I go up, I try to stand on my toes to make me taller so that when I bow the sensei can see me. But I fall over instead. And he comes around to the front of the counter and asks me if I'm all light?

My sister is cool. She's a night receptionist for an escort agency up in Auckland. My mother does escort duties too as part of her job. She takes people to the hospital to their outpatient appointments. But she works during the day. My sister's agency does it at night for people who work. Night-time is the only time they can keep their appointments.

Once I heard my mother telling my sister off about working at night because it's dangerous up in Auckland. She told her to get a decent job, but my sister said she can make more money in one night than my mother does in one week. I wish my mother would get a job like that. One day when I was up in Auckland having a holiday at my sister's some of her workmates came over. They go to Paris Texas for their clothes too. They drew lines on each other, like the ones Madonna has on her hands. And they did it in my sister's bedroom. She asked them if they wanted to do some lines, then they went to into her room and drew on each other. Stay in here boy, she said to me. I don't think they liked those drawings anyway, because when they came out, their hands were clean. They must have washed them off. Then they started to talk about their clients. And my sister told them to shush and looked at me. There was no need to worry. I told her that I knew about the Privacy Act, and confidentiality and that, Mum'd told me. My sister said for me to go outside, because I suppose they needed to discuss stuff about their clients. But gee, I'm not gonna say anything. Who wants to know about glass eyes and hearing aids ? When I was up there, I went with my sister and her mates to their R&R day at the Waiwera Pools. When I got home and told Mum and Simon, he said to Mum that he bet they stood out from the rest of the people there. And when Mum asked him why, he said they would have been the only ones standing up and fully clothed. And he asked me how they ate their ice creams. Clown. One man pushed in front of my sister at the ice-cream stand. And she said to him, excuse me sir but I was here first.

And he ignored her, so she said it again but louder and she added, perhaps you would like me to handcuff you to that pole over there, and she started opening up her handbag and continued talking ... of course ice cream isn't as good as whipped cream but I'm sure ... the man stepped back and let us go first. The next time I saw that man he was leaving with his wife and kids I supposed, and the kids were crying because they hadn't had a swim yet. My sister and her mates laughed at that. I think he must have been in trouble with the law or something, but don't know how my sister knew. You should have seen his face when she said about the handcuffs. I saw my mother taking a ring off her finger once, so that's what the ice cream would have been for. That was a neat day.

One night, Mum and Simon were having some beers and listening to music. I was watching videos because there was no school the next day. They were real old Bruce Lee ones that my brother gave to me. He did kung fu. He was the man. Simon asked Mum if she wanted to do a bit of kung fu, and Mum laughed at him. She said he wouldn't know the first thing about it. Then Simon said that one day he was walking down the road and a tomato hit his head, and he yelled out, who the kung fu that? They laughed. But they're always laughing at dumb things. The clown.

In my sleep that night, I could hear Mum and Simon doing kung fu because she was making noises like she was in pain. I wished he wouldn't do that to her because he's much bigger and she doesn't know about blocks and keeping her guard up. I wished I had shown her stuff, but I was too tired then. Any way she must have been alright because I heard Simon saying I love you, I love you, over and over. So I guessed she was okay.

The next morning I looked at my mother to see if she had any bruises from the kung fu. She had some on her neck. Simon must have been doing illegal moves because you're not supposed to hit there, unless you really know what you're doing. I don't think he hurt her too badly though because she was all smiley and gooey like when she talks to my brother's baby. And every time she walked past Simon he patted her bum. Egg.

At school, we're doing media studies. We've divided into groups and we're going to visit media places. One group is going up to Auckland to visit TV and filming places; another group is going to visit radio stations in our area, and my group is going to visit newspaper places. I chose to be in the newspaper group because I read our local paper every day. Mostly the ads and that's how I found out about when PS2 was coming out. I can't wait for that. I can do a lot of the crossword too, sometimes without using the saurus. You can find out a lot from the newspaper. One day my mother told me that she had to take my little sister to the rapist about her speech problems. I know that rapists are quite bad people, they go to jail with murderers. I read about that in the paper too. I hope the rapist is good to my sister.

It must be a lady rapist though because my mother calls her, 'she'. I suppose that's alright, it's only men rapists who go to jail in the papers. We're allowed to wear mufti when we go on our trip. My sister's left some of her Paree gear at home so I wear her jacket. I look cool, and we got a neat lunch. No sandwiches. We're going to have it at the lake and Mr Chan has promised us a very special treat at the end of the day. The bus is going to drop us off at our homes too, because Mr Chan said we might get back to school too late to catch our usual buses. We're on my street now. I thought we had one more place to go to. Now I'm gonna get home too early and Mum won't be home yet.

Oh man, this is our special treat. Of course, Mr Chan's Chinese, he's related to the sensei he's arranged for us to visit the dojo. Oh thanks, Mr Chan. I'm going in, choyyyce. Hey guys, this is the dojo I was telling you fellas about. Good one, Mr Chan. In my head I practice what my brother told me. Feet together at the ankles, hands together at palms as if in prayer, bow from the waist, head up, look at sensei when you bow, don't take your eyes off your opponent. Show your respect for the centuries of knowledge, skill and expertise for this art and the culture it belongs to. Man my heart is beating in my ears. I'm the first off the bus. It's a bloody advertising paper. Like the one we used to get up in Auckland. A bloody paper. The *Loot*.

Simon, the clown. I'm gonna tell my mother. And I hope she gives him a good knock. No thank you Mr Chan, no ice cream for me.

And I said, What about Milos at Nanny's Place?

Eru J. Hart

Sitting down with his nanny two things occurred to Jeremy Manawa. First: he wasn't her favourite mokopuna. He knew that. Everyone knew that. But then there was the other thing.

Second: His nanny would lie down on a bed of hot coals for him if he were going to walk across.

Yes, Emma Materua would've growled like nobody's business afterwards, with her puku all blistered and weepy, but Jeremy was right. She would have cast herself down onto this imaginary coal bed in a flash. No doubt she would make a martyr out of herself, all dramatic and woe-is-me, arms a-flailing, like Vivien Leigh in *Gone With the Wind*. But, oh Rhett, she would do it, in a heartbeat.

And that made the boy feel very special.

Apparently Nanny Emma's mother was an Anglican. Strict by reputation and severe by nature. But this was, of course, all family gossip.

He'd seen pictures of her, sitting all la-di-da with her tight bun and her straight back and that smooth, smooth skin. Because of those pictures and Nanny's reputation he'd always associated Anglicanism with Severity. He guessed one day he'd like to find out just how right or wrong he actually was about that. But Jeremy had given up going to church a while ago.

'Too much keeping up appearances for me,' he'd told his mother, with a bit of 'snotty' in his attitude.

People were often surprised by just how proper Nanny could be, just like the ladies in the old American movies about the Civil War. Southern belles? Yeah, that's it. She may have never used the phrase, 'Good silverware and china tonight, thank you, Hetty,' or anything as polished as that, but no one felt uncomfortable or unwelcome in Nanny's house. Nobody questioned her hospitality. Nobody. Jeremy knew, though, that at times she could have benefited from a gentle reminder that she was no-part southern American, and all-parts South Pacific. He began to study her weathered face, and decided that even though in places it looked like leather, leather was actually very pleasing to look at. People pay a lot of money for leather jackets, he told himself. He gazed upon those heavy lines while Emma continued speaking.

'Aunty Charmaine Osmond, you know from out Bridge Pā, well she says....' Nanny paused for some time, and then continued. 'She says that her granddaughter, Cheyenne, who I think is Cheyenne Rata – yes 'cause that's right, her dad's a Rata – Cheyenne Rata....'

The boy scratched his left ear softly, and took a deep breath, losing a degree of his posture.

'Well 'pparently, this Cheyenne Rata is at Queen Victoria University with you too, moko, down there in Foxton, with you,' said Nanny with a sigh.

Oh no, he grimaced, not this again.

'Victoria University, Kui, Victoria, not Queen Victoria.'

Nanny looked a little bit bummed out, but was obviously determined not to show it.

'Oh, hmm, OK,' she said, very matter-of-factly.

'And it's in Wellington,' Jeremy added.

'What did I say?'

'You said Foxton, Nanny.'

'Right. Well Charmaine – no, sorry, Aunty Charmaine – would like to know if you've ever bumped into her Cheyenne.'

Thing is, Jeremy had never bumped into anybody at Queen Vict – sorry, Victoria University, ever. There was quite a strict protocol of keeping one's eyes unfocussed on the ground three or four feet in front of oneself. This meant you could still deftly dodge the blurry objects, in this case people, before any 'bumping' became imminent.

'There are twelve thousand people at Vic, Nan, and so, um, no I haven't bumped into Aunty Charmaine's Cheyenne, amongst those twelve thousand Nanny so, hmphf ... sorry.' Jeremy was very serious, yet beneath, could feel a giggle coming on.

'Oh, twelve thousand, gosh, well, no you wouldn't have then.'

Nanny got up, asking on her way out of the sunlit front parlour, 'Hot drink, moko?'

The options – Earl Grey tea, beer, herbal tea, coffee – went through his mind, in that order, but he finally decided on Milo.

'Milo thanks Nanny.'

There were, of course, no other options; Nanny was a Mormon, and an active Mormon too. But she was sweet; she was cool, in an elderly-churchy kind of way. Thinking about all those heavy lines nestled into Nan's face the boy's thoughts turned to his mother. His direct matriarch, e whaea e, his mother. True, amongst the lines on Nanny's pretty face there were glimpses of his mother, Moana Manawa, née Materua, but Pāpā's genes had also come into play, tampering with the pool, to create a woman of striking features: Moana Manawa.

'Ko Moana Materua Manawa tōku whaea,' he whispered under his breath, taking his Māori lecturer's advice to use simple sentences whenever they popped up. Moana, the woman who was the biological link to this wonderful relic, taonga, presently making Milos in her clean, white nineteenth-century kitchen. The whānau is linked generation to generation, umbilical cord to umbilical cord, Jeremy found himself thinking. He really liked that. He would have to write it down soon as he got home, and make it into some kind of story, or a poem, yeah, a poem. Poets pull the honeys, he thought. Hmmm, he liked that too.

One of the good things 'bout Nanny, he guessed, was she always smelled really good. 'Cause everyone knows a lot of girls her age do not. As a young nine year old, Jeremy had been involved in cub scouts. Here was the catch: his big sister, who was quite a bit older than him, was the akela. During one of their goodwill missions to an old folks' home, young Jeremy had registered one odour, coming seemingly from a near-motionless elderly gentleman. An unforgettable mixture of mothballs, cough medicine, camphorated oil and dead-something. One unforgettable fragrance. But Jeremy did have a healthy respect for the elderly, odour and all; it was just nice that his Nanny wasn't one of the stinky ones.

Nanny's house rested at the end of a small cul-de-sac, deep in the thickets of New Zealand suburbia. Whatever that might mean. He knew all her neighbours by face, and they knew most of Emma's family by decibels. This was the kāinga where, as children, cousins were met with most often. For the boy it was nice to be here alone with Nanny for once. Her time would become a little precious when heaps of the young ones were around. Jeremy wondered if her neighbours were a little puzzled as to why an elderly widow pushing seventy, whose children were all adults with children themselves, always had a steady supply of under tens at her house.

But that was just the way it was with him and the whānau.

The boy heard a succession of clink-clink-clinks, the noise of teaspoon meeting porcelain mug.

'No sugar thanks Nanny,' he called.

Bang-whoop-floow-whoop went the cupboards rhythmically and surely.

There would be no say on milk levels here. Jeremy would just have to subsist on the Nanny standard: a large tablespoon, approximately, of skim milk. Still pleasant though. Just.

At that moment Nanny glided back into the room, like some patupaiarehe, her silky scarf giving the impression of translucent fairy skin. And yes, Jeremy supposed, there must be brown-skinned fairies. Must be.

She was in good form today, old Kui; her posture seemed a little surer. Jeremy grinned from ear to ear. She lowered his Milo, still steaming, being of course mostly boiling water, onto the Milo table. The Milo table that had not a single Milo-ring on it, despite its antiquity. Not a valuable antiquity, just an oldness.

'Have you seen Waiona, Kui?' he asked.

'No, not for about a year, still in Australia though.' She gurgled through half a mouthful of Milo.

'Anyways,' she said swallowing, 'you've got your aunty's number. Give her a call and ask her yourself.'

Jeremy and Waiona. They were quite the inseparable cousins as tamariki. And while everyone in the family went around calling her 'Why-owner', Nanny would be very careful to say 'Wa-i-ohh-na' whenever speaking to or about her. He thought someone had said the original Waiona was one of Nanny's friends. That made sense. Jeremy recalled the way he and Waiona would bike to school every day, each trying to edge their own front wheel just slightly in front of the other's, without being real obvious about it. That sense of power first thing in the morning was a great substitute for breakfast. Waiona had even offered to beat up this one girl – Rhiannon –who'd wanted to go out with him. Now there was a true cousin. Thinking about it he realised that Waiona was probably the first girl he had ever kissed. A fact both sad and haunting. The boy remembered it vaguely; they would not have been any older than four, and in an innocent and almost sweet way they pecked each other for about ten seconds, giggling all the way. Aunty Lena however was not giggling, and Jeremy remembered getting a little smack. Jeremy had heard Waiona had turned lesbian. Hopefully all unrelated. A Māori lesbian in Aussie.

Go cuz, he thought.

'You know, moko, we have that reunion coming up.' Nanny spoke with her honey-brown lips still cupped to her hot drink. 'Only me and Nanny Iti left now.' She spoke in a philosophical manner. Then another sigh.

In her safe little cul-de-sac, Nine-Oh-Five McLean Street, Emma Materua had raised most of her children in peace and safety.

And now the last fear the Manawas had was the only fear that really matters: that of her Death. She wasn't even sick though, not yet. You couldn't've said that Nan was healthy, but she certainly was vibrant.

Perhaps a little big, some crueller ones may have said morbidly obese. But, he mused, only other people have fat nannies ... and mothers ... and sisters. Not the Manawas though, not Jeremy's family. They were simply ... naturally generous.

Immediately the boy thought about a book he had read, and one passage in particular. On his first endeavour to these shores, Cook – Captain J. Cook, that is – had encountered a waka of woman, on the coast of Nanny's area. The ship's log leaves a description of these wāhine as being 'very jolly ... having large breasts'.

Mr Manawa had chuckled, perhaps inappropriately.

'Those were her ancestors alright,' he said, near silently.

'What was that moko?' she asked, only a little interested.

'Nothin' ... nothin' Nan,' said he, adding, 'have you lost a bit of weight Kui?' for extra irony.

Nanny hailed from Nuhaka, a small East Coast township. As a town it was a shave too insignificant for a movie theatre, yet was large enough to sustain the unwritten rural standard of fish and chip shop (owned by a local man, with a local-sized fishing boat), post office-cum-general store, and a miscellaneous opportunity shop, stocking what the townies call kiwiana and the locals call rubbish. As children it was their Camelot. An area of pure oral legend, until of course he'd visited as an adult, and it turned out the streets did not happen to be painted with gold.

It was a legendary location, so the stories go, where Māori child after Māori child jumped for pennies from a bridge. It was imagined that this bridge was three or four storeys high. And it sounded like there were no shortages of tourists, pockets heavy with pennies.

The tourists, as the imagination goes, would have been from the farthest-away places, the mythical Timbuktu perhaps.

'Gosh Maude,' foreign husbands would say, 'do you see those mow-rees jump?'

There would of course have been a lot of clapping. And as for the bravado of the natives, well, Jeremy and his cousins had themselves believed. It must have been a world-famous place.

At one stage it sounded like his mother had spent her entire childhood jumping from that bridge.

Nuhaka was also the place referred to whenever Nanny locked her doors, or read of a burglary in the newspapers.

'We never locked our doors,' she would begin. 'In Nuhaka,' she would end.

All this, however, was before Nanny became part of what history describes as the great Māori Urban Migration, capitals not added.

It was, as Jeremy recalled (by now deep into the 'contemplation phase' of a Milo high), given a lot of focus in history class. Less than the Great Migration to Aotearoa, he thought, congratulating himself on this insight.

'The victors write history,' his teacher would say.

'Just going for a mimi Nan, 'scuse me,' he muttered.

'Ka pai,' she returned.

Walking past the faded orange wallpaper and scuffing across the fluffily worn loop pile, he re-noticed one of the photos hanging lazy on the wall to his left. It was in the same position that it had always been, flanked by the same pictures that had always been its neighbour, but today the boy took special notice of it. There were four figures in the photo, all of them instantly recognisable though thirty years younger than they appeared today. The original must have been a small black-and-white print, taken in a studio of the period, with a camera that could not have been better than the disposable ones of now. This, though, was an apparent enlargement, and not only that, it had been coloured in one hell of a gaudy fashion. In the back row was his mother and then there was Uncle Whetikei, the bus driver. He noted how beautiful and fresh his mother looked. Even Uncle looked pretty handsome, considering he's no Don Juan now. And in the front row were Nanny and Papa. Very Ma and Pa Kettle, thought he.

The last thing he noticed, before speeding up to catch the toilet in time, was the colour scheme. Whoever had coloured the print had added a creamy grey-green, fanning out toward the borders. This artiste had also left a mellow white area around the figures' outlines. This gave an angelic effect, an amusing angelic effect. But it was the clothing that made Jeremy Heremia Manawa laugh the most. They were like the clothes found in pull-out dolly books. Lacking all texture, the one-toned pinks greens and browns (all those browns) added outfits to people who would never have worn them.

Jeremy was still laughing when he returned to the sunroom.

'How's Mrs Paraire?' he asked.

'Elva? Oh well, yes, she's looking after herself,' Nanny commented rather succinctly. 'I miss my piano, moko – damned arthritis.'

Her fingers were gnarled like the roots of a kahikatea tree. Grainy and as old too. Clean white nails, neatly trimmed, capped her fingers, and they were all but useless for the really small movements. Movements like playing the piano.

He had only asked after Elva because of a rumour that was doing the rounds at the moment. Apparently Elva Paraire had asked one of her nephews to pull the plug on her. Auē, euthanasia. Elva was a very robust woman, with thin, tight pink lips and a saggy androgynous face. Just a little older than Nanny. Jeremy had wanted to know for sure, and you didn't get any closer to the horse's mouth than Nanny. But today it was she who would be the tight-lipped one.

Many of Nanny's friends had already died. That prospect chilled the boy a little. It must be pretty trippy, he thought, to watch all your old mates die of old age.

'Nanny, I just wanted to say that I've found myself a girlfriend, she's real nice too,' he said. 'One of those good ones, a Cook Island girl.'

Nanny pondered this; it had definitely interrupted her avid Milo session. She returned her cup to the table and a cheeky grin looked about to erupt.

Jeremy fumbled for the next sentence.

'These are my wishes.' She cleared her throat for a long one. 'As the eldest son of my youngest daughter I would like your first child, if a girl, to be called Emma, or Materua, I leave that up to you.'

How democratic, the boy thought.

'And your second child, boy or girl, after Pāpā.' That was it.

'Jim, Kui? Even if it's a girl you want us to name her Jim?'

'Āe, or James.' And that was definitely that.

Jeremy pondered and decided if it came to it, he liked James much better. Just in case Nanny left some kind of clause in her will cutting him off unless his second-born was named Chanikra, for example.

'Kui, I've just met this girl last month. She may be a little frightened off if –'

But then Nanny interrupted him. One of those important interruptions, he could tell. Nanny took a big in-breath and settled herself down into a very wise and secure position. She wobbled her lower half nestingly into her squishy chair.

'A month moko,' she said with rehearsed profundity, 'is a very long time for a kaumātua like myself. Anything else?'

'She's got beautiful long hair Nan, takes real good care of it too,' he commented, feeling a little foolish for having said so. 'Always smells pretty clean, anyway.' Oh god, that was worse.

'Good. Too much moko. Strange though....'

'Why's that eh?' he quizzed.

'Nanny Iti and me always thought you might be gay.' With that she could hold it back no longer and she laughed, and then they both laughed. For ages and ages. Though he did hope she was joking.

Uncle Alex's Tangihanga

Vicki-Anne Heikell

'KIA ORA my whanaunga!' she yelled, waving her hanky at me.

'Uh-oh – what's she doing here?' I asked my cousin. 'Did she know Uncle?' We were sitting out the back of the wharepuni skiving off from Uncle Alex's tangi.

She closed in on me and pulling me toward her squashed my face against her belly.

'Pēhea ana, Boy?'

'Pai,' I replied, punching my giggling cousin.

'Your Uncle Alex was a lovely man ... lovely man. It's good your family brought him home from the city.'

I was freed from her headlock as she spied another victim – Uncle Brownie.

'KIA ORA my whanaunga,' she yelled.

My cousin and I burst out laughing as we watched her waddle toward my uncle.

'Man, talk about rent-a-crowd,' I said.

'Yeah, Mum says when she sees the cars up here she's gotta come up and have a jack. Anyway, I better get back to the kitchen. I'll catch up with you later.'

A group had arrived and my uncles were about to welcome them so I headed for the front of the whare to check it out. Loud wailing was drowning out Uncle Brownie's speech. I could see the rolling of eyes, and raised eyebrows between members of my family – they were mad!

'Auē, auē ... au no! au yeah!'

It was HER! She had managed to work her way up to Uncle Alex who was lying on the porch. He was surrounded by the tangi brigade in their blacks and with their hankies. Some were giggling into their hankies, some were whispering to others from behind their hankies; and others were trying to wave 'Aunty' away with their hankies.

As Uncle Brownie finished his speech he turned slightly and signalled for the waiata. 'Make it loud eh,' he muttered

As everyone stood I headed to the kitchen. Helping my cousin set the tables, I told her what had happened. 'Do you think she's a bit pōrangi?' I asked

'Dunno – maybe.'

People had started filing in. Uncle Brownie waited until each table was full before banging the table with his knife and saying grace.

He sat down and spooned potatoes onto his plate, and then cabbage.

'Hōmai ngā rīwai, my whanaunga.' Uncle Brownie turned and there she was, right there, right next to him. He looked and looked again, and cleared his throat – and then, and then – he passed her the potatoes. He looked across the table at Aunty Mina who just shrugged and dished up her potatoes.

'Kapu tī – milk?' I asked.

'Ah, yes please! Boy, can you get me another steamed pudding; and some corned beef and potatoes?'

I left my teapots on the trolley and trudged back to the kitchen and asked the cooks. They pointed to the far bench and a small cardboard box with little wrapped parcels of left-over kai – corned beef, potatoes, pumpkin and steamed puddings.

As I returned to the dining room, 'Aunty' pushed out her chair, leapt up and grabbed the box.

'Don't you want your kapu tī?' I asked.

'No, no, no – I had better get home – it's late, very late now.' She headed quickly for the door, and was gone.

'You'll catch flies with that,' piped Aunty Mina.

'Is she pōrangi, Aunty?'

'Kao – just hungry.'

Maui me Tama-tere-i-te-rā
Te takenga mai o te tikanga

Darryn Joseph

Ka hōhā te iwi, ka hōhā ake ki te rā. Ka puta te rā i tōna rua, ka hī, ka tō, ka hī, ka tō, ka kore e roa ka tau te pō. He rā te rā, ka paku haku, ka pīki amuamu te iwi, tētehi ki tētehi, rātou ki a rātou, i te mea, kāore rātou i te whai wā kia mahia ngā mahi i te awatea. Hāunga te haruru, te kekē o te pō! Mai i te haruru, te hoihoi o te iwi ka tīwaha ake rā tētehi toa, 'Kāti rā te tangiweto! Wā koutou nei! Māku e rapu, ka kitea! Māku e mea te rā kia āta haere.'

Āe e hoa mā, ko wai atu tērā, ko Māui. Ko tana ingoa roroa, ko Māui-tikotiko-o-tarau.

Nā, ka whakaaro a Māui-tikotiko-o-tarau, me aha ia i te tuatahi ki te hopu i te rā. Ā, ka puta te whakaaro, me haere ia ki te āporo nui, ki te auahi nui, ki tēnei tāone e kiia nei ko Pōneke. Nā, e ai te kōrero, mā te huruhuru te manu ka rere. Nā reira a Māui i huri ai hei manu, ka rere atu ki Pōneke, ā, ka tau ki tērā tari Kāwanatanga, Te Pune Kōkiri. Arā, ko te tari o te *Charged Spoon*. Ko te tūmanako, mā te pīki pune nei ia e whāngai ki te kōrero, homai he mahere, homai he huarahi kōkiri hei whaitanga atu.

Whakatata atu a Māui ki te T.I.O.[1] a Ngā-tata Aroha, 'E Nga-tata Aroha, aroha mai, pēhea e ngata ai taku nei hiahia?'

Whakahoki kōrero atu a ia, 'Me whai pūtea i te kāwana, whakatū hui, huri atu, huri mai, pātaihia ngā pātai, kōrerohia ngā kōrero, hoki mai ki Pōneke, kore nuku, kore neke!

1. Te Ingoa Ongaonga

Noho ki te tūru me te kore kūru, ui atu, ui mai, tuhituhi, ā, ka pai!'

'Mmm, pēhea te roa o taua whainga?'

'Ē, tekau tau!'

Ka puta a Māui i te te tari o Te Pune Kōkiri me te whakaaro, *ee iee, me kaua rawa e waiho mō te ara a Taihoa.*

Heoi, kāore tēnei toa i waiho ki reira. Ka toro atu ia ki tōna kuia ki a Muru. I tētehi whare okioki mō ngā kaumātua a Muru e noho ana ki Porirua. Ko te ingoa o taua whare okioki rā, ko Te Tōnga o te Rā.

Nā, ko tōna ingoa roroa, ko Muru-rongo-whānau. I tapaina pērātia a Muru i te mea ko tāna, he whakarongorongo ki ngā nawe, ki ngā kotiti, ki ngā hara a te whānau. I te mutunga o te whakarongo hara, kua murua! Heoi anō, kotahi noa iho te mate o tērā ara whakaea hara, he turi rawa ōna taringa. Nā, hāmama atu a Māui ki tōna kuia, 'E kui. Māku e whakaata haere te rā!'

'Ka pai e moko he tere tō motokā!'

'Kao, kao, kao! Ka patua te rā ... kia whai wā.'

'Mao, mao, mao, whiti whiti ora?'

Tata puta a Māui-tinihanga i te whare okioki, ka kitea iho ngā niho o Muru i roto i tētehi kapu. Ā, ka tangohia, ka kawea ake. Ka whaiwhai haere te reo o tōna kuia i a ia, 'E moko, ka kite! Patua te rā kia whai wā, he he he!'

Nā, ka aro a Māui ki te kimi hoa haere mōna. Ka whakaarohia ōna tuākana. Heoi anō, kei tētehi hotēra rātou e noho ana. Kei te hotēra nei a Pāremoremo rātou e mauheretia ana. Heoi anō, ka huri ia hei kāhu, ka rere atu ki reira. Ka tae atu, ka kite ōna tuākana i te iari e hiki rino ana:

ko Māui-mua-kaikai,
ko Māui-muri-kai-huare,
ko Māui-runga-noa-atu,
ko Māui-raro-e-putu-ana,
ko Māui-waho-i-te-tika,
ko Māui-taha-wāwāhi-tahā,
me te nanakia haere i te pō,
a Māui-pae-mate-paipai.

Ka ohorere ngā poi e whitu nei i te tau mai o te kāhu, matihao koikoi me te āhei ki te kōrero, 'E koutou mā. Ho-ho-hoake tātou ki te whakatō-tō tō i te rā kia āta haere.' Ka wahangū ngā tuākana, heoi, ka taka te kapa ki a Māui-pae-mate-paipai,

'E Māui-tikotiko-o-tarau ee! Te pōtiki, te whakapākanga, te ihu hupē, tiko tata nē! Tokowhitu mātou. Kāore mātou i te wehi i a koe, nē whara mā!' Ka huri ia ki ōna tuākana, tēina hei āwhina. Ēngari ko tā ratou he 'mm mm atu', tino ngoikore nei. Kātahi ka pupuke te tinana o Māui. Ka nui, ka rahi, ka pīki whara. Ka huri a Māui hei arewhana. Toro iho tōna ihu roa, ka hikitia a Māui-pae-mate-paipai ka whiua ki te rangi. Ka rere whakawaho atu i te whare herehere. 'Hmm, mmm' te piukara a Māui-arewhana-ihu-roa, 'Ka pai tērā whakaaro. He kōrero, he pātai atu anō?'

'K, ka, kaka, kā, kau, kao,' ngā whakahoki a ngā poi e ono.

Ka pātai, āwangawanga nei a Māui-waho-i-te-tika,

'Engari... me pēhea tātou e puta atu ki waho...' I mua i te mutunga o tana kōrero, ka rerekē anō te āhua o Māui. Ka huri ngā waewae tīwai kia porowhita te āhua. Aī, auē! Ka whai wīra te arewhana! Kāore i paku huri te ringa karaka, ka huri a Māui hei pīki taraka!

'Eke eke! Eke eke!' Ka eke. Kātahi ka oho ngā tūtei hiamoe. Kāti, kua tūreiti ngā tūtei. Haere ana a Māui mā, ka pakaru te pakitara, ka puta atu. Ka kitea a Māui-pae-mate-paipai e iri ana i te rākau. Ka tōia mai, ka haere tonu i tā rātou haere. Ka haere ki Te Tairāwhiti, ki Tūranga-nui-ā-Kiwa, ki te putanga mai o tērā nanakia e huri kakama ana i te rangi.

Heoi anō, i te tere o te haere o te rā i te rangi, ka hī, ka tō, ka hī, ka tō, ā, ka hī, ka tō, ka hī, ka tō, kā hika, ka pau te toru wiki rā anō ka tae atu rātou. Arā ki Tūranga-nui-ā-Kiwa, ki te hīnga mai o te rā. Ā, ka tae, ka āhua atua-tangata anō mai a Māui-taraka-wīra-nui.

Ka tūpou iho ngā māhunga o ngā poi me te pātai ake, 'Me aha tātou?' Ka kī a Māui, 'Tēnā tātou, ka here i te rā nei kia āta haere ai, kia roa ai te mahinga a te tangata i tētehi oranga mōna.'

Ka mea atu a Māui-raro-e-putu-ana me tana maumahara ki a Māui Arewhana Ihu Roa, ki a Māui-taraka-wīra-nui, 'Ā, ē, e kore pea e tata atu te tangata i te nui o tōna wera.'

Ka kī atu a Māui, 'Kāti! Kua kite rā koutou i te tini o aku mahi. Ka huri hei manu, ka huri hoki au hei arewhana, hei taraka. Ko Māui-tikotiko-ō-tarau ahau, ka taea noatia! Kia pēnei tā tātou mahi!'

Nā, ka kamakama ngā tuākana, tēina ki te whai i āna tohutohu. Ka whiri taura, ka hanga waka, ka whatu kākahu. He kākahu rerekē. He kākahu whakaārai i te wera.

Kāti, ka hī, ka tō, ka taka te pō. Ka waihoe rātou mā runga waka ki te rua o tērā *Whara-nui-i-te-rā*. Ka whakamaua ngā kākahu ārai wera, ka tatari. Kīhai i roa, ka toro mai ngā haeata. Kātahi ka puta ngā hī o te rā, ka tukuna ngā taura kia mauheretia te rā.

Ka kuhuna e Māui ngā niho o tōna kuia ki roto i tōna waha. Ka peke ki runga. Whakatata atu ki ngā taringa o te rā. Ka tīmata tōna waha ki te komekome, ki te patupatu, ki te ngaungau i ōna taringa. Ā, ko ngā hara katoa i rongo ai tōna kuia, a Muru-rongo-whānau, ngā hara o te whānau, ka rere katoa atu i te waha o Māui ki ngā taringa o te rā.

I te tuatahi ka kata te rā, engari mau tonu a Māui i tōna taringa, mau tonu. Ka whāki atu, ka whākana, ka pūkana mai i ngā hara, ka tō te rā, ka pō te rā, ka pōuri te rā, ehara, ka pīrangi ruaki te rā. Ka pōtaitaka, ka pōauau, ka pōrangi, inā ka pō rawa atu.

Ka tiro mākutu te rā ki a Māui, ka karawhiu atu, 'Pokokōhua, pokotiwha, kai a te kurī, a te ahi, pūrari paka, hamapaka, koretake, tiripaka, tikotata, tō kaka! Kāti te kōrero! Kei turi au! Pūrari hamapaka, he aha rawa te tikanga i patua a Kanga-nui-i-te-rā?'

'Ā! Tēnā, *Kanga-nui-i-te-rā*. Ehara i te rā whatiwhati kō! Kāore mātou e whai taima ki te mahi i ngā mahi. Me āta haere koe, e Kanga, ka tika!'

'Ē kī, e kī,' te kī a Kanga, 'Tō hamuti! Hei aha koe māku?'

Ka toro anō a Māui ki a ia, anō nei ka kōrerohia tuaruatia ngā tini hara. Kāti ake, ka tere whakaae mai a Kanga-nui-i-te-rā.

Heoi anō rā, ka toko ake te whakaaro o Māui. Me noho mai tētehi taonga hei paihere i a rāua, hei hohou i te rongo, hei whakaāio i te whenua, hei tatau pounamu anō hoki mō ngā uri whakaheke me te rā. Ka mea ake a Māui-kerewa-tiki, 'Oi! Kanga-nui-i-te-rā, hei paihere i a tāua, anei te tohu hohou i te rongo, te taonga whakaaio i te whenua, te tatau pounamu, te taonga tuku iho ki ngā tamariki....'

'Kia tere Tiripaka!'

'Koia nei ... he kapu.'

Ka puku te rae o Kanga, tata karawhiu anō i tōna takariri. Engari ka puritia āna kupu kangakanga, ka pātai iho, 'He kapu? He kapu *aha*?'

'He kapu *aha*?' te kī a Māui, 'He kapu *tī*. He Tī, Kanga!'

Bargains

Darryn Joseph

A taonga tuku iho. Born of an antique dealer and a bushman-come-hunter, the familial trait tended towards 'collect the collectable'. Over the years, gala days, op shops, auctions, church fairs and the many sales – private, garage, car boot and estate – were all fair game to the modern-day hunters. Eight kids with eight hobbies, we were into comics, cutlery, crockery, clothes, stamps, ornaments, bits and bobs, and odds and ends. Galas, more so white elephants, were the best. A stampede of kids, like baby piranha, would descend onto the school hall and in two minutes flat we'd pick that elephant's bones clean. Dodging the flaying arms of the treasure's first line of defence, the grannies, we'd edge in and make our dollar last the distance. All our mates would be getting tractor rides and charfing floss but this was the sweetest rush, the pump of adrenalin on the first sighting, the twist and turn through the throng, the jostle to grab it first, then the haggle.

'Fifty cents? It's broken/chipped/cracked/dirty/old/only rubbish!'

'Five cents?'

'OK.'

Ā, the halcyon days, but everyone grew up, except for me. While I watched my older brothers and sisters collect boyfriends and girlfriends, babies and the dole, I stood firm on tradition. As the youngest I'd get spoilt by either Mum or Dad or my bros and sisters, and they'd continually build onto my main collection – comics. Comics were my world. My mind was stretched and vocabulary expanded by *Spiderman*, *The X-Men* and *The Fantastic Four*. It didn't really matter which title, publisher, superhero or even the comic's condition; it was the words, the words that I really collected.

I remember one of my sisters giving me shit for reading 'baby books'. It was an early issue of *The Incredible Hulk* and he was fighting mutated prehistoric dinosaurs.

'Why do you read that sissy-baby shit for?'

'It's not sissy ... I learn stuff!' I yelled, defending the Defender.

'Like WHAT?'

'Dinosaur names....' And with that I rattled off the Latin names for ten of the finest and most ferocious mokoweri that had ever stalked the Hulk. She stopped giving me shit. Kind of.

I moved from comics to *Reader's Digest*. Well, not so much the lame-oh survival stories, but the 'enrich your vocabulary' section. Every waiting room, aunty's house or supermarket, I'd flick to the twenty words or so and go for exceptional:

Kāhui (k.i.) a. manu, e. tangata, i. kararehe, o. rōpū

Dad spoke Māori as a child, but something happened. He was sent down south and put in a foster home, an English-speaking foster home. Twenty years later, by the time we came along, he'd lost his mother tongue, but he still would break out into spontaneous song and sayings that we all thought were gibberish:

'Ā titoi tiko tata ee. Ish da patari, ei poi. That's how the old people spoke, eh boy.'

It wasn't till later on at varsity, in an immersion class, a Tūhoe lecturer told us that 'tiko tata' was a phrase used by kids to taunt each other. 'Ish da patari' turned out to be kaumātua car maintenance, pidgin style. After that I collected as many phrases and kupu that I could from Dad.

The real taonga tuku iho, though, came from my parents' love of books.

Mum left school at eleven, Dad at twelve. That didn't stop either of them from educating themselves. Dad went bush in his mind. He did the old trails and bushwhacked with eighteenth-century warriors, hunted with Crumpy, and went on many adventures in Maoriland. Mum went west. To England, odorous monarchs, zinc foundation that ate the skin and seasonal castles 'cause of smelly toilets. It wasn't the stories though, it was the words, the words and their food store, books. Books meant bookshops – much to the dismay of my wife.

Bookshops lie on the fringe of good business. Out of the polished business district there are the second-hand, tarnished bookshops. Unlike its modern counterpart that excels in selling felt tips and crayons, these booksellers specialise in rare goodies. Goodies, where I find treasure my wife calls junk. To a collector, any collector, a place that sells your treasure is a holy place. To a non-collector it's purgatory, a place to watch paint dry.

'I'll meet you back here at the gate in an hour.'

'Yeah –'

'One hour!'

'OK bud.'

I'm off. One hour of decadence. One hour to indulge the primal urge instilled by family mania ... must meet at gate, must meet at gate....

The sandwich board does its magical karanga, calling my car to a stop and beckoning me in. *Hara mai rā e tama ee, mauria mai tō pūkoro hōhonu hei painga mā mātou nei ee.* No trouble getting a park here, and, making sure the car's locked, I go through my first ritual of encounter. I almost hongi the dollar bargains, crusty jackets, wrinkly covers, with a dusty shake I greet each one, pausing respectfully. Even though they've been relegated to their final resting place – before cremation – the dollar footpath bargains beckon me on. Confidently scanning the colours and textures I quickly identify the old from the new, the 'past it' from the potential, but nothing today. A ripped, dangling cover blows a raspy whēterotero, laying down the challenge to enter the bookshop. That's where the real gems lie, hopefully. The chorus from the bookshop is deafening, story upon story, crying out to be read:

Hei runga, hei runga,
Hī hā, hī hā,
Piki mai e tama,
He tupua he pukapuka,
He pukapuka, he tupua
Hī, hā, hī, hā!

Climbing the stairs the sentries follow my creaky ascension. Oversized books too recent to be of much interest vie for my attention, alerting their relatives on the shelves above:

Kia hiwa rā ki tēnā pae, kia hiwa rā ki tēnā pae,

Kia ohooho, kia pīata, kia mataara!

My eyes pick up the pace and scan ahead. They've wallpapered with floor-to-roof books. Shelf upon shelf, books crammed and old floorboards creak as I gingerly take the final step up. Masking my excitement I let out a casual 'hi' to the local inhabitant, an elderly woman, slightly balding with a gappy smile. A croaky hello is my whakatau.

'Looking for anything in particular?'

'Māori language books....'

'Ah....' Rising to the sound of opera in the background, her chair heaves a sigh of relief. Lips upturned she says, 'We don't have many ... in the Maari language ... but there's Ti Rang-ga-tehi, a few others, and of course the older regional histories are in the cabinet.'

Glassed iwi histories are a long-term dream, too pricy today.

'Thanks.'

Returning around the corner to her control centre, she sits, left ear arched toward the oscillating opera voice, ignoring the secure quadraphonic surround mirrors, humming to herself.

The books in turn go an octave higher and begin to natter. Their spines throwing challenges back and forth, retorts and rebuttals abound. The fat ones garbling out their message with a chunky font size, the thin ones a bit more styley, but still just the same bookshop rhetoric. My fingers quickly pass over the usual textbooks, *Te Rangatahi* one and two, *Modern Māori*, pre-loved, pre-battered compulsory texts, the constant of bookshops up and down the country. I flick on, not heeding the old cries of classroom learning. Dictionaries, dictionaries ... a hint of yellow between red and green, trained neurons force the phalanges back between Williams and Ngāti. I part the two monoliths and a faded lemon softcover greets me. A diamond in the rough, I hit a gem.

MAORI–ENGLISH, ENGLISH–MAORI DICTIONARY

Carefully holding book in right and turning with left, I open up the book.

VOCABULARY FOR SCHOOLS

MAORI-ENGLISH, ENGLISH-MAORI

For several years teachers of Māori blah, blah, blah ... vocabulary based on Whare Kura ... blah, blah, blah ... any suggestions or additions ... blah, blah blah ...

Fuck me.

Rev. P. Ryan

St Peter's Māori College

Fucken tīhei mauri ora! It's Pā Ryan's first draft of Ryan's dictionary. Top right-hand corner, hand scrawled in pencil, five bucks, score!

I put it back. There is a protocol to follow. Guarded by its counterparts I finish the Māori section and circle the room, clockwise. New Zealand fiction, New Zealand non-fiction, New Zealand reference, a litany of histories, true and false, come cascading down.

'Ā.'

Heinemann Dictionary of New Zealand Quotations.

Quick flick to the middle reveals:

MOO103

On dislike of the Māori (c. 1870).

The Maori race will be extinguished because they do not now fit into the present state of things now existing on the globe – wank, wank, wank ... turn the page – They did very well long ages ago to eat the black fellows – oh please – who were created before them and who were only a rudimental Papuan sort –

Sweeet. The first dictionary of bad-arse quotations: you are mine. I pop it back....

Circling on: Military, History, Philosophy, Art, Hobbies, then English Literature. Nah, nah, nah, nothing here. I spiral inward to the display table. Curio books, odd shapes, sizes and ages, face up, laid out delicate delights. Skim, scan, slurp ... cute. Undersized, faded cornflower-blue cover matches Ryan's lemon in my head.

Ivory trim, onion-domed lithograph bottom-right quadrant, the title, Middle Eastern in character saying *Rub—* something. Honing in, right hand, left hand opens. My left hand's digits move in trained unison; thumb, index, pinkie, years of reading precious comics, thumb, index, pinkie: *Rub— of Omar Kh—* something, something. I thumb, index, pinkie my way to the next page. Fucken sweet!

Omar Khayyam:

The poet-astronomer of Persia, died in AD 1123. His verses are famous for their supreme beauty, hamana, hamana, hamana, translated by Edward Fitzgerald, hamana, hamana, hamana ... rhythm and melody, hamana, hamana, hamana ...

Omar Khayyam rings a bell ... this is one of the works Pei Te Hurinui translated. Thumb, index, pinkie:

Awake! for Morning in the Bowl of Night
Has flung the Stone that puts the Stars to flight:

What the hell does that mean? He had a big dump in the middle of the night in a bowl and pissed a kidney stone? Pausing, I take a breath. Keeping my reptilian fight-or-flight brain in check I reread the passage, through Pei's eyes:

Awake! for Morning in the Bowl of Night
Has flung the Stone that puts the Stars to flight:

Ā, he pō tangotango. The stone's a metaphor for Tama-nui-i-te-rā. Oh that's good. Man, if it was good enough for Pei –

I put it back. Spiralling to the end of the table, I turn around.

'Do you have the time?'

'Quarter past one.'

'Thanks.'

Oh, shit! Spiralling back I pluck up the little book of poetry, back past *The Merchant of Venice*, Van Gogh and *The Whole History of Bi-Planes* I grab the thick quote book, then back to the beginning I pull out sweet Father Ryan's draft copy, whā that's good. Looking over, I look to see whether the woman is watching me through her mirrors. The bookkeeper, the guardian of the word, leans far left, lifting off her seat. I think she's swaying with the music until her opera and the cacophony of word music in my head is broken by the sound of a large fart. Almost toppling over she sways back down and the chair lets out its second sigh of the day. Waiting an appropriate amount of time, I take my buys up to the desk.

'Ā, I'll have these please.'

'Great....'

'Yeah, they're great finds. Pei Te Hurinui Jones translated this poet's work and this one appears to be the original draft of Father Ryan's dictionary.' What a bargain!

Her liver-spotted claw spears my knuckle:

'EFTPOS?'

'Ah, yeah, tā.'

'It'll take a few minutes to warm up.'

Bugger.

New technology in a musty room, oddly out of place, I shake hands with the EFTPOS arm, sliding my card across the palm.

The exchange is made. The touch of the brown bag, reasonable weight, holy communion.

'Thank you.'

'Thanks.'

Shit, shit, shit, ha'-past and I fly down the stairs, into the car and make my way to 'the gate at one'. Oh, well, I'll have my hākari later when I feast on the kupu, the whakataukī and the mōteatea. Fucken beaudy!

'Hi buddy....'

Sauces

Fitzgerald, E. (Kaiwhakapākehā) (c. ages ago) *Rubaiyat of Omar Khayym*, Whitcombe & Tombs Ltd, Aotearoa.

Orsman, H. & Moore, J. (1988) *Heinemann Dictionary of New Zealand Quotations*, Heinemann, Aotearoa, pp. 439-440, around the middle.

Ryan, P. M. (c. some time ago) *Māori-English, English-Māori Vocabulary for Schools*, some publisher, somewhere.

Tomlinson, K. Y. (ed.) (1995) *The Reader's Digest Word Power Quiz*, Reader's Digest, The U.S. of A.

The Land of Ooze

Phil Kawana

It was the arse-end of the world. The kind of place you ended up at, never intentionally went to. When the rains came – which was often – shit would seep up out of the paddocks and speckle the fields with Lilliputian mounds. Some said it was just grass grub, but most of us knew better.

Everything came up from below. Even on a good day the sky would hover overhead, afraid to come too close. Sometimes we'd take our bikes down to the dump and leap them off the dirt banks like pubescent Evel Knievels. If you did it right, if you had the balls to give it everything you had, then for a split second you could leap up into that hovering sky. You could stand on your pedals, nothing below your wheels but several feet of grey air, and take a mental snapshot of the reticent blue. Sometimes you could travel out of yourself, and you'd see the dust melting into the sweat on your face. And you'd yell. You'd yell loud enough for the trees to fold up their branches in fright, sending the scavenging gulls scraarking across the gully towards the old dam.

Hep reckoned the dam pond was bottomless. It was so narrow that we could throw stones across to the far bank by the time we were eight, but even when we were twelve, Hep was the only one who would swim in it.

'They even brought one of those diving bells once,' Hep called as he clambered, naked and dripping, out onto the far bank one afternoon. 'They had scuba gear and everything. And they still couldn't get to the bottom.'

Just then Tama scored a bull's-eye with an overripe black doris plum, right on Hep's exposed butt. It splattered all over his cheek like bird shit on a windscreen. Even from our side of the dam we could see the juice dribbling into his crack.

'That got to your bottom!' Tama howled, before fleeing into the pines for safety.

That was the day Hep showed us the tunnel.

'Me and Tai found it last holidays,' he told us over his shoulder as he pushed some kawakawa branches away to reveal the opening. 'It goes way back, all the way under the hill.'

'What's at the end?' I asked, hanging back a little. Tunnels aren't my thing.

'It comes out in the gully behind the dump. They must've dug it for drainage or something.'

The tunnel was just big enough for Tama and I to stand upright. Hep had to stoop as he led the way. We were out the other end in about five minutes. We went in as three horis on holiday. By the time we got to the gully, we were commandos deep behind enemy lines. We could hear a car pulling into the dump above us.

'It's the Gestapo! Drop down!'

Tama and I did paper-scissors-rock to decide who'd get recon duty. Tama lost, so he had to creep through the rubbish and peer over the lip. Me and Hep held our breaths as we listened. A car door closed. I looked to Hep, waiting for orders. He seemed about to say something, but Tama came skidding down the slope as fast as he could.

'It's Mr Thompson, and he's got a rifle,' he whispered urgently.

'Shit. He's rat hunting – run!'

And we were gone, squishing garden cuttings and rotten food under our feet. We were already well into the tunnel before the first crack of Mr Thompson's gun chased after us. We ran on, all the way to the dam, bursting through the kawakawa and out into the dank smell of pines.

On Sunday mornings Hep and I both had to go to church with our families. It was boring as, but at least it was better than helping Tama clean up after one of his parents' parties.

Because we were too old for Sunday School, we had to sit through the main service. Reverend John wasn't all that old, but his attempts at jokes were. All the grown-ups thought he was marvellous, but Hep and I knew better.

Near the entrance to the tunnel, under a drift of pine needles by a fallen tree, we kept our secret stash of old *Playboy*s. Someone had thrown a whole box of them over the lip of the gully, and we'd carted them through the tunnel to safety.

'D'ya think anyone in our class is gonna have tits like that?' Tama asked with a mouthful of plum, waving a picture at us.

'They're not real anyway,' Hep answered, barely bothering to look up. 'Tai reckons it's all Sellotape and fancy lighting.'

'Whaddaya mean, Sellotape?' We were both curious now, poring over the photo like it was the plans to an ice-cream factory, or something equally important. We couldn't see anything that didn't look like it should, but then we weren't really sure what they were supposed to look like anyway.

'They use Sellotape to hold them up, and have the light shining down so that there's shadows and they look bigger.'

'Bullshit,' Tama said, but sounded a little uncertain.

'True,' Hep assured us, still not looking up. He was sitting cross-legged down by the water, skimming stones across to the far side of the pond. 'They do that to give ya bigger stiffies.'

'Like this ya mean?' Tama asked, slipping his pants to his knees and waving his chubby at us.

Hep looked up this time, but only for a moment.

'Put it away, ya pubeless wanker,' he said in a bored voice.

The following Friday, Hep and I won the table-tennis doubles at the church youth club. Our prize was a king-sized bar of Dairy Milk each. Hep reckoned it was because we won it almost every week that he already had his first pimple.

Reverend John presented us with our prizes.

'You boys should think about playing more seriously,' he said, one hand on Hep's shoulder. 'There's a club in Wanganui that you could join. Who knows, you might even make the rep side.'

Hep shuffled about, looking at the floor. Reverend John's hand had slipped around, and was now softly patting him on the back.

'Nah,' I said. 'Too far to go.'

'Oh, I'd be quite happy to drive you. I have to go through there the evenings they meet anyway. I'm sure your parents wouldn't mind.'

'Thanks all the same, Reverend, but we're happy with the chocolate,' Hep said, twisting away and heading for the door. He tugged at my shirt as he went past.

'Well, if you ever want to give it a go, just let me know ...' Reverend John called out after us.

Outside, the night was warm and still, and we could make out the Southern Cross pointing lazily towards the dam. With our chocolate stuffed inside our shirts we rode our bikes down the dump road and went and sat by the pond. Hep pulled out his chocolate and laid it on the ground next to him. Then he reached deep into the front pocket of his jeans and pulled out a small package. In the dim starlight that managed to creep through the trees, I watched him flip it open and pull out two cigarettes.

'Here,' he said as he passed me one. I took it and held it awkwardly between thumb and index finger. Out of another pocket, Hep produced a lighter. With a flick, the shadows around us slithered away behind the kawakawa. My first puff on a cigarette didn't get past my mouth. I just held it there for a moment, then spat it out like a mouthful of water. Even though I couldn't see it, I could feel Hep watching me.

'No, take it right in. Like this.'

An ember-red glow didn't quite light up his face. When Hep inhaled, it sounded like the beginning of a sigh. I gave it a second go, and collapsed in a coughing heap.

'Useless bugger,' Hep laughed.

After my third failure to smoke properly, I had to stagger off and be sick. I was so dizzy, I only barely managed not to trip over. Hep grabbed my discarded cigarette, pinched it out and returned it to the packet.

'Maybe you should just stick to chocolate until you've grown up a bit more.'

I didn't feel like my chocolate just then. The mere thought of it made me feel queasy. Hep finished his fag and then abruptly stood up and started stripping.

'Whatcha doing?' I asked, before trying to spit the disgusting taste out of my mouth.

'Going for a swim.'

'But it's dark!'

'So?'

Hep stood there for a moment, naked, looking down at me. Patches of starlight decorated his skin like pale badges. Then he turned and ran to the pond's edge. The water erupted as he dove in, echoing amongst the trees. When he finally surfaced, he was out near the middle of the dam.

'How do you spot a queer?' Hep called.

'I dunno, how do you spot a queer?'

For a few seconds there was no reply. Hep trod water silently. I couldn't see his face. I could only make out the shape of his head and shoulders, bobbing in the shadows.

'Reverend John will like you,' is all he said. He rose up a few inches, then folded forwards. I saw the starlight shimmer on his back, bum, thighs, and then at last his heels as he disappeared like a dolphin down into the bottomless dam.

Welcome to Funky Kingston

Zion A. Komene

Jerky rubbed his fist over the thin layer of ice frosting the window of his stepfather's van. His face screwed up at the grime and cobwebs smeared all over his hand. He peered out the window at the gloom of a late afternoon sky. Thick grey clouds loomed above the Bottom Pub, aka the Hui House. Probably because anyone who entered usually walked out crying. Uncle Haki did that when he lost his week's wages at the TAB – Auntie Miriama threw a garden gnome at him. Uncle Lawrence sobbed when he won four hundred and fifty grand on Lotto – after spending a decade on the dole. Janie cried when she married Benji – after fifteen years and five kids of living together. Her little sister Elva wailed after giving birth to baby number seven – this time swearing that it was an immaculate conception.

They all gathered in the Hui House. They all wept, too. They wept at the scale their lives played out on. Maybe this realization let their emotions swim to the surface. Whatever. All Jerky knew was the realization created a near certainty – that each and every one who entered the Hui House would eventually stumble out past the bottle store, their sobs spreading over the footpath.

Jerky had heard that bawling since he was seven years old, when he first found himself in the Hui House car park waiting for his mother and stepfather. Five years ago. These days the cries blended into a symphony in his ear.

Jerky saw figures walk towards his van. He slithered down so no one could see, but he could sight them. The figures took on shape; four males wearing leather and denim, steel-toecapped boots. Jerky watched. One man passed another a bag, palming a wad of bills in his hand. Another rolled a cigarette, cracking a flame with a lighter, dragging long and sharp before passing it around. Jerky pressed his head on the van wall, listening closely.

'Cher, good shit man.'

'Cher, buried it last season.'

'No shit bro? You throw it in the back garden?'

'Nah, threw twenty keys in a drum. Buried it under my kurī's kennel.'

'Cher, security eh?'

'Yeh, but the fucken mutt dug it up and ate half of it. When he barks it's like a spacey woooooffff. Hahaha.'

Jerky knew the joke. He liked the way his people laughed – a collection of humour from mountains and valleys, rolled into one big ball over the ocean and through every one of his peoples' homes. It ran up feet, through legs, gathering momentum in stomachs, exploding in full throaty laughter all over Papatūānuku. Kind of like how stars explode into fragments after spending eons burning energy, leaving the debris as building blocks of future celestial bodies. When Jerky's people dumped their laughter over Papatūānuku, they left tiny shards of humour all over the place, the building blocks of future chuckles, jokes and cracking up.

So Jerky laughed. The van rocked and swayed. Jerky tried to stop, but too late, he opened his eyes to see heads staring through the window. Jerky bolted upright, hitting his head on the roof. He lost his balance and fell into the spare wheel for the van.

'That you Jerky?' said a voice. Jerky looked closer. 'It's me, little bro, how you doing?' It was Shirts, Jerky's cousin. Jerky opened the van door and stepped out. Shirts and his mates were all the same height. Which meant Jerky was chest height. Jerky sighed. Sometimes he wished he could skip 1982, being twelve years old and jump right over being a teenager. Just go for broke as a grown-up.

Jerky locked his eyebrows in greeting to Shirts, tilted his head towards the Hui House. 'The Old Lady and The N are in there.' Jerky never called his stepfather Dad. No one who shattered beer bottles over a woman's head deserved a name. So he settled on The N. The first letter in his stepfather's surname. Jerky thought it caught the right mix of loathing and resentment. Whenever he said it, it seemed hollow. Like how he felt the night The N kneed Jerky's mum's face in. Or when The N floored his van into Jerky's mum's car. While she was still in it.

Jerky remembered the little things his dad used to say. 'Anei te kaupapa: hold onto truth, son, no matter what.' Jerky remembered being four years old, his dad holding him, telling him to hold onto truth. 'Let your mana work for you, son. Let it do the mahi.'

But as the years stumbled on Jerky struggled to hold onto the memory. He felt hollow. No matter how hard he tried, he couldn't work the mana in the car park. It was too empty. He could sniff it in the air, taste it on the breeze. Jerky knew Shirts breathed in that truth too – it echoed around them. Even the sunlight felt cold as it turned a rich orange in the sky, ready to farewell day, welcome in night.

'Just you here bro?' Shirts didn't believe it.

'Yeh.'

Shirts shook his head, 'You got money? Kai?'

Jerky flicked his eyebrows at the van. Two bottles of warm lemonade, two cold meat pies, some peanuts and a Buzz Bar poked out of a paper bag in the front seat. Jerky reached in and grabbed the peanuts, offered them to Shirts. He knew his cousin loved peanuts.

'You going in the Hui House Shirts?' asked Jerky. He hoped his cousin would stay. Jerky liked Shirts. They walked their homes together, around the hills indented in tilled grooves. Like thick koru. Our tūpunas' mahi, said Shirts, as he and Jerky climbed them. Shirts would tell stories his grandfather had told him – how one woman rode from Hawai'iki on the back of a whale to their home; how she let her voice catch the wind as she chanted a waiata to transform her whale into a taniwha before gently carrying it, on karakia, to its new home in the lake up the road from Shirts' house.

'This hui house sucks bro,' muttered Shirts, gesturing at the pub. Shirts' mates agreed. They hated it too, but were too staunch to say so. Walking into the Hui House was like stepping into a crazed 1930s nightmare, full of dusty pinstripe suits – but no one person ever wore the full complement. Jackets, trousers, shirts and vests were scattered amongst the patrons who mixed and matched the dresswear with tracksuits, denim and swandris.

Shirts detested the way his people licked their lips as they almost ran into the Hui House. He hated the silent desperation on the faces. But most of all, he reviled the message he got from school, on the street, in the paper and on TV – that he and his family and friends would all march into the Hui House, forever and ever, ake, ake....

'Stick around Shirts,' said Jerky, 'we make our own fun here.' Jerky nodded towards other vehicles in the car park. James and his sister Kalia were in their Kingswood. Marty and Maui were perched on the hood of their car, eating hot chips. Kahi was stretched over the hood of his dad's car, trying to sleep or look cool, no one really knew.

One of Shirts' mates laughed at Jerky. 'What you little arseholes gonna do eh? Hehehe.' Jerky opened the back of the van, revealing a long rectangular wooden box. Old shoes and newspapers were scattered over the top. And lots of dust. Everywhere.

'Your coffin bro?' laughed Shirts and his mates. The box was so big it could fit two people in it.

'Well actually bro,' said Jerky as he forced the lid open, 'this is the entrance to Funky Kingston.' And he pulled out a large tarpaulin, which proclaimed in black and red, gold and green spraypaint 'WELCOME TO FUNKY KINGSTON!'

After helping Jerky secure the tarpaulin over the fence, Shirts stepped back, admiring the work. No. He admired his cousin's audacity, the way he carved the world into his own. Jerky pulled a small barbecue out of the coffin and a bag of coal. James and Kalia laid out cuts of meat from a beast their dad killed. Leeanne and Toni pulled out their boombox, and hit the play button. Everybody started chanting to Toots and the Maytals, *well she's such a beautiful woman, yet she have so many ugleh men....* Marty and Maui strung torches and candles on cars, lighting each one carefully, before joining in with Toots and the rest, *but when she goes to the market place, she leave all character at home, ohhhhh....* Kahi stood on top of his dad's car, slow grooving, proclaiming to all that this was the chocolate hour just before darkness creeps in, creating night. And he demanded that everyone join him in singing along with Toots, *oh sweet beautiful woman, beautiful woman, beautiful woman, will drive you crazy....*

Shirts' mates surveyed the scene, moving to the beat and sniffing the beef sizzling on the grill. One of Shirts' mates smiled. 'They got some aroha goin' down here alright, cher? Let's spread more around.' And he jumped into Funky Kingston to touch the jah love, made him feel alright. Like so much eyreeye kotahitanga going down.

When the sun set, torches and candles burned bright at Funky Kingston. James passed bottles of DB Bitter around, while Kahi cracked open some Black Heart Rum and traded shots for drags on joints being handed out. The smoke rising above the crowd made the flames from the candles and beams from the torches glow with an orange sheen.

Kalia and Jerky tended the barbecue, the hot coals crisping the beef to a dark golden brown. Shirts fumbled around in the coffin, stumbling on a guitar with three strings. When everyone yelled out and James killed the volume on the boombox, Shirts went to work, plucking out some rhythm and lyrical dedication from the melodious Tyrone Taylor.

From a little cottage in the Negril,
I wrote these lines, to you
From a little cottage in the Negril (ohhh babeh)
I realise I love you still
From a little cottage on the hill,

Way down west of Negril,
This man sit, pining,
For your love...

Everyone sighed appreciatively, while kids from the billiard hall came out to join the fun, and shopkeepers busily scratched their heads before running to call the police.

Jerky climbed the roof of The N's van and looked down on Funky Kingston. 1977 he'd first entered the carpark. A cold, wet night. The N had just got paid. Jerky and his mum rode with The N into town – to buy food, pay bills. But The N had other ideas, swinging the van into the carpark, aiming his wairua straight for the Hui House.

'I'm just going to get some money from him,' said Jerky's mum. 'I'll be back.'

Jerky wrapped himself in an old jacket he found in the back, and waited – he believed her after all – until the only light in the carpark shone from the Hui House. Jerky watched people come and go, hoping one was his mum. His heart pounded, adrenaline pumped. And his head smacked the van roof when Mangu Kaha gang members ran up, splattering their faces all over the windows, lips flattened against the glass, long wet hair, flailing wild fists over the doors, feral screams and laughter as they jumped on the roof, while more Mangu Kaha rocked the van to and fro, chanting together, 'Come out leedle boy!'

Jerky remembered curling into a foetal position, like a little pounamu tiki his grandmother used to wear. She told him it gave the wearer good luck. That night Jerky wanted so bad to be a tiki. So bad.

Much later Jerky had opened his eyes and let himself listen again. He heard his mum singing. He saw The N looking at him, spitting at his face. 'Little bastard. Fucken pub closed 'cause of you.'

Jerky heard his mum, voice all syrupy. 'Leave him alone. He's had a good night eh, haven't you? Here's a mince pie. Go on, eat it. They go gluey when they're cold.'

'Bro, you okay?' Shirts looked at his cousin. He was worried. His grandfather had told him a story about Jerky. Everyone wondered about his real name. It couldn't have anything to do with the wairua. It wasn't spelt right.

'Kāhore, no,' said Shirts' grandfather, 'He is named after the capital city of South Korea. His father and I went there as soldiers. No, we went there as boys. We did strange things, some of which frightened us. But that tamaiti, well his father kept my spirits up. Until he got hit. A mortar blast. He went to hospital in Seoul. There he made friends with an old Korean man, who told him his youngest tamaiti would be born late in his life, in a time of hardship for him. He would never see his tamaiti become a man eh. So he would have to teach his tamaiti as much as he could as fast as he could, so he could have a chance eh.'

Shirts pondered this information. He knew it was custom, since the Two Eight Māori Battalion came back from kicking Nazis, for soldiers to name children of their family after places they had fought in, or for exemplary deeds in life. That's why his cousin was named Alamein and his sister was named Bastion. Maybe now was a good time to find out how he got his name.

'So Matua, I was named after the biggest city in Australia because that was where you made your test debut for the All Blacks right?'

'Now that's a good beginning to a story, Boy,' chuckled Shirts' grandfather, 'I'll make sure to remember that one.'

'Is my cousin special?'

'Kāhore. We are all special.'

'Then why you telling me?'

And Shirts' grandfather ruffled his hair and laughed. 'Because. One day you might want to awhi him. Manaakitanga. If he's been taught well, I'm sure he'll help you too.'

'I'm cool,' said Jerky. He helped Shirts climb on the van roof. They looked out over the Hui House. The windows were all frosted. No one could see in or out. But Jerky and Shirts saw shadows, drinking and talking, spluttering and laughing. Jerky closed his eyes. For a moment he imagined his Mum's voice rising above the Hui House din, above Funky Kingston. He wanted to charge into the Hui House, pull his mum out and burn the place to the ground. But convention held him back – the very same rules which said the Hui House carpark was for patrons only. The same rules he broke to create Funky Kingston, but couldn't repeat to save his mum.

'Time to eat. Haere mai ki te kai!' yelled Kahi over UB40 on the boombox telling anyone who would listen they're a one in ten, a number on a list, and how they're a statistical reminder of a world that doesn't care.

And right then, with Kahi leading the way, the whole of Funky Kingston proceeded to punish the mess of barbecued beef something bad. Bread and butter, Coke and Mello Yello, hot potato chips and coleslaw from Aprea's Pizza House. All on the menu.

Kids ate like it was a decade of Christmases in a row, minus the presents and the drunken fighting. After licking the grease off their hands, they danced to a UB40 slow groove, *ooh, you say you're gonna leave me, I'm begging you stay, but babeh I can't get through anyway, no I can't.* Kahi lifted Kalia onto the hood of his dad's car and held her like he always wanted, while UB40 drifted on, *and when I wake up in the morning you are gone, little pretty thing you know I'll be all alone.* Everyone stood mesmerised and watched the young couple sway in and through love, all over each other as UB40 played on, *you'll hear me crying, oooh please don't make me cry....*

And the whole of Funky Kingston stared, transfixed at the etching of Kahi and Kalia bonded on the car. Everyone remained locked in their tight embrace, until the screeching of sirens and the flare of blue lights exploded into Funky Kingston, turning it once again, into the Hui House carpark, where parking is for patrons only.

Jerky drank in the panic. He yelled at Kahi and Kalia, 'Look after everyone!' And Marty and Maui jumped on a car. Maui pulled his grandmother's violin out of his bag. His uncle gave it to him after they buried her. His whānau knew she wanted Maui to have it.

Maui bent the violin strings into sound, while Marty strummed the guitar. The music seemed to swirl, wrapping everyone in harmony, hiding them from police scrutiny – those adults who wanted to intervene and damage Funky Kingston. Forever.

Jerky jumped off the van roof. He rummaged through the coffin, pulling out two large fire extinguishers. 'Here, grab this,' he said to Shirts, throwing a fire extinguisher at him. And they ran through the crowd, towards the police car. Jerky unravelled the extinguisher hose, yanked the release pin. And he darted around the police car, enveloping it in waves of creamy white foam, while Shirts stuffed his hose through a back window, filling it like a chocolate éclair.

Jerky and Shirts stood back to survey their handiwork. They had brought their friends just enough time to disappear into the night. The Hui House would be closing soon, and people would be exiting the doors. But Jerky and Shirts smiled at each other. Funky Kingston was closed for the night. Shirts helped Jerky wrap up the tarpaulin, dampen down the barbecue, close the coffin. They watched Jerky's mum and The N stumble through the crisp cool night, while cops struggled out of their car, handcuffs at the ready, too embarrassed to radio back to HQ for backup: 'Unit one-five to base. We have a ten-ten alert. We've been foamed!'

Shirts looked at his cousin, knowing he had more to learn about him, a lot less to take for granted. 'You wanna come home with me bro? You don't wanna stay here eh?' And Shirts locked his eyebrows, feinting to his right, towards The N and Jerky's mum.

'Sweet as bro,' said Jerky. He helped himself to a pair of the cops' handcuffs. A keepsake. 'I better cuff them before they start scrapping. I'll drive them home myself. Drunk drivers are killers.'

'Can I get a ride back with youse?'

'Geez how were you gonna get me home if I had gone with you?'

'Dunno, probly hitched eh?'

'Cher, you may as well drive then. I'm underage.' And Jerky searched his mum's pockets for the keys, before carefully placing her in the back seat. Shirts went to help The N get in.

'Bro, just kick him in,' said Jerky. And he did just that, booting The N on the arse so he went flying head first into the car. He tossed

Shirts the keys, while The N grunted about the indignity of ending flat on his arse, in the back seat of his car, even though Jerky's mum bought it. Jerky said nothing – just squeezed the fire extinguisher trigger into The N's slack mouth.

Shirts shook his head. 'Cher little bro, you got this down to a fine art eh?'

'Yeah, I wanna be the Salvador Dali of Aotearoa bro.'

'What?'

'Salvador Dali. He paints freaky pictures like hands full of eyeballs and stuff. Some say he's pōrangi. I think he's colourful.'

'Cher. Well bro, you can paint my whare anytime.'

And Jerky and Shirts cracked up. They didn't stop laughing until they had pulled out of Funky Kingston and hit State Highway 1 for home.

Mother

Mahinaarangi Leong

Black. The Finishing.

She was in the water again. Waitangi. Higher.... Higher.... Pulse beating, ears roaring. Breathless. Then the water again. The garden. Fighting for air. Accretions of age. Karakia. The tree. The earth ... and something older; harder. Hesperides voiceless, standing like sentinels. Barren. Our song is still, e hoa.

Auē ... auē ... auē.

Black. The Stirring.

She breathed the rarefied air. She was being pushed too fast, too high. Unseen hands ... an aphonic hymn meticulously, insistently sliding her from Tangaroa nearer the sun. She needed to climb, poised and poignant. Icarus-like, she began to fall away; away from everything. The choice. That had always been the problem. It was now.

Something in the earth shifted. Rimu felt the transposition. Dark ... but soft hues. Our waiata is moving now, e hoa.

Auē ... auē ... auē.

Black. The Rising.

She saw her home, only it wasn't. It was someone else's. Sterile. Banal. A life woven from hers. Arachne's eulogy. Kahikatea like a mirror. Refraction. Recognition. She thought she saw herself – insular, sentient – in the water. Charybdis waiting. Out of her depth, gasping. No reflection now, no shadow, no sound. Something? She knew it was there again. It barely breathed, it lay absolutely still. Languid. Feigning. Acquiescent. Lichen on rock. Then it was inside. A fingerling offering antipodean spawn. She felt it exorcise itself … talons of silk, butterfly wings, whispering … caressing … slipping into her subterranean regions and lower, oh much lower. Intussusception. Our voices must be strong, e hoa.

Auē … auē … auē.

Black. The Understanding.

She was trying to remember … something. Far out, she could hear whales singing. A prayer soon to be lacerated. She probed, prodded, pommelled. Her memory, a prison. The tide was out now. But she continued to be drawn. Āe, never once recognising it for what it was. Te Reinga – penultimate repository. Wild within. The oldest of pohutukawa yawned. Its roots pirouetted, dilated. Demeter inhaled. One day she would have to swim back to shore. Soon. Our words need meaning, e hoa.

Auē … auē … auē.

Black. The Diminishing.

She heard the voice. Something. Reminiscent of a psalm. It had happened again. Just time to focus. Noiselessly, she was there. Aphrodite. Approaching the headland from the sea. Pure. Pacific. One siren singing. In Rangi's arms, she levitated, caught her breath and swooned. Tawa from Isis' seed. One again. The homecoming. Hers. Our karakia is softer now, e hoa.

Auē … auē … auē.

Black. The Silence.

She saw it. Heard it. Smelt it…. Something crouching left of her soul. Bifurcated. Focused. A speechless invocation. A parody. It watched its Persephone. It breathed her. Moving for that first delicious time, it came. The tide rushed in. The matai stood its ground. Scylla satiated. Lost. Our wāhine do not sing, e hoa.

Auē … auē … auē.

Black. The Irony.

She remembered. But it was not her memory to have. She, of the tribe. She, the Psyche of her hapū. Ngaio. Odin, Cronos, Amon-Ra … where were they now? Submerged? Absorbed, mute, asphyxiated. Her eyes shone, her mana held. She understood the kinship of her true species. A serpent treed. A pathology upon its haunches, poi astride mere, breathing into the mouth of Tāwhirimātea. Retribution. The chill blew early and long across the Tararuas. A litany – half expressed; half answered. Ephemeral; immutable. Some-thing. No-thing. Hera … Zeus … sister, wife. Absolute relativity. Pitiful. Pitiless. Our people smile through their songs, while their hearts break, e hoa.

Auē … auē … auē.

Black. The Starting.

She – no longer in the water. She – not drowning. She – surviving. She – insistent that the water keep her afloat. Resurgence. Renaissance. Restitution. Poseidon's epiphany. In him, every man. She saw him. Rākau. A muchness. Then she was with him, inside his head. She reached in and sucked – exquisitely. He could feel her. In his marrow. She was too deep. Everywhere. Not letting him breathe. He could do nothing. She moved softly at first and he shuddered; ached. Wanted. She made him wait. Then she very slowly crucified him. Such a small death, really. Expunged. Expiated. Our poroporoaki is our beginning, Gaia.

Ake … ake … ake.

April the fourth. You came. A singularity. One suitcase. A kahu. No preamble. Predatory. No one home that day saw the pervasive sweep of your approach. Encroachment? Rapprochement? My mother's freesias, assiduous in their attention, would have been the first to sense you, then the little ponga, the pūhā through the asphalt; and finally all the others – a garden full of trees that bore no fruit.

Mum asked you in. You talked about 'the war' and all the medals you had won. You talked about the sea (that formed your backyard) and your favourite tree. Mum introduced the boys then me. You pronounced my name – slowly, easily; water off the tongue. You knew my identity, so totally. You, who already had the foreknowledge. Were you listening Mum? Dad hadn't come home yet. The six o'clock swill took its toll (and our men) in Matapouri.

Mum showed you to your room (my room) – yours for the weeks that were to follow. Why did you two not talk? You never lingered. Just surface bubbles. No posies, no ihi, no aroha. Us kids just kept playing. And after the Sunday roasts had come and gone – you were too; Mum's engagement ring in your case. Another medal, but for what battle, Uncle?

Shadows rabid and charred in their desolation move like apparitions in and out of my mother's life. Crab apples. You were one of them, nē ra, Uncle? She only let us kids see one or two of the old silhouettes – kēhua. We never understood the Valkryies who took our warrior-mother away. We just knew she never came back. Not really. In fact, she had never been back (not anywhere) since the time she left her mother's care three months shy of that first tender iridaceous decade. Ripples.

Mum says you raised her. Helped her family. Helped her age. You and Aunty. She loved Aunty. I know what Aunty looked like. I never knew what you looked like, Uncle, until you came to stay. Aunty died eh? Mum's mum gave Mum to you to look after, so she could help you. Did she help you, Uncle? Mum says you were lonely. You fullas had no kids, that's not our way. Mum's mum had too many kids. She didn't miss my mother, but I know how much my mother missed her. At night, almost every night, she remembered ... cadences cascade through the years. Generations on, they still do.

You were stuck Mum, eh? A 6 a.m. to 3 p.m. kitchen hand. A life snatched between the Frigidaire, half gees, and pints of milk. A brown girl's cantos ... or a tirade, Ma? A sad little blossom, ripe for the plucking. Incarceration takes many forms. And day by day, I saw a sunburnt Shirley Valentine pace out the confines of her suburban cell. Papillon has wings. Kia kaha, e Kui. Entrapment of the small and beautiful is part of the nature of whānau; but you'd understand that, Uncle.

Mum told me she hated the farm. Couldn't even stand the sea. Your farm, Uncle ... your sea too. Nine and prematurely free from school. A succulent. Succumbing. But not free. There's no childhood if you know only work, eh Uncle? Too much to do and a child doing it. All. But what we do to others, we do to ourselves too.

You weren't a bad person, Mum said. Just tough, the way land people are. She said she had a lot to be grateful for. Couldn't be blamed. Hard times and all that, Mum said. She always (nearly always) went to bed with her belly full. She had you to thank for that.

My mum has these kind of gaps in her life. Like cloth that's got all frayed or has rot or something. Her life has indents. She's not whole. And a madonna not whole has children and moko with holes. The blow-out from the humdrum of a working-class melancholy. Internecine penetration. Perforation. Bit of a worry for the phenomenon we call the fabric of society, eh what? No rainbows here. Only ennui and a chocolate Artemis, nē Uncle?

Mum said you do everything well, Uncle. Mum says Dad does too. Every Friday, us kids got Woolworths jelly beans and Catholic fish and chips. Every day, you got the vacuity of chrome, Formica and linoleum. The pay packet came in and you pocketed most of it along with your pride. A kept woman awash with four kids, none of them his. Like pale Ngā Puhi, anaemic – armed with the casuistry of burgeoning manhood, your kind never came south for cloaks or flax, your errands were more insidious, more basic. Plastic bouquets. Bloodlines. Regeneration. And so our mother went north. Sow in heat. A ring on her finger. A good Māori sheila. Yours ... Polydectes.

Thirty pieces of silver or Charon's fare – it's all so much easier when your soul's not yours. Obsidian. You do the perfunctory. Automaton fulfilling a set task; unvarying. Not a dream blower in sight. An Assyrian vanguard into battle – high tech, weak ethics. Perfect. Patriarchy ... sexist, fascist, racist ... ist! Old kūmara. A temperate genus waiting to seed.

Because of you Uncle ... but not entirely because of you, I am coming to understand who my mother is. Not affranchised yet – slowly, though. She told me once how she, coming directly from working the sea, went to communion and had to clear the confessional first. Easy when you're fourteen and there's nothing to confess. A life of beatitude and utility – pūhā never pulled except to eat. Eucharist style, eh Uncle?

On the odd occasion we spoke, you said you knew my mother well. Most of her life, as it turns out. I liked the smile on your lips and in your eyes. You said she was stubborn right from the start. And when did it start, Uncle? She was in standard three when she came to you and Aunty. But what did that mean? In the manner of our tīpuna, time was neither absolute nor uniform. Āe! Whatever life threw at her, she could wade through, never really minded. She, appearing like a spectre in the middle of it all ... but really on the periphery, in the nimbus, on the edge of a sixties Ford, and a bach at the beach. Embourgeoisment. White man's bondage, Ma. And years on.... Yours. Mine. Ours.

Where are our photos, Ma? Whānau have photos. Nah, not just those on the mantelpiece. Something. Proper ones more. Connections, e Kui? Everywhere smells Pākehā, Mum. In us too – the meeting ... the parting, nē ra? But I think it's going to be alright. Has to be, eh! In the pre-dawn everything looks OK. I guess that's what happens when you look from inside a doll's house or you open your eyes and gaze up through water.

When you left Uncle, we did not wonder about you. Cui bono? But I gave you the freesias because you said you liked them. They were the crème de la crème of our garden – fragrant, fragile; gestalt in bloom. And with the malleable symmetry of the gullible, I allowed myself to be divided neatly then put back whole. But not quite. What does it all mean, Uncle?

I saw what you did. The little bodies – all white and yellow, strewn on the gravel not fifty metres from the soil that swaddled them. Crushed like some ventriloquist's dummy thrown down in pique. The flowers lay at oblique angles, wretched in their repose. A gutter garland.

I tried hard not to see them. But such a nefarious and nondescript death is ironically difficult to ignore. That day, I saw what becomes of the vulnerable uncle. The spoils of war. When did growing become a sin? When did it all get so mixed up? Aotearoa – a white land long clouded. Paralysis. Genesis.

You say that when you were a younger man nothing gave you greater pleasure than watching Aunty or Mum ironing. Even now, you say you love the smell of freshly laundered and ironed clothes. Just to let you know: I never iron! I see you there, with your nice middle-class white shirt. I've never seen you iron. I look at my mother who is all ironed out.... Has she told you her tale? Have you not, then, a life levelled? Power has a gender, eh Uncle?

Shuffling between the sink and the washing board – a jet visage. I know it's important not to stay still. Stay still and you get caught. The water catches you. Drowning – Me. Her. Us. Keep moving! Your time to be still is soon. We are watching. Your family is near. Do not let the terror hold sway. We are all around you now. Within. Go inside now. Not a branch moving. Cry not, for the child you hardly were.

Between the gingko and the turnstile synapses, your reality remains precarious, e Kui. Cocooned in a forgiving forgetfulness, we know that one lets slip what one must. You never came home, Ma, because you never left. Āe, now I see. You have our cunning, old one. Here all the time, but in our preoccupation we overlooked the obvious. In order to hide something, you hide it close (atu: mai – away and to). Ultimately, you engulf it. This is our lingua franca.... And it is total.

We sense each other, you and I, sniffing at our being like snakes, tongues to-ing and fro-ing, feeling the scent. The heat. But the others? She stared down millennia at her ancestors. She looked slowly into their faces – a biology of universal grammar, wordlessly exposed. Unity. Prediction? Predilection? Words, expressing a myriad of themes but foreclosing on the same story. Māori mythology. All mythology, Uncle.

Each day. Eternity. Forever. Never. Ghosts, a surfeit of enemies ... where are they Ma? They are charcoal chimera we carry inside. They are the everythings and the nothings we put between ourselves and the world. What remains is what we have given away. And we gave it all away, eh Ma? Deciduous, we are a cataract in flood.

No, don't go away Ma. Don't turn your face from mine. Don't go back to your garden, what is there for you? Do you see me, Ma? Am I you? Have I not been you? Am I not you now? Are not we two one? Too alike, nē? The water will come again – to take you – and I shall let it? ... as you let it take me. The vagaries of intercession. No longer evergreen.

And is not each passing much like the others? But when did you really go Ma? The real one. The one before the obituary. Why did you let him? J'accuse! Oblivion. The void. Cessation. Row upon row of headless flowers. Our urupā, like our whakapapa, cropped with deliberation. A kind of castration, Uncle.

I wither you grow, Mother. You join, I break, e Kui? Some kind of injunction, or perhaps a seduction? The mind infiltrated, the body made corrupt – the carnage and the apperception, e whaea. Our whānau's innerscape. An ecology of loss. The colour of the earth.

I understand why I have no grandmother; and so it must be. I also understand how it will be for your granddaughter ... your seed. Our women are unforgiving. But oh god, the night is vast and Hine Nui te Pō, the primeval, quintessential Eve, awaits. Expurgating. Inexorable. A visitant.

You said, 'Swim,' and then turned to walk away. Stillborn, you never heard my reply, Ma – 'Kāore he wai.' (But mother, there is no water.) What tortured creature sits in your mind e Kui; hissing and howling at windmills? Ma, I don't want to go in the water. I can't swim, I'm frightened. He is in the water. No, much worse – he is the water! Preternatural. Primordial. I am not yours to share, Ma. I am able to be whole. Indivisible. Inviolate. You're not listening, e Kui. The bunch of flowers I hold in my hands is now separate and limp. I weep for the flowers. They suffer under the misapprehension that they are in bud, when in fact they will never be, Uncle.

Who is our enemy, Ma? Is it us? Art thou that? Art thou him? Such sanguine and sordid duplicity. Blood seeping into tissues, the ultimate adultery. A done deal. Before my birth, eh Ma? History allowed to repeat its kind of watered-down gendercide. The pīpīwharauroa still tells its tales. A mother's collaboration. Betrothed and betrayed.

Ours is a kind of shared dementia Ma – an intergeneration quid pro quo ... and thus the sins of the mother.... Is it my duty to do someone else's bidding? Was it this you raised me for? Servitude.

Generation. Degeneration. I think I understand now, Ma. Women of our whānau ... transmutated ... transmogrified. Pūrerehua. What a desperate fraud we partake of.... My mother. My diablerie.

You are looking at me again, Ma. What do you see? A nigrescent childhood? Layers, weeds, a Gordian knot – tied we two – all convoluted and indecipherable. A vicarious life, nonetheless. Debris the pallor of deep mānuka. Your colour, Uncle.

I watch your seed like a myopic worm burrowing through the foliage to reach the empyrean – only to find true reality – inter faeces et urinam. Te Rā was always here on Earth – kaikōmako, tōtara, māhoe, pate and pukatea, our witnesses. Another woman to immolate on the pyre. But water is a deadly serpent and there is nothing you do not know about me. Here I stand, my mother's daughter. A succubus. Et tu Brute? The end is the beginning. An overflowing. A realisation that the water never goes away.

It was then, I looked up. It was my birthday Mum and I saw you raise your hand like a benediction. You were smiling, Ma. Te tīmatanga. Black vistaed, indehiscent – about to take the first bite from a lovely, red-green apple – my favourite: Pacific Rose.

A Small Cultural Problem

Pierre Lyndon

The two boy-men hopped in. The Transit van sidled off with the Old Man driving. An hour later they were parked outside the post office. While the Old Man disappeared off to the loo by the taxi stand, the person they were there to meet arrived. She wore a scarf on her head and glasses, like the ones you buy at the Warehouse. She handed Paapu one of those plastic kits, popular with old ladies at church. 'Hang on to that for Aunty,' she said.

The Town Hall clock struck 9 p.m. when they set off again for Auckland. It had begun to rain and only one of the wipers worked. Paapu drove while Billy fidgeted with the wiper control. Half an hour later he announced that it was not working.

The Old Man spoke non-stop to Aunty Awhina the whole way. 'If Hone's pigs come into my garden one more time, I'll give them both barrels,' he said. Two chooks tied up at the back of the van gave a little squawk.

They had to stop to gas-up and the Old Man went, again. Aunty gave twenty dollars toward the petrol and Billy took over the driving. A meat pie each and a big bottle of Fanta kept the boys quiet. The chooks got the scraps.

'We'll have to see about those tappets when we get home boys,' the Old Man said. 'They're making a hell of a racket.' One of the chooks answered with another squawk. Aunty Awhina chomped silently away on her Big Ben pie without the aid of her dentures. These she kept in a small hanky somewhere on her person.

A yellow neon light blinked in the night. In daytime it read "Arohanui Funeral Services". At night the Arohanui part didn't work.

The Hetarakas said they would be able to fix the light, if all the Māoris and Islanders paid their bills.

Mr Hetaraka emerged from a room marked Staff Only with a roll-your-own hanging out the side of his mouth. A sign above him said No Smoking. He apologised once more for the delays.

'There've been some complications,' Mr Hetaraka explained. 'There is a big build-up of fluid. That's the cause of the swelling. We won't be too much longer,' he lied, for the fourth time in five hours.

The whānau filled the waiting room. Outside the young ones, and some not so young, smoked and talked about the Warriors' chances of winning on Saturday. Inside the surgery, a small mouse scurried across the floor. Mr Hetaraka's sister worked with no visible sign of urgency. She had one eye on the clock. The moment the clock struck 1 a.m. it would cost the whānau an extra five hundred dollars on top of their fee. At 1.10 a.m. the Hetarakas wheeled the body out, apologising once more for the 'complications'. Uncle Johnny looked smug inside a brand-new deluxe casket made by an Access Training Scheme in Dargaville.

Even though Uncle Johnny had lost both legs to diabetes eighteen months ago, the whānau still opted for the full-length deluxe. It would look odd for manuhiri to attend the tangi and see Uncle Johnny in a four-foot eleven mini coffin.

The Transit van wheeled into the Whaiora Marae at 2 a.m., and a couple of minutes later they headed straight for the wharenui.

'Back that van up to the front door Billy,' the Old Man ordered.

Aunty Awhina slipped her false teeth in and headed out with a brolly in hand. The Old Man carried his carved walking stick.

The lights were on in the wharekai as some people were having a late cuppa.

'Can you wait for the kaumātua to come back?' a woman said. 'He's just gone home for a shower.'

The Old Man brushed her aside and headed for the wharenui. 'You should be ashamed of yourself,' said Aunty Awhina, 'attending a tangi wearing lipstick and a miniskirt.' The woman yelped as Aunty Awhina drove the point of her brolly at her arse.

There was a hushed murmur as people in the wharenui recognised the Old Man and Aunty Awhina. 'It's the body snatchers,' shrieked a Pākehā man near the body. 'Grab that lid Billy, and put it on.'

'We have a legal and binding will,' said the widow, thrusting the papers at the Old Man. Aunty Awhina took the papers and tore them to shreds. The children began howling. An educated type stood in the way of the Old Man and announced that his cousin would only be moved 'over my dead body'. The Old Man pointed the two-kilo walking stick at him, and his momentary outburst of courage vanished.

It was front and back, as Paapu and I eased the coffin into the back of the van. The chooks squawked as their territory quickly became a confined space. Inside the wharenui everyone just looked at each other and stared at the blank space that was meant to be Uncle Johnny. In the morning his mates from the bowling club were coming to pay their last respects. The widow was beside herself, the kids sobbed and everyone was speechless.

The educated type slowly got to his feet. The experience of the past half hour had not been covered in Māori 101. 'It's OK!' he said to no one in particular. 'In the morning I will ring the Otara Neighbourhood Law Office. They'll know what to do.'

At 3 a.m. we were over the harbour bridge when Paapu spotted the blue lights. 'Drive on,' the Old Man ordered.

'Mr Paraone, we have received a complaint from a distraught family that you have stolen their father in the middle of their grieving. May I look in the back?'

'Can I borrow your mobile, officer,' said Aunty Awhina. Two minutes later we heard her say, 'Good morning prime minister, it's Whina here. Sorry to ring you at this ungodly hour. We've got a small cultural problem. We're taking our nephew home to bury. They were going to cremate him tomorrow at the Puhinui Crematorium. Here, you speak to the officers.'

Ten minutes later the van groaned its way along the windy ridge just past Waiwera. Paapu drove the whole way. At 5 a.m. we arrived at the wāhi tapu and started digging. At 10 a.m. the Old Man was sitting in church when the whānau arrived from Auckland to find their husband and father already buried. Paapu sauntered in to give the Old Man an update.

'Tell them to go down town to the fish and chip shop and buy a feed,' the Old Man said. 'I'll be finished church at three o'clock.'

A Man's Gotta Do What a Man's Gotta Do

Pierre Lyndon

The manuhiri are gathered by the gate. Unbelievably, they are gathered before the home people.

'I wish these Māoris would get organised,' someone says.

It's past the appointed time. The manuhiri are restless. They are shifting around. They've decided to plough on ahead. There is no one else, so Midge, a man, has to do the karanga. What can he do? All the women are off elsewhere. What a situation. How extraordinary. Midge launches into it.

'Haere mai rā, haere mai, haere mai.'

He's heard Aunty Tiki do it a thousand times before. Actually, it's quite easy when you have to do it. It's quite empowering.

While it's not a woman per se doing the karanga, it's the next best thing. The manuhiri notice the swing of Midge's hips.

They are all safely inside. Uh oh. Where are the kaumātua? Never around when you need them. Now Midge has to be the speaker too.

'Kia ora huihui mai anō tātou,' he starts out. The manuhiri are unperturbed. They just want a hot drink and to settle in for the night. They've come all the way up from Auckland. Their speaker responds. No waiata. It's too late. No one's got the energy or the inclination. That's it, mercifully.

Midge takes a peep outside. The tribe still haven't turned up and only Taro in the kitchen. Midge tells the manuhiri to get their gear and to dump it all in the wharenui. He heads directly for the wharekai. Yep! Taro and Midge, the two silly fools, left holding the baby, again.

The manuhiri wander on in.

'Help yourselves,' says Midge. 'The tea and Milo are over there. There's no coffee, I forgot to call into Pak n Save. Take it easy on the sugar, we're running low.' Midge takes a seat and has a cuppa of his own.

After a cuppa tea, it's back to the wharenui. Taro sails into it. Bedding and linen are her department. 'Did you find the mattresses? They're up there in that back room. It's not locked. Get them out after karakia.'

Everyone is in the wharenui. Uncle Hare, the kaumātua, still hasn't arrived. There's a nasty suspicion that he's on the turps, being a Friday night. Midge rings the bell.

Everyone knows it's time for church. The bell rings for the third and last time. All they need now is a minister.

Taro looks at Midge. 'Looks like you're it.'

'Kia ora huihui mai anō tātou,' he says for the second time in two hours. It's the favourite opening line at Tau Henare Marae. Midge has been brought up with it. When in doubt, let it go. 'Kia ora huihui mai anō tātou.' It has a certain ring to it. It has its own appeal. Kind of like, peace of mind. 'Kia ora huihui mai anō tātou,' Taro says too.

In the morning, it's self-help. The manuhiri wake up to porridge and toast. They make the porridge and they make the toast.

No kōhanga reo today. They share the marae too.

Someone goes past on a tractor. 'What time's kick-off ?'

'One o'clock this afternoon. Women's match, Auckland versus Pipiwai.'

The rugby boys are down on the field with spades. They're collecting cow crap off the field. 'Someone left the gate open again,' one of them yells out.

The Aucklanders are wandering around. 'Where's the showers?' they ask.

'Down the river bro,' says Taro. 'Make sure you keep your shorts on mate, the eels might bite,' she laughs.

'Hey Midge, you playing this afternoon?'

'Sorry honey, I'm a netballer,' Midge says. 'I play for the Southern Sting. I've got to watch myself, I might get injured.'

It's 1.30 p.m., Auckland lead 13-3. 'Hey, you got a few big Islanders in that team. They're on steroids,' yells the Pipiwai coach.

Kare is sin-binned. She's clothes-lined some poor woman from west Auckland. Ten minutes later, the whistle blows. It's all over, a draw.

'Funny how a lot of these marae games end up a draw,' Midge says from the sideline.

The music starts up. It's Len's disco. Len loves the Bee Gees. *Staying alive*, the music blares. The place is packed. People all over the place.

'Looking to score tonight Midge?' says Len.

'Sure am, doll,' he says.

Unbelievably for the Aucklanders, the music stops on the stroke of midnight. 'Church rules,' the DJ says. 'It's now Sunday – the day of rest. Can't break the sabbath.'

The Aucklanders can't believe it. 'You're kidding,' Aunty Elsie says.

'Them's the rules,' Midge says. 'It's in the constitution.'

Everyone makes their way back to the marae to sleep. Some head off to the nightclub in town.

In the morning the locals put on bacon and eggs. Tomorrow, Uncle Henry will be looking for where one of his pigs has disappeared to. He'll come up to the marae to collect the scraps not knowing that some of the scraps are Dolly the pig.

At 11 a.m., like clockwork, they farewell their Auckland relatives. 'See you next year. Ka kite anō.' A puff of black smoke, and the yellow bus heads off.

It's OK

Michelle Manning

It was as if the night had opened its mouth and swallowed her up, without chewing, just one complete gulp and she found herself in the pit of its stomach. It was dark, still and warm. A thick sweaty warmth filled with her own body odour. Cocooned in its belly she felt safe, protected. She never wanted to leave, but the thumping above her head, thump, thump, thump, was like a large hand reaching down the night's throat, grabbing her roughly by the scruff of the neck and hauling her shivering back into the real world. She sucked in the cold, crisp air of her bedroom and cursed the need to crawl out. The blankets were her only way to escape, but the stale air became thick and unbearable after a short time. It wasn't nice out here. The monster was waiting and she was scared. Thump! This time the wall next to her bed shook, rattling the cracked picture of Jesus that hung on it. Those before had left it behind and her mother had never bothered to remove it. The girl shivered again and thought that if it got any harder He would topple onto her. Having Him angry with her as well was all she needed right now. A faint whimper trembled into the room. It wailed and wobbled, and then choked to a halt. Her sister twitched uneasily beside her and her soft breath warmed the girl's cold cheek. At the end of their bed the large window gaped. Without curtains, the room lay exposed to the pale rays of the moon. They pushed through the trees outside and cast broken shadows around the walls.

Thump! She jerked as her spine convulsed. It was getting louder now. The girl clamped her eyes shut and ground her teeth. The slow crunching circles were like someone dragging tin across concrete. It echoed harshly inside her head and she tried to bury herself amongst the sounds, searching out another dark place to hide.

It was my job and I forgot. I'm sorry!

When her teeth ached painfully from the effort, she gulped into the cold air of the room again. Her stomach clenched and unclenched and the acrid nausea burned her throat. A slow roaring filled her head and she wondered that if it was allowed to keep growing bigger and bigger, louder and louder. Would it just explode and leave her head empty inside? A dark, black space filled with nothing. She could stop hearing then. She could make up good noises to match silent moving lips. But the crying next door was like a hot knife. It sliced with ragged strokes through her head. It forced her eyes open, forced her back into the shadows of the room and made her listen to what was happening next door.

'Please Matt! Leave me alone. Just leave me alone!'

A pause and she held her breath but it came again.

'Don't. Don't! Please!'

The cry cracked through the thin wall. He was hurting her too much now and there was no way her mother could keep it quiet any more. Sharp hard slaps like snapping twigs followed. Again. Again. He was hitting her face. The girl flinched at each sound and covered her ears. She pushed her face into the pillow.

Rub the ears until they ache. Make some noise. Don't listen. Don't listen.

'It's your fucking fault!' She could feel the air hissing.

'It's no one's fault!'

Her mother's voice stumbled. Her defiance wavered. The girl knew this part and dreaded how it ended. Her mother would try to stand up to him, but he was bigger and he knew that.

'They're only bloody chooks Matt! For heavens sake, just chooks.' Her voice lost its strength, ending in a shaky whine.

'Don't fucking answer back!' The wall shook from the weight of a heavy body falling against it. Some help you are! the girl scorned up at Jesus, and the tears made wet puddles on the sheet.

'Make them stop Sam. Please make them stop.'

The voice wobbled at her through the dark. Her sister's breath trembled on her cheek.

'Shh Kyla, shh,' the girl soothed. 'It's OK. Mum will be alright. You know that. She's always OK the next day. Shh. Go to sleep now.'

Sam breathed in deep, feeling her lungs expand. The cold air hurt her chest. She swallowed the fear.

'Sleep Kyla. It's OK. It's OK,' she whispered, forcing her voice to be calm.

Another thud next door startled her sister. Kyla rolled over and curled up, tightly pushing her head below the blankets. Sam reached out and gently pulled her hair. Kyla would learn to shut it out, Sam reasoned. That's how it worked. Sam pulled the blankets up and pushed her head beneath the pillow. Her breath seemed to echo loudly into the musty space. This was a good noise and it nearly worked.

Like an interlude in a bad movie the room next door went silent, but Sam knew it wasn't over. He was on a roll, he wasn't going to stop now. Her mother's sobbing would really rile him, piss him off in a major way. Sam's stomach tightened and twisted as she heard him start again. He was using his fists now.

'No!' her mother cried out. Sam knew she was trying to cover her face. 'Please stop it Matt, you're hurting me!'

It was her cry, high pitched and sudden, that startled another into action. The new voice frightened awake screamed into the night. It shuddered, stopped and then began again.

'Look what you've done now! Stupid bitch!'

Sam could hear her mother's frantic clucking to soothe it, but the baby felt the tension in her stiff jolting arms, heard it in her shaking voice. It wouldn't stop. The baby's squawk continued, acting on raw nerves like nails down a blackboard.

'Shut that fucking kid up.' The bed springs groaned as a weight lifted.

'Don't you touch him, Matt. Leave him alone.'

Sam hit the icy floorboards at a run and skidded to a halt outside her parents' bedroom. Instinct had made her brave, but fear tugged at her nightie, begging her to come back to bed. She shivered, uncertain now. The loud crash and then her brother's panicked cries jerked her into action. Sam pushed open the door, the room's light catching her. She stood still and blinked adjusting to the sudden brightness. Her mother had backed herself into a corner, shielding the baby. The chair had become her unexpected ally. It now lay broken against the wall. Sam didn't know the man by the window. He wore so many faces. Over the years Sam would see many more and never see the true one. Calling him Dad was a learned response and meant nothing. This man sometimes gave her mother money. Just enough to keep them hungry. To make her mum cry alone in her room. Tonight it was an empty face with pit-black eyes. The skin was drawn tightly across his jaw where a muscle twitched, then jumped erratically. The stale beer and smoke were nauseating.

The baby, out of breath now, opened his mouth and filled his lungs. Sam darted a quick look at that face again and knew it could change. The baby would break him, and become the focus.

'I'll do it, Mum.'

She kept her voice steady and walked swiftly into the room. She took the baby, hitching him up over her shoulder. He took up almost half her length, his solid legs brushing her knees. Like a running tap shut off in mid-flow, his cry dried up and he bunched chubby fists into her hair. Sam kept her face impassive and turned towards the door. Her movements were deliberate and unrushed.

Don't look at him! Look straight ahead! Look straight ahead!

'Don't fucking bring him back!'

Her father kicked viciously at the door slamming it shut. The force shook the frame and startled the baby. He jumped in her arms and his face crumpled again. He pulled at her hair dragging her head back and she gasped from the sharp pain.

'Shh,' Sam soothed, bouncing him gently as she hurried back to her room. 'Shh. It's OK now, Sammy's here, it's OK, shh.' She sat him in the large double bed next to her sister's sleeping form and scooted in beside him. The room next door had fallen silent. The baby cooed into the dark as she gently bounced the bed. Sam had faced the monster. She had never done that before. She pulled her knees in tight to her chest. She pushed her face down between her arms and knees and rocked back and forth. Fear waiting in the corners crept out and stroked her. Her brother gurgled at the shadows moving across the wall as her shoulders shook with sobs. He squealed at Sam and rolled to snatch at her nightie. She wiped her face across her knees and slipped down beside him. The monster had gone to sleep and the room was fresh with relief. Sam thought it was a good silence now. She watched the silhouetted branches sway back and forth as the baby giggled at the soundless ballet.

Thick pudgy hands tugged at her tangled hair. Sam winced. Sloppy baby bubbles dripped onto her cheek. Sam used her sleeve to wipe away the baby drool and burrowed deeper into the warm bed. 'Too early,' she moaned. But she felt the first rays of daylight intrude beneath her eyelids and groaned. The baby squealed as sunlight tangled in his outstretched fingers. He reached higher and tried to catch some more, blowing bubbles at the lukewarm rays. Her two brothers shivered into the room and crawled under the blankets at the other end of the double bed. A cold blast of air chased them in and the icy contact of their feet sent shock waves up Sam's legs. She gasped and wiggled away but when she lost the blanket war with her siblings, Sam decided that breakfast was an honourable retreat. She picked up her baby brother and sought out her slippers. By eight thirty she had everyone ready for school, had the baby fed and the kitchen tidied. A routine perfected by the age of ten. It gave him one less excuse to use. Her mother shuffled into the room and eased herself into a chair. Her father had started work before dawn, taking the fear with him. He always made it to work on time. Always looked after his mates and hated being reminded that he had a family to take care of.

Mother and daughter acknowledged each other silently, without eye contact. Sam put the dishcloth in the sink and dried her hands on the tea towel. Her mother lit a cigarette and winced as she forced it between her swollen lips. The smoke drifted upwards and hung in the sun's rays above, framing her head in a false halo. She sat at the kitchen table with her back to Sam, and looked out the window. The street had already shaken itself awake like an old dog stretching and yawning to start the day. Old Mrs Pike stood at the end of her driveway, waving her grandson off to work.

'I've got to walk the boys to school now,' Sam said quietly into the sink. 'Stevie's had his breakfast and his bottle is warming in the jug.'

Another trail of smoke drifted up, a nod indicated her mother had heard. She was watching the boys chasing each other around the clothes line outside. Although aged five and six, they were similar in height; well matched, great mates. They had slept through last night and their laughter echoed into the still kitchen. Stevie sat at Sam's feet chewing on a rusk. He waved his biscuit up at her and squealed. His face was cheerfully smudged with soggy biscuit and his bib damp with drool. She picked up her school bag and headed for the door.

'Sam?'

Sam stopped at the door and stared straight ahead. If she turned around she would see it all again in her mother's face.

'It wasn't your fault, hon. You know your father after a few drinks. Any excuse. If it wasn't your chooks it would have been something else that I should have done.'

Before breakfast Sam had coaxed the chooks back in, then pushed the drum hard up against the door and filled it with bricks. It wasn't going to move at all. Sam blew a sigh and looked around now. The welts on her mother's cheek had started to discolour, the cut on her bottom lip still bled a little. She nodded down at the baby.

'He has to sleep in my room from now on, OK Mum?'

Her mother's hands shook as she dragged on the cigarette again. She drew it in deep, tilting her head back and savouring it before shooting it back out.

'Move the cot into our room. Please, Mum?' Sam persisted, 'before Dad gets home?'

Her mother nodded, stubbed out the cigarette and reached for another. As her daughter left she blew out the thick smoke. She followed the thin trail up towards the ceiling. It twisted and coiled and faded into the brown stained roof. She dragged on the cigarette again, but it became a sob and tears dripped down her cheeks, stinging her welts with salty trails.

Sam gathered up her siblings and herded them out through the gate. The two boys clambered ahead like puppies in play, pushing and shoving each other. They picked up handfuls of dry brown leaves and threw them over each other. Mrs Pyke waved from the letter box. Sam offered a small wave back. She knew. Sam blew another sigh. Hell, they all knew and no one did anything.

'Is Mum OK now?'

Kyla was only eighteen months younger and she still remembered the things that happened. Her eyes had started to take on serious shadows. She had to work it out, Sam thought. She had to learn to keep it at home.

'It's OK now. Everything's alright.'

Sam dropped a crooked grin from the corner of her mouth. The comical look got the smile she wanted.

Kyla nodded and shrugged. She squinted into the sunlight as a voice hailed her. She smiled at the small figure waving and ran ahead to meet it. Talking about it made it too real. A look, a nod, perhaps some small talk. It was all they could handle.

Sam looked back in through the kitchen window. Her mother had nearly finished her second cigarette. She would go through two packets by the day's end. When they came back from school, tired and hesitant, the house would have settled back into its uneasy stillness. Washing would applaud them from the line and the cat would purr at them from the front step. Inside would smell of disinfectant and wood oil. Scrubbed shiny and clean. Even the postman often said that anyone could eat off that floor. Then the rowdy noise from enthusiastic boys would fill the quiet. Tea would drift delicious smells around the kitchen and the baby would scuttle across the lino to greet Sam with a sticky kiss. Her mother's smile would be too forced and a little overbright. She wouldn't go out for a few days and Sam would run her errands until make-up worked well enough on casual eyes. A fresh batch of biscuits, still warm from the oven, would be offered in apology. They would sit around, biting into the sweet softness, and make small talk.

An Irrefutable Law

Dale Moffatt

There's a valley in the south that surely must have been a resting place for the gods. A place of beauty and bounty. A river winds its way down through it from its source high above the bush line in the mountains, through virgin beech forest and lush green farmland. About mid-way down, on a rise beside the river, nestles a pretty township, content with its place in the world.

It was where I was born, on a winter's day during a raging storm. Mine was an idyllic childhood, sheltered from life's furores by protective parents and valley life that was sufficient unto itself. My view of the rest of the world was from books that I lost myself in, soaking up every word.

The summers are long and full of sunshine in this little slice of heaven deep in northern Murihiku. The kids and adults alike savour the harvest of greengages and raspberries; breathe deep the scent of hay and wild rosehip bushes. The pristine mountain waters of the river and creeks turn a swim into an adventure of discovery.

One Saturday early in the summer of my twelfth year was the beginning of my first real grasp of the essence of the place I lived in.

We had finished our work then eaten lunch. The other kids had scattered to the four winds while I, as usual, had my nose buried in a book, waiting for my friend Ani to arrive. We were going for our first swim of the summer at the river by Rangi's Rock. This was a popular swimming spot as it had a deep hole for jumping into from the rock. It also had a sandy bank on the paddock side where you could drive your car right up and unload your picnic or barbecue.

My mother had a rule about not allowing us to swim before the snow had gone from Te Wakaroa, the mountain that crossed the top of the valley, because until the waka cleared the white water it wasn't safe to enter the river. She had rules about everything and drummed them into us with other similar stories to that one. With the disdain of a voracious fact-gathering eleven year old, I knew the rational explanation behind Mum's fairytale and took satisfaction in telling anyone who would listen. While snow remained, the spring thaw had not finished and rain in the mountains could cause the waters to rise with alarming speed, literally catching the unwary, or foolish, in its fury.

Mum would look me in the eye after I would relate my facts and say, 'Well, don't you be the foolish one that gets caught with her pants down!' and she wouldn't look away until she saw that I knew who was boss. While I thought I knew everything, the one thing I knew for sure was that we didn't dare disobey the rules.

Therefore we had learnt that the riverbed changes constantly. It had become second nature to find the holes and avoid them, check which banks were undercut while assuming they all were, and to read the currents before venturing into the cool clear water.

I couldn't concentrate on my book as the day was really hot. I heard a car stop outside, then a murmur of voices. Recognizing Mr Smith's voice I jumped up to see if Ani was with him. Mr Smith looked anxious. Dad was putting on his old sneakers as Mr Smith told me Ani was only allowed to go swimming at the creek swimming-hole today – why don't I go to their house and pick her up on the way.

Dad brushed past me into the wash-house and came out carrying his oilskin. He told me I wasn't to go to the river if I wanted to swim, then he and Mr Smith left in the car. A chill had passed over me when I saw that old coat. I hated it because it scared me and I didn't know why. It hung in the wash-house, had hung there ever since I could remember, but I'd never seen Dad actually wear it. And I couldn't fathom why he would need it on such a hot day.

Ani and I had a glorious time finding heaps of neat stones, skipping flatties, swinging out on the rope to bomb everyone, floating down the creek on rubber tubes and scoffing our hastily made picnic. It was after six when we made our way home. We were not worried that our parents would wonder where we were or whether we were safe. There were still families at the swimming-hole, in the water or cooking tea on their barbecues. People had come and gone during the afternoon, all of them from the valley, and it didn't take much of a detective to find out what any kid was doing in any part of the town, at any given time.

Wandering along our street after leaving Ani at her house, I saw Dad arrive at our gate. He looked tired. Something was rolled up under his arm as he walked to the house so distracted he didn't see me. By the time I reached the house he had discarded his shoes and was inside talking to Mum. I took my wet togs off in the wash-house, shaking the sand out of my clothes so I could put them on, catching parts of their conversation all the while. I noticed he had hung the oilskin back up on its hook. It looked damp. My eyes kept going back to it as I dressed and tried to listen at the same time.

'Always happens. Why don't people....' This was from Mum moving about getting tea ready.

'I know. They never listen. They come here and don't take any notice of the locals,' replied Dad. His voice was weary. 'It's too late now –'

He broke off as I walked in. When I asked, too late for what, he said never mind, it's not for little girls to know. His look and mood were unlike any I'd ever seen from him, kind of serious and sad, so I didn't say any more. I felt sad myself as did the rest of the kids, although most of us didn't know why and those that did weren't saying anything.

The pall stayed over our house, indeed the whole town, for about a week. People talked, but not where little kids could hear, so I never got to find out what actually happened. I asked Mum but, in her frustrating way, she made out she was telling me everything but, in fact, was telling me not much at all. 'It's just a tragedy that should never have happened,' she said. 'People not listening to folk who know. A family from the city came to stay for a holiday and their little boy drowned. Don't concern yourself about it – you just do like we've always told you and you'll do fine.'

I couldn't help thinking it had something to do with Dad's coat. I went to the wash-house and looked at it long and hard. It seemed tired and sad too. Something about it made me feel so uncomfortable, but still I looked. Tentatively, I reached out to pull open the front. It was damp, smelling oily and wet at the same time, and some other smell.

I saw the hair as I was carefully letting go of the front flap – just a glimpse, but unmistakeably a hair. It was a single short strand of light blonde hair, curled like a crescent moon. I ran from the wash-house into the bright sun and spun around till I was dizzy. I didn't think about it any more.

I avoided the coat as much as was humanly possible.

The season moved on and soon it was autumn. This time of the year brought the winds and nature's greatest display of colour. The yellow, red and rusty splendour of the leaves are reflected in the sunsets which seep out of the sky and paint the land so the eye doesn't know where earth ends and heaven begins.

Mum says it is a time of death and dying as the old makes way for the new. One of her rules was that we were not allowed to wander off around the countryside by ourselves during the mornings and evenings at this time of the year. This was because Papatūānuku missed her Rangi and mourned for her dead and dying mokopuna alone, without him to comfort her. You could see her tears in the form of the mist that clung to the ground in the morning and evening light. Papatūānuku may well be tempted to take an earthly child to replace those she was losing.

I knew the rule was because the fog was so thick at this time of the year you can't see a foot in front of you and many an accident or worse has happened because of that fact.

And so it was with no real surprise but much regret that we learned a car had missed a bend on the road and gone into the river just outside of town. Dad joined the other men to do what needed to be done.

It was a teenage boy of about seventeen. He was from out of town so it didn't really touch me except for the shiver that went up my spine when I heard Dad tell Mum that where he went off was the highest point of the road and the car had rolled a few times down the bank before going into the water. 'Can't have even seen the corner – there were no skid marks, just tracks on the gravel verge,' he said, shaking his head. 'Probably couldn't see two feet in front of the car and still didn't think to go slow!'

Being so isolated, Dad and the other townsfolk got called to all sorts of emergencies and events throughout the year. He would rush out in his coat and hat, gumboots and gloves to rescue people, animals, fight fires, sandbag riverbanks, and do many more communal duties, but I never saw him wear the dreaded oilskin.

Winter came and went without mishap. The weak sun brings little respite from the bone-chilling cold, and hoar frosts lie for days at a time. The land retreats under a blanket of blue-white ice to rest. The river appears to be resting also, its colour deep and dark. It was my favourite season.

Ice-skating on the frozen ponds in the eerie, frosted landscape at night with a floodlight to see by, a bonfire to warm the hands, hot cocoa to warm the insides and with music echoing through the valley on the chilly air to warm the soul, I was provided with all the magic ingredients to make this a season of enchantment for me.

Mum said it is a time of renewal and rebirth. The children of Rongo and Tāne lie under Papatūānuku waiting for the life-giving warmth of her body to give them life. For once I didn't regale her with the whys and wherefores, because a time of enchantment needs myths and legends; not cold, hard facts. She smiled and looked me in the eye. 'Some things defy explanation smarty-pants. And even if you could explain everything, some things need a story because the reality doesn't touch the soul.' She didn't look away until she saw that I knew.

Soon the weather warmed slightly and the snow came, softening the outlines of nature and turning man-made ugly into pure white mystery. Long after the snow melted in the valley it sat on the mountains waiting for the spring thaw.

It was a fine spring day when Dad collected his oilskin from the wash-house like that day in summer almost nine months ago. Mum saw me staring at the coat under his arm like it was a kēhua, come to spirit me away. I didn't see the look of understanding that passed between my parents. Dad rushed out to the gate where Ani's father soon appeared in his car, and they left.

Mum ushered me to a seat at the kitchen table then sat quietly till I looked at her.

'Someone's in the river, honey,' she said. 'I don't know who, but Dad said it was a little boy. They've gone to look for him. For the body.'

She placed her hand on my shoulder for a short, comforting time then went about the business of preparing for the worst. For Mum this consisted of cooking food, checking everyone was where they should be and generally keeping herself busy, with one eye on the clock, one on the gate, one ear on the phone and the other listening for something beyond my experience.

After an interminable wait, Dad returned. Once more he was carrying his coat rolled up under his arm. He went to the wash-house then came into the kitchen where we were waiting for him to tell us about it.

'It was Jeff Burn's nephew, Sonia's little boy. Just three years old.' Dad stared at the floor, gathering himself. 'They think he followed the dog through a gap in the fence. They thought he was fenced in and safe. It's only a short, sharp drop to the river through that fence. They thought he was safe.' He ended on a note of helplessness.

'Oh my god, such a beautiful little boy!' Mum cried. 'I saw him with his mother up the street just yesterday. A head of golden curls and the biggest blue eyes I've ever seen.'

'Yes,' said Dad, 'they were here to see Jeff before heading back to Aussie. Sonia had never been here before, now I doubt that she'll ever want to hear of the place again. Jeff's so cut up – blames himself. He didn't expect this when he moved here.'

'None of them ever do,' replied Mum. 'They have no idea!' She sat in disbelieving silence.

'You know, when I was carrying him to the car, I just wanted to wrap him in a nice, warm, cuddly blanket instead of that old, smelly oilskin. He looked so much like the others, it was like a dream. Just like that little boy at the beginning of the year. Even the boy that slid into the river in his car. All of them, fair-headed, blue-eyed, innocent kids.'

'Well,' muttered Mum, 'that's a rare coincidence, but I'll tell you what isn't – every one of them isn't from here.'

She paused, staring out beyond us to some place far off in her mind, then continued almost angrily. 'They all come here with their families to enjoy the place and not one of them realizes the danger that exists. Taking the river for granted because it looks so clear and inviting – so harmless. Taking the bush and the hills for granted because they seem so serene and taking the weather for granted because the days are long and seem so settled. They see our kids enjoying a freedom they want for their own but they don't realize ours are born and raised here. They live with the nature of this valley and they grow up respecting it.'

'I know,' responded Dad with resignation in his voice.

I had sat there without saying a word, piecing together the puzzle. I knew now why the oilskin had scared me. It had carried the bodies of the river's victims in its ugly folds. They had left part of themselves with that unlikely shroud. I could feel it as surely as I knew the sun would set tonight. This time I could find no fact or any other rational explanation to explain it away, or why that knowledge took my fear of the coat away. I wandered outside and contemplated the enormity of what I had learnt this day.

I had been born into this valley as my parents before me had been. It was part of who I was. My parents were passing on to me the ability, and the necessity, to read the river, foresee the weather and understand the hills and mountains and I had unwittingly been learning.

They have been teaching me how to exist with nature, to respect it and to know my place in the structure of it. In my smart-alecky ways I had not really noticed the lessons. But today I had learnt an irrefutable law. We are given the most beautiful gifts, but they come with a barb in their hidden recesses so that we don't take them for granted, or use them carelessly. I promised myself to ask Mum to tell me her story about that.

I sat on the gate in front of our house to look at the river winding its path over Papatūānuku. It shimmered in the evening light, fairies dancing along its silvery smooth surface. Clouds gathered in the dusky sky, warning of more unsettled weather before the long hot summer days came calling.

I mused about lessons learnt, the wonder of nature, and the mystery of the river, in whose depths lurked a taniwha with a penchant for golden-haired, blue-eyed boys.

Cartography

Kellyana Morey

Fra Mauro, a Renaissance cleric of a Venetian monastical order, pauses in his frantic scribbling to replenish his pen. Although the industry he is presently engaged in is that of a diary, a book of lamentations, confessions and questions, his most usual trade is that of map-maker. *A few centuries earlier he would have been burnt at the stake as a heretic for this pastime, but as luck would have it …*

Fra Mauro is cartographer to the Queen, and a learned and pious man of the cloth. His life's work is the tabulation of the definitive blueprint of the world. A chart that encapsulates the large and the small of experience, the yin and the yang, the zing and the zang of living. He dreams in topographies and territories, borders and perceptions, traversing locale, dominion and mandate, fathoming the world's truest nuances, dimensions, harmonies and demeanours.

Fra Mauro has to travel in the idiomatic languages and texts of the incubus because he has never left these shores. In fact it is rare that he ventures far from the city of his birth at all. There has simply been no need. All that he has desired has been contained in this wondrous drifting jigsaw puzzle of unsolid lands and infinite interlocking canals. Venice, the monastery, the tower and the self are contained only by the borders of his imagination.

The glittering city of Venice which in the mid-sixteenth century was at the zenith of its social, cultural and political rebirth resounded with knowledge both old and new. Worthy practitioners of lucid scholarship became lodged in the rectories of the faithful, a fact to which Fra Mauro's presence has already born testament.

However, the debris of humanity that seethes and swarms – reproducing at will like a multi-headed hydra – is submerged in the fetid waters, fighting for the next breath and the next. Invisible and silent, but for their guttural cries of survival, they twist and turn through the maze of sewers, bridges and into the inexplicable dead ends that city planners had thoughtfully designed for the detriment of the well-heeled visitor from the phlegmatic north. Those dour and unimaginative people with their abhorrence of display, masquerade and the delicious pleasures of the flesh, their wallets all the heavier for their proud conservatism and all the more enticing for the stiletto-twirling pickpocket at the next corner.

When our topographically tortured cartographer first embarked on his task to create his definitive chart, he used the finest paper made from Egyptian linen which lower-order monks would carry to the tower. With the abandoned feather of a migrating godwit, the monk paints the hills and valleys and peoples of which he is told. Soon the shelves and chart-hanging frames of the tower are overflowing with maps, collapsing from their piles and onto the floor, inching closer to the door and windows. Each day someone new arrives at the salt-bleached door of the tower to speak of lands not yet determined.

Throwing up his arms in despair, Fra Mauro petitions the Queen, who duly summons the tonsured and tongue-tied cleric to her. She grants Fra Mauro his stammering request with a barely discernible dip of her fair head. Henceforth he takes delivery of swathes of white cotton on the first Tuesday of the new moon. This in no way solves the problem of containing the banners once painted, but Fra Mauro has already contemplated this dilemma at length and formulated an audacious plan. On his knees in his cell he begs and cries, pleads and cajoles until God himself finally agrees to the monk hanging his geographies from the heavens where sun will bake them, rain can flay them and time change them.

Thieves and adventurers, the poor, the excursionists, the nomads, the dispossessed, the hungry, pilgrims, colonists and opportunists alike spread to the furthest reaches of the globe in the creation of a chart, a single consummate articulation of the world and all its experiences and meanings.

It is time to leave Fra Mauro now, his contemplations are for his and God's eyes alone.

Surveyors with furrowed brows arrive in horse-drawn carts. The sun is much hotter than they are used to. Sweat trickles down their faces as they strike camp overlooking a white sickle of sand and the endless restless blues of the sky and the sea. From where they stand they can see islands where flax rattles, unquiet and constant, in the winds that drift in as constant as sea birds.

Marta, young and fearless, approaches the tents that are arranged on the dry coastal grasses with the precision you would expect from men who see in numerical configurations. In her arms she carries a bundle of firewood to add to the meagre pile that the men managed to gather before the call of the card table and whiskey bottle overcame their good intentions. The days are long and the four men play poker in the fading evening light, wagering not their salaries but naming rights of the lands that they expect to discover in the course of their travels. Marta, who reads, writes and speaks English, listens to their outlandish bets openly. They have not acknowledged her presence although she has stood only a few feet from them for some minutes. A thin man with distressed red skin and yellow hair flutters his cards importantly at the other three men and announces portentously,

'I wager that that mountain, as poor a specimen as it may be of a mountain, is a camel shape, therefore henceforth it will be known as Mount Camel, against your Mount Wellington. So, what do you say to that, Charlie old boy?'

Marta doesn't stick around long enough to find out whose bluff is called in this particular hand. She finds her father working in the kūmara garden.

'What are they doing?' she asks him.

'Making maps so you and I will always know where we are when we look at the land,' he replies.

The desire of man to measure, determine and plumb every inch of the land has survived, it seems, the vagaries of time and place. We will return to Marta

of the uncharted lands soon, but first we need to know more of our map-maker. The dawn is restlessly tapping at Fra Mauro's window, he has slept well in his nocturnal travels.

Three ships have recently returned from far-off lands and the captains have been eager to bring the monk small treasures and stories that they have procured with him in mind. By evening the cartographer's head aches with knowledges and he has opened the window of the tower to set the maps dancing and soothe the dull pain that has settled into the corners of his heart. The moon is a cold sliver, a scimitar in the hard, bright sky. It is a night of might-have-beens and random second thoughts.

A drunk sailor finds a woman with a few coins outside the gates of the monastery. Fra Mauro hears her diseased cackle and the clatter of their retreating footsteps fading into the labyrinth of doorways and quiet deaths. Our creator of maps of the new world follows the whore and her trick with a navigator's instinct. The smell of her syphilitic breath makes his task all the easier. He sees her in a moment of clarity in future winter, her face eaten away from the infection she sells for the price of her survival. The woman's revelry echoes in the emptiness of his chest and the fullness of his testicles. Alone but for the clamour of the voices mapped into the swathes of cloth that hang from where the roof of his tower once rested. Enough cloth to wrap the universe and all its experiences.

Tonight the banners are peaceful. This is unusual – most often they are shouting and cursing, hurling obscene abuse at each other in their loudest voices. These maps have no manners. The smaller locales are out-roared and outrageously bullied by empires and kingdoms. But tonight they are the soft caress of a mother's voice heavy with sleep, the soporific lull of a warm bath, and they have the look of contrite children. Fra Mauro scolds them gently, and they giggle and promise to be friends and share. Always. The rare spasm of regret that the coarse hilarity of the whore sent coursing through his body is quieted by the lullabies that his choir sings, and his eyelids grow heavy.

The day that Jacob first sees Ripeka she is riding her father's prized thoroughbred mare. Six years ago, Wiremu had purchased the mare and her unborn foal at great expense from an English bloodstock catalogue. He sold a three-thousand acre block of land in order to obtain the mare and her passage to New Zealand on board a boat carrying sheep and cattle to stock paddocks carved from forest and scrub.

The horse had arrived but skin and bone from her voyage, her belly distended by the foal that kicked impatiently at her prison. Ripeka, who was twelve, was given the task of leading her father's newest acquisition the three miles from the wharf to her new home. Ripeka whispered the names of the hills and streams into the horse's long narrow ears. They twitched at the sound of her voice. The mare grew fat and glossy, rewarding Wiremu with a filly foal for each of the past six years.

The current foal is a leggy bay with a fine head. Ripeka is riding bareback with a leg hooked over the wither so that she is side-saddle, like an English lady, when she sees Jacob. 'Hallo Pākehā,' she says, looking him up and down before kicking the mare on. Her laughter tumbles out of her mouth and onto the road. It melts at Jacob's feet.

Evensong has many hours since past and the summer twilight has deepened to midnight blue. Fra Mauro re-dips the pen. We have startled him from a daydream and the ink has dried during his reverie. The page of his processes and procrastinations is marred by a blot shining wetly in the candlelight. He clicks his tongue with irritation.

Fra Mauro ponders his most recent visitor's revelations of a land not yet imagined, beyond the island they call Serendipity. This weary and salt-lashed sorcerer of the sextant and the sail, with a beard that grew red and wild, spoke of people who talked about their territories with their bodies, as if the land itself lived, cried and gave birth. Every breath and heartbeat articulates their own and their ancestor's cartography of connection. 'How,' ponders our genteel and imaginative cleric, 'do I draw such understandings into my map?'

When Ripeka and Jacob's oldest child opens her eyes, mouth and bowels for the first time, what she sees are the rivers of ink that flowed over the faces of the women who give her life, give her history and belonging. Marta strips off the boiled mutton-cloth that swaddles her thirty-first grandchild, and holds her up like an offering to the sky and earth, before sniffing the child from head to toe much to the agitation of Jacob's spinster sister Madeline, who looks nervously to the kitchen were a great cauldron boils in ravenous anticipation. Madeline's fears of her first niece ending her day as a tasty supper pass as the kuia hands the child they will call Katerina back to Ripeka. 'Smells like Pākehā,' she states, and never discusses the incident or her favourite granddaughter's choice of husband again. Being a resourceful woman, Ripeka makes the best of both worlds and gets on with living, wanting to believe that her children and Jacob's will always feel the earth beneath their feet.

I wonder, though, how much Marta told that child, barely minutes old, in that brief exchange of breath.

Jacob is king of all he surveys, though if the truth be known his castle has its support pillar sunk deeply in the mana of his ink-painted consort. The black ribbons that grow from Ripeka's chin are her map of these lands that her husband proudly calls his own.

Katerina is dawdling as she hangs out the week's wash up on the hill behind the homestead. She looks out to sea, never tiring of the movement of light, the endless manifestations that she knows better than her own face. The wind from the coast sets the laundry cracking like a whip and tugging at the wooden pegs that anchor it to the earth. At her feet, three siblings play. She is throwing lengths of dazzling white cotton over wire that Jacob had strung on the hillside for that purpose. Katerina returns to the wash-house where Ripeka oversees the boiling copper and concrete sinks. She refills her basket again and again until the entire hillside is filled with the flags and their joyful songs of praise.

Ripeka has become a grandmother and a great-grandmother, her descendants like an unfinished mat covering the land, draping golden and saffron down to the sea. She looks across her fields of children and ancestors to the pure white slabs of the sandbars where the godwits, fresh from the salt marshes of Siberia, replenish their empty bellies. With a contented 'humph' she packs her memories into a flax kete woven by her youngest granddaughter and journeys northward towards the islands.

Fra Mauro dies peacefully in his tower in his eighty-seventh year. He had breakfasted frugally, as is his habit, before sitting with his maps in the tower. He looks to the sky, reaching his hands upwards and into the sun even as it blinds him with its brilliance. The pennants relinquish their grip on the celestial city of God, as Fra Mauro cries 'Hosanna' to the heavens, cascading to earth in ribbons of silky white ash. Ivory castles crumble to dust between his outstretched fingers. His mouth is stained with sun.

No man, or indeed woman it seems, is an island or a tower.

Today I look out to distant black and gunmetal shadows anchored in light silvered oceans, seeing Ripeka, Marta and Katerina in the distant undulations and brooding forms. Because if people wear maps of land upon their bodies, then land clothes itself in people. These are lands rich in blood and bone.

Many Mansions

Paula Morris

Although Barbara Mackenzie's funeral was not till three, they started filling stainless-steel trays with peanuts at nine in the morning.

Her daughter-in-law Ra had left her home in Matakana early that morning, when it was still dark and damp outside, to make the drive to Auckland Airport. Peter Mackenzie was waiting for her at Dunedin, leaning against a pillar with the morning paper folded in his coat pocket. He wore a sweater Ra had never seen before, and his face looked pale and tired. He reached a hand out to take her bag and they walked out to the car park without speaking.

On the way to his father's house, Ra asked what the hospital had said, exactly, when he went to collect his mother's belongings, and Peter asked about the twins. It had been nearly three months since he'd moved out of the house up north.

'It's just as well you didn't bring them,' he said, looking straight ahead. 'I don't think they'd know what was going on. I don't think they'd remember her.'

'I suppose,' Ra replied, embarrassed that she was yawning as she spoke.

'I don't think they *will* remember her,' said Peter, suddenly fierce, and they didn't speak again for the rest of the journey.

Peter's two sisters, who had driven down together from Christchurch the day before, were still in bed. Ra set to work laying out cups and saucers on the table in the breakfast room. By the time his younger sister Jennie wafted downstairs, wet hair pinned high on her head, asking in a half-whisper if there was anything that she could do, it had already been established that they were short of everything – cups, plates, forks, teapots. Ra surveyed the numerous wine glasses and tumblers, hired yesterday, arranged in orderly regiments on the glass-topped coffee table. Peter was looking for the other bottle opener. 'One won't be enough,' he said, rifling through the dresser drawers, spilling napkins and tea towels onto the floor. Jennie sat drinking coffee, watching them fall. Ra stooped to gather them up.

'You can have my mug when I'm finished,' Jennie offered, speaking to Peter.

The older sister, Susan, descended in time to answer the door to the third flower delivery of the day, a canoe of yellow carnations. She carried it mutely into the kitchen and balanced it on top of the microwave. Peter's aunt Anne appeared at the end of the drive, dropped off by one of her sons in his new snub-nosed executive car. She walked up to the front door clutching a box of cutlery and a tired-looking black hat. 'Why is everyone arriving so bloody early?' Susan muttered, her mouth full of toast.

'God knows,' replied Jennie, stretching her arms above her head. 'Get the first go at Mum's things, perhaps.'

Both sisters arched their eyebrows. Barbara had always widened her eyes in the same way when she was telling stories. Ra had never noticed this resemblance before. The sisters had never seemed like their mother in any way.

Aunt Anne's arrival brought Peter's father down from his room to discuss whether the occasion warranted releasing the Royal Doulton from the dust-free depths of the china cabinet. Ra left them all in the kitchen and walked to the living room window, pressing her shins against the low sill, gazing down the long length of the garden. The pond was covered with a net of wire for the winter. Frost still gilded the lawn and the early morning sun illuminated skeletal rosebushes and the dense, dull green of the hedge. Ra squinted beyond the garden shed at the rhododendron at the end of the garden that never flowered. She remembered Barbara pointing this out to her the first time they walked around the garden together. Wrong kind of soil, she thought, wrapping her arms tightly around herself.

'Because I'm not really happy about using them,' Peter's father was saying in his loud, deliberate voice. There was a flurry of agreement in the kitchen, and more flowers arrived at the front door.

'I mean, would you use your Wedgwood?' he continued, walking into the living room with an empty plastic bag in his hand, speaking to Ra's back. 'I suppose you would. You don't need to worry if someone broke something. But I'm on a strict budget. This is all very expensive.'

He was walking out the back door into the garden, still talking.

'I mean, I have to put my hand in my pocket every day.'

Aunt Anne was on the telephone to the other aunts, asking them to bring more teacups. The sisters got dressed and drove out to the funeral home one last time. Ra placed a peanut tray on each side table and sat down on a footstool to rest. She felt hot, as though she were standing too close to a radiator.

'Susan said you could have a lie down on her bed, if you're tired. She's staying in the front room,' said Peter's gruff voice behind her. 'There's plenty of time. The car's not coming till half past two.'

The front room had been the girls' bedroom when they were young, and their school pictures still stood on the dressing room table. They were both dark-haired now, but then they had long sandy-coloured hair, tied into pigtails with blue school ribbons. The first time Peter took Ra home to Dunedin to meet his parents, Barbara had touched her hair with a soft, uncertain hand.

'You have such lovely thick hair. Not like us,' she told Ra, and took her out to the garden, warning her not to step on the paving stones. Peter had laid them one summer holiday when he was at college. He had meant well, Barbara told her, but they were constantly collapsing into the pond.

By the time Ra woke up, more people had arrived, uncles and cousins and old friends who lived far away and had given themselves too much time to get there, just in case. She put on her only jacket, which happened to be black, and the pearl earrings that Barbara gave her as a wedding gift, and went downstairs.

Everyone wanted tea, if it wasn't too much trouble. Ra stood in the kitchen boiling water and filling the dishwasher with dirty cups, carrying out fresh trays every fifteen minutes. People asked her what the children were called, and told her that she and Peter should think about living down south for a while, especially after this, especially now, and said how miraculous it was that the weather had cleared; you couldn't wish for a better day. Aunt Anne was looking peevish because one of her sons had arrived wearing jeans and a short-sleeved shirt. Jennie and Susan were smoking outside on the patio, shivering without their coats on. Peter's father was upstairs, dressed, sitting on the edge of his bed until the car arrived.

Peter walked up to Ra as she tapped tea leaves into the sink and asked her shyly, sullenly, if his tie was straight. She turned to look at him, her face flushed with the steam from the kettle. The sun poured in through the kitchen window and she began sneezing helplessly, stung by the bright light and stultified by the overwhelming scent of flowers.

The car arrived and there was not enough room. Ra locked up the house and rode to the church with one of the neighbours, arriving just in time to slip into an aisle seat near the back. Four undertakers in grey coats carried in the coffin, with the family, hunch-shouldered, filing behind. The vicar – young, plump and entirely unknown to them – read the introduction. Barbara never went to church, even on Christmas Eve, when everyone else in the family tumbled off to midnight mass after the pub shut. She told Ra that she always felt cold in church.

Barbara's was the only service that day, so the building was chilly. Everyone sat in their coats, standing and kneeling and singing and praying as instructed, dragging on the hymns, stumbling on the psalms. Lines of technicolor apostles crowded the windows like spectators. Beneath them, stone heads jutted from the walls, strange gaping faces of men with sunken cheeks and worker's hats, ugly and ordinary below the feet of the stained-glass saints. These heads, their pumiced skin the colour of sand, gazed wild and astonished at each other across the ranks of pews, stranded in an eternity of commemoration.

Ra heard a small, stifled sob somewhere nearby, the sound washed away by the braying chords of the organ, beginning the second hymn. The taut, restrained bodies in the pews around her, propped like cardboard dolls, fenced her in. Barbara lay trapped and sealed in her narrow coffin. Tears sluiced the sides of Ra's nose, running into the corners of her mouth.

The stone faces suspended above her on the wall had witnessed more than a hundred years of these ceremonies, she thought. A hundred years of stiff backs and colourless eyes, promises, pledges, and processions, countless sung evensongs and holy communions, the monotonous ebb and flow of christenings, confirmations, weddings, funerals. The dour hymn echoed off the walls, resounding around their frigid ears. Ra wanted to wail. She wanted to throw her head back, open her mouth wide and wail. She wanted Barbara to hear her – hear all her sorrow and regrets, hear her love and respect. And would they wail with her, in anguish or deliverance, these stone men trapped in the wall? How would it sound if suddenly, after a century of masonic torpor, these petrified labourers came to life?

In the cemetery, the sun was setting beyond the ragged outline of pine trees in the next field. People stood scattered around the grave, waiting for the vicar to begin talking. The gang of undertakers lowered the coffin into the ground, making an ostentatious, synchronised bow. Ra walked over to Peter and placed her arm loosely around his waist. His head was bowed and his heavy winter coat hung perfectly still. The vicar spoke, his words carried away by the breeze, and then turned away, trudging along the path towards the church. The four undertakers each gathered up a handful of pale soil and in turn let it fall gently into the grave. Everyone else stood watchful and motionless.

'You should throw some soil,' Ra whispered to Peter, and without looking at her, he bent down and scooped a little in his hand. His father tried to follow his example, but there was barely enough to fill his fingernails; the mound of earth next to the grave was sealed with a thin coverlet of artificial grass.

'I don't want to do that,' snapped Jennie. Susan was coughing, her eyes trickling tears, one hand clinging to her sister's arm.

An undertaker had lain his black silk top hat a few feet away on the ground, beside a pyramid of waxy white lilies. The flower arrangements were placed in a long line, like entries in a competition, their cards peeping out. Everyone shuffled past, admiring and awkward, bending over for a closer view.

Ra could hear voices asking who was Peter's wife.

'No, not me,' said the cousin who had been sitting next to him in church. 'That's her, over there, with the dark hair.'

A pale, wiry woman grabbed Ra's arm.

'Two soup plates,' she said, her eyes teary. 'We were the two soup plates.'

Ra blankly watched the woman walk away before she realised that she'd been talking about the wedding.

'Thank you,' she called. 'Thank you very much.'

There had been twelve soup plates altogether, and Peter had told her that, as far as he was concerned, she could keep all of them.

Back at the house, people were sitting outside in their cars waiting for someone to let them in. Ra ran down the driveway to unlock the door, leaving it ajar behind her. In the kitchen she switched on the kettle and then the oven, tearing open packages of food and tipping the contents onto baking trays. Soon every room was humming with mourners, drinking tea and sherry and wine. Old ladies crept up to Ra, wanting a little more hot water or diffidently offering to help, asking if she were Peter's wife – asking if she were Peter's Māori wife, as though he had several of different races.

The aunts ferried platters in and out of the living room, and Peter brought her a glass of wine. Susan leaned her head in, and, without looking Ra in the eye, asked why the savouries hadn't been put out yet. The smoke alarm went off twice because the kitchen door was open, and one of Peter's friends whacked it silent with the back of a wooden spoon. When at last nobody seemed to want any more tea, Ra ventured out to collect dishes. Although it was generally agreed that nobody knew what to say at a time like this, everyone in the living room was talking very loudly.

'The weather held,' someone said.

'A lovely day for Barbara,' another voice agreed. 'She would have been out in the garden on a day like this.'

By seven o'clock most people had left, except Aunt Anne, who was hovering anxiously in the kitchen, her forks trapped inside the dishwasher. Peter impatiently jerked open the door and rescued them, steaming hot, cramming them into their plastic-covered canteen. Ra carried one of the flower arrangements out to a cousin's car and laid it carefully on the back seat.

'They managed to get through eight bottles of wine as well,' said Peter's father, clutching the empties to his chest on his way out to the garage. 'I suppose I shouldn't complain. This isn't something that happens every day.'

Peter offered to drive Ra back to the airport that evening.

'Thanks for coming,' he said in a small, tight voice. They were sitting at the table in the breakfast room, drinking coffee and picking at the leftover ham. Ra looked up at Barbara's cookbooks lined along the countertop, covers torn, spines broken, scraps of paper sticking out. Peter followed her gaze and silently passed one down, a notebook with handwritten recipes and menus ripped from magazines.

'This is it!' said Ra, her eyes widening.

'Yup,' he said. 'The famous Christmas pudding.'

Ra thought of Barbara's face, flushed and happy, on the other side of the dining table, dolloping servings into the Royal Doulton bowls, laughing when it fell onto the cloth, annoyed when it dripped onto her new silk blouse. The recipe was listed under 'G'.

'Why G?' Ra asked, squinting at the page.

'It was Granny's,' Peter replied, pouring some more coffee. 'She gave Mum the recipe.'

Ra shrugged her shoes off. There were peanuts ground into the carpet under her toes. She had to strain to read Barbara's handwriting through the stains, and the smudges, and the watery ink.

'Remember when I tried to make it without the recipe?' Ra asked him. 'It fell apart.'

'You should take it,' said Peter. 'Keep the book.'

'Really? What about your sisters? Won't they want to keep it in the family?'

Peter tipped back his cup, hiding his face.

'Look at this,' she said, holding the book open so he could see. 'No wonder we couldn't move after eating it.'

'Seems like an awful lot of suet,' he agreed, and they both started to laugh, opening their mouths wide, smiling at each other for the first time that day.

Douglas Street, 1968

Paula Morris

The wooden gate swung open and the child tore up the pathway towards her grandmother, who was waiting, as usual, on the verandah.

'Two nights,' she announced, pressing her nose into the soft folds of the old woman's face, bent low to meet hers.

'My mokopuna,' whispered the grandmother.

The child leaned her cheek against the old woman's hip and felt something hard and smooth, like a flat stone, buried deep in the pinafore's pocket. It was sewing chalk.

The gate creaked again and her father loped towards the verandah, balancing a small bag in one hand and a tricycle in the other.

'We'll see you on Sunday,' he called, but the child, fizzing with excitement, was already across the threshold and into the endless dark of the hall.

The indoors world began where the stained-glass panels of the door threw a sickly light onto the floor. It ended at the back door and the rickety set of stairs tumbling down to the yellow hibiscus tree in the back garden. The child could hear her grandfather cursing the noise. She pounded along the thin carpet, waiting to be found.

The grandmother stood outside talking for a while. A draught skimmed through the open front door and whistled down to the back door, slamming it shut.

'Mary!' her grandfather's voice bellowed. 'Shut the bloody door!'

The child ran towards the sound.

Since her husband retired, Mary had kept to the back of the house. John liked to sit in the front room, watching the television or surveying the street, but she considered that part of the house to be cold and uncomfortable. Her son and his wife had lived for a while in the other front room, across the hall. But now that was just an empty room with a lumpy double bed covered in worn candlewick. Halfway down the hallway a pair of curtains hung, one wing hiding the telephone table. This marked the beginning of Mary's world, of the big bedrooms, the sewing room, and the expansive kitchen where everyone ate and talked and listened to the radiogram.

The front room had so much furniture that it felt like a museum lined with neglected exhibits. It looked worst in the summertime, Mary thought, when the sunlight searched out the long streaks of dust on everything, and the sofa seemed more faded and shabby than usual, and the Christmas tree wilted in the corner next to the television. Even when he wasn't sitting in it, John's armchair had a reproving look.

Guests were expected tomorrow night for cards, so this afternoon she'd make a start on some housework. Mary drifted into the front room, holding the brown feather duster, idly wondering what kind of bird the feathers had come from. They looked like ostrich, because they were so thick and brown. Perhaps they were moa. No, that couldn't be right. Moa had been extinct for years. But still, they had that look to them. She'd seen pictures.

Mary passed the duster under her chin, wondering why it didn't tickle, wondering why the moa had died out when the kiwi hadn't. Moa were too big, she supposed, and couldn't hide as well, which was hard on the moa but lucky for the kiwi. When she was a girl, her grandmother had given her a cloak of kiwi feathers. The cloak looked just plain brown from a distance, but up close it was speckled with the colours of sand and cream and mud and treacle. Up close it looked like heavy rain. It bristled, breathing as you touched it, as though all the birds that had given their feathers to make it were still alive, huddled beneath the fabric. Mary wore it once, a long time ago, when she met the Queen, but never again: when would she have occasion? Mary splayed the feather fingers of the duster against the sideboard and wondered, for a second or two, where that cloak could have gone.

Outside the window the child was chattering and John was laughing. Mary flicked the duster down the doors of the sideboard, across the dull top of the piano. A vase of frazzled flowers in water brown as gravy stood at one end. Mary looked down at the seat of the piano stool, which needed a new cover. She raised the lid of the piano and the keys grinned up at her, yellow and black, still straight and even. She dropped the duster, her plump fingers straying across the keys, hands drifting like dark clouds. There was sheet music under the frayed seat cover, bundles of it. June used to belong to the Light Opera Society, and in the old days she was always bringing songs home. There was that one she used to sing all the time. What was it called? How did it go?

Mary sat down. She couldn't remember the name of the tune but even so, it seemed to flow from her fingers. She still had the touch. The song filled the room with sadness and sweetness, and the memory of it made her smile.

June could hear the music as she opened the gate, and she could hear her father and her niece, their voices floating up from the side of the house. They were exclaiming over something shiny that he'd dug up. She resisted the impulse to join them.

'Is that you, June?' her mother called, still playing. June dragged the door shut and tugged off her headscarf.

'Mum?' she said, scowling into the semi-darkness of the front room. It was so damn dusty in there. Everything looked like it was coming to pieces.

'That song,' said her mother, without looking up. 'I've been waiting for you to come home and tell me what it is.'

'I don't know,' said June. Really, this was too much. All she wanted was some peace and quiet, after a long week of queues and impatient customers. But here was her mother making a racket, her father getting the child over-excited, and a whole weekend of their clamouring and noise ahead.

The heels of her shoes drummed down the passageway. The noise echoed slightly; it made her headache worse. She'd taken her umbrella today because the radio had predicted rain. But it hadn't rained yet, and the umbrella was just one more thing to carry. She'd wrenched it free of a closing bus door this afternoon and bent a spoke.

'Damn,' she said, frowning, and dropped it into the umbrella stand behind her bedroom door. June had five umbrellas. They seemed to accumulate, like earrings or pantyhose. She'd bought one of them in Sydney: that she remembered – a soft dove-grey, the handle was very delicate, like mother-of-pearl. It was a smart umbrella, the kind you'd tuck under your arm to give an outfit that finishing touch. She never used it anymore, not since she'd come home. It would be ruined in a week in the gusty Auckland rain.

The house stood on the corner, facing east onto a broad, busy road, studded with shops, which stretched like elastic in both directions. The side gate opened onto Douglas Street, which dipped into the gully and flattened out far to the west. Beyond the back garden was an unbroken view of brick chimneys, red corrugated iron roofs, lean-to sheds and washing-lines.

John Knight, hands on hips, slightly out of breath, surveyed the ragged back fence. The back portion was being wrestled to the ground by next door's misshapen grapefruit tree. The street sides of the fence were still erect, more or less, but their buttery yellow paint was curdling, flaking away onto the flowerbeds and the asphalt pavement.

He'd been sent out that morning to clear away the rubbish drifting in from the road. So far he'd found three ice-cream wrappers and half a broken bottle. John stumped round the house grumbling, brandishing the bottle like a club.

John had bought the house the year the war began, when they walked off the farm and moved back to Auckland with the two children. The three-storey building next door, its sheer brick sides like a thin slice cut from a loaf of bread, cast a perpetual shadow onto the house's north-facing rooms. In the winter, Mary stuffed thick sausages of newspaper into crocheted covers and rolled them against every door in the house, trying to trap the heat.

When the Knight family first moved in, the Indians didn't run the grocer's shop and the Yugoslavians hadn't taken over the restaurant on the opposite corner. That had come after the war. But John didn't mind them. They all worked hard. They washed their windows and swept the pavement, and their children wore shoes to school every day. The Indians invited them to weddings where John and Mary pinned dollar notes onto the bride's sari and ate rice, just like everybody else. John often walked over the road to Dino's, to sit in the steamy kitchen and talk about the economy.

It was the Polynesians he objected to, creeping up the hill from the shacks in Newton Gully – dozen to a house, he'd heard, and more arriving by the boatload every week. They weren't like Māoris. They didn't belong here, and they didn't try to fit in. Never worked, but there was always a crowd of them at the pub and the bookies. You could hear them staggering back along the road on Saturday nights, big drunken gangs of them, singing and fighting.

The sound of voices in the street always woke him. When the child was old enough to visit, she slept in her father's old room. John checked on her once, twice, three times a night. Every time he climbed out of bed, the creaking floorboards disturbed Mary. He knew his nocturnal patrol got on her nerves. After a while, she began putting the child to bed in their room. He kept the curtains open a little, so he could watch her tiny face in the moonlight, soft and trusting, oblivious to everything.

The day had flown, just flown. Everybody would be arriving at any minute and Mary wasn't ready. John was in the way. He'd checked on the child so many times, she'd never get to sleep. Some of the glasses weren't clean, so Mary was giving them a quick rub-over. Pretty glasses, etched with Greetings from the *Orsova*. How long was it since June sailed to Sydney? It sounded exotic, Mary thought, possibly Greek. She'd seen pictures of Greek statues, postcards her son had sent from Europe. All the statues were nude. Nude! That was the kind of word that shouldn't be said aloud, especially around the child.

June wandered in and out, not settling to anything. She wasn't going out tonight, she said, but wouldn't be joining the party. She worked too hard, Mary thought; didn't get out enough in the evenings.

June had fried herself eggs an hour ago. She'd eaten them at the kitchen table with the child on her lap. The child leaned over the plate, June feeding her as though she were still a baby. The child had wriggled around and kissed her aunt's face with wet yolky lips. They sat snuggled on the creaking chair, curled together like the fronds of a fern.

Later, Mary had carried the child into the big bedroom. They paused, the way they always did, to look at the photograph hanging near Mary's side of the bed. It was of Mary and her two sisters, taken just before she married John. All the girls had long dark hair, great waves of it. Mary's fell below her hips.

Meri, she'd been then. Meri. John used to say it in a soft voice, tender; he'd whisper it like a secret. He'd called her that just the other week. Mary was squeezing into bed next to the child, who was sound asleep and spreadeagled across the pillows.

'Be careful, Meri,' he'd murmured, and she remembered the first time she heard him say it, a breezy spring morning, sitting under a pine tree in her father's back paddock.

June sat smoking on the back stairs. Some of her mother's friends had already arrived. She could hear their cackles and the chime of chinking glass through the open windows.

Perhaps she should have gone out to the pictures this evening. She wouldn't have felt so alone in the darkness of the Regent. Most of her old gang were gone, married and scattered through the suburbs, or still in Australia. It was ten years since she'd set off on that great adventure with some of the Light Opera crowd. Maybe she should try it again, alone this time. She could go somewhere else: Australia was a big country. Ten years was a long time ago. She was still young enough, almost, though not young and silly anymore, thank god. Not so bloody wide-eyed and naive.

She'd met him on the boat. It was funny, really. After all those years of saving every penny, after all her dreams of escaping this sodden, dreary town, she'd ended up in love with someone raised a few streets away. She'd sailed away to see life in a real city, the kind that bursts with people and high-rise buildings and neon lights that stay on all night. And instead, all she saw was him. It took a long time for his face to go away, to quit her memory and her dreams, to stop staring back at her from train windows or the other side of a bar. Even after he was physically gone, headed for Perth and new adventures, she could see his round face and quizzical expression every time she closed her eyes. She saw it in the face of the baby she held for half an hour before they carried it away to a real family. Half an hour. It was just long enough to hear it cry, and to trace his outline in its squashed little features. He was long gone by then, and who could blame him? He hadn't come all that way to settle down with a bushy-haired girl from Douglas Street. He never knew about the baby. Nobody knew about the baby – nobody here, anyway. She'd left that part of her life behind her when she came home.

'June!' someone called from the gate. It was Mrs Leaf, who lived further down Douglas Street. She had twisted her hand through the rungs of the gate and was groping for the latch. 'Can you let me in?'

June stubbed out her cigarette with the toe of her sandal and stood up, brushing off her skirt. Mrs Leaf's hand was flopping like a fish in a trap, skinny and veined with silver. Hanging from her wrist was a heavy bracelet of half-sovereigns. Mrs Leaf's father had brought them home after the first war, to make up for the leg he left in Europe. The coins, scraping against the peeling wood of the gate, had shaved off a sliver of paint.

'Mind your hand,' said June, grimacing.

'Someone should bring that in before it rains again, or gets stolen,' said Mrs Leaf, gesturing towards the child's tricycle, which lay upside down outside the wash-house. Her bracelet glinted in the last of the sun.

'I will,' June murmured. She closed the gate with her hip and leaned up against it, her back to Douglas Street.

The noise woke everyone, even the child.

There were shouts from outside, and a cracking sound, and then glass breaking. Her aunt was at the door of the bedroom, with curlers in her hair, saying stay there, just stay there, but her grandparents were up and looking out the window. The child began crying, and her grandfather picked her up out of bed to make her stop.

Her aunt was already out on the verandah by the time the three of them got there. A group of men was standing on the corner, big men with dark faces, so many she couldn't count them. The fence had collapsed, and one man was lying right on top of it. His face was red with blood. The child inched her way out of her grandfather's arms and stood next to him, one hand on the dangling cord of his dressing gown. She wasn't afraid.

'Just be on your way now, boys,' her aunt was saying in a loud, deep voice. The child had never heard that voice before. 'And we won't need to call the police.'

Everyone was standing very still, the men on the pavement and her family on the verandah. They were all looking at each other.

The child gazed at the wild faces of the men. Their eyes were red and streaky, like raw bacon. The man who had fallen rolled back and forth on the toppled fence, like he was rocking in a cradle. Maybe he was sleeping. She stretched to her tiptoes to see if his eyes were shut.

Her aunt's back was straight and strong. She stood facing the men and spoke in that loud voice again, calm and measured. The child loved her aunt's voice. It sounded brave. The men liked it too; they were listening intently. Then one of them pulled the sleeping man to his feet and they lurched off down Douglas Street. They weren't shouting anymore. Her aunt was still as a statue, watching them leave, but her grandmother was already walking back inside.

The child turned to her grandfather. He stood stiff and tall, his face a pale grey in the moonlight. She tugged on the cord of his dressing gown, but he didn't look down at her. He didn't move at all. She reached up to take his hand, and felt it trembling.

Geraniums

Paula Morris

A package was waiting when she got into work that morning. She opened it before unwinding her scarf. In it was a brown envelope; within that was a small white envelope, with a note and six tiny packets. Each contained seeds from his garden, marked with his careful, clear handwriting. He had told her to grow them in containers out on her fire escape. If I could, he wrote, I would send you a garden with a wall around it.

Yesterday, not much had been said. His voice was tired and nervous. He was calling from a public telephone. He told her the baby's name, weight and length.

'Is that long?' she asked.

'I'm not sure,' he said, laughing.

She asked him if the baby was OK and he said yes.

'Everyone's fine,' he told her.

Snow had been falling all morning, skimming the windows of the tall building in which she worked. In a meeting, sitting around the long table, she absently watched it drift by. Some days when it snowed the streets below were clear and black; the snow turned to rain before reaching the ground. Someone was asking her a question and she walked over to the pass to look down.

'It's snowing,' she replied.

'Yes, it was snowing when I arrived. But they say it'll stop this afternoon. Should be a good weekend.'

The snow would stop. The sun would come out. Everyone around the table nodded in agreement.

'I got the seeds,' she told him.

'Good,' he said. The line seemed to go dead, but he was still there. 'It's been a long day. I'm exhausted.'

'I can imagine,' she said.

It was still snowing when she left the building early that afternoon, her face damp, threading through the late lunchtime crowd clogging the corner. The snow was already turning into thick brown sludge, engorging the gutters like fat-veined gravy. Waiting to cross Park Avenue, she stood ankle-deep in it, not noticing that the hem of her black coat was dragging in the slush, flecked by the taxis turning north.

In his note – which she'd re-read again and again, as if seeking clues – he told her that the seeds were not shop-bought. He had been saving them for her, putting them aside. In one of their conversations, he'd told her that she should have a garden. He couldn't believe that she could be happy simply overlooking someone else's. He collected the seeds so she'd be able to grow something herself.

She'd grown up a long way from here. Behind her parents' house was a vast, wild garden that tumbled down a hill towards a mangrove-filled creek. Under the dank pongas, there were hundreds of places to hide, to shelter from the sun. It was always cold beneath the thick thatch overhead.

Her brothers and sisters had wanted a tree house. They talked of monitoring the creek's progress out to the harbour from halfway up the giant pine. Together they all cleared a dirt space near the base of the trunk. Deep in the garden, they couldn't hear anything but the twitching of cicadas and sound of the wind shaking long grass on the bank that was too steep to mow.

Every front lawn in their street opened wide-eyed to the footpath, each house dull and uniform with bedroom windows and venetian blinds. In the hot weather, from driveways smothered with hose pipes and skateboards, children drifted into the street to play softball on the hot asphalt. In the winter, when the rain poured, gutters swelled with drowning worms, and armoured wetas materialised outside the front door. The garden grew sodden and impenetrable. The creek flooded, and glossy eels circled the trunk of a dislodged tree. The whole world was a dark, dull green.

His call had come exactly at noon, as though it were the appointed time.

'Everyone's fine,' he told her.

'Good,' she said.

'Are you OK?'

'Yes, I'm fine,' she said, wondering why he asked, as if she were the one in the hospital, as if she were the one having a baby.

Geraniums, pale pink and pungent, filled the front border. They'd been transplanted from her nana's garden. Every spring, daffodils poked their way through piles of grass clippings. Her mother hacked red-faced at the bank with blunt cutters and trained bougainvillaea up the crib wall, where it flourished, bright and determined, behind wildly sprouting pongas.

'I didn't plant those,' said her mother, defeated. 'They've flown there themselves. Things just grow in this country wherever they like.'

She pulled her hat down over stinging ears and walked up Fifth Avenue to the bookstore. At the foot of the escalator, a small audience had gathered around a dais to hear a man describe, in droning monotone, the urinary problems of cats. She fingered the candy spines of the children's books and found the one she had decided to get months ago, when it had seemed just the thing. Just the thing for a friend to buy. Upstairs, all the cards sprouted floral Easter greetings. She wanted something blank. She wanted something as anonymous as the notepaper he had wrapped around the seed packets.

She had congratulated him, as friends do. 'You have a good weekend,' he said.

'You too.'

'I'll be at work for a short while on Monday. I'll try to call you.'

The baby had come early. She had hoped for a few more weeks. She had hoped for a month, for what was left of the winter.

When she was small, she'd found it hard to breathe outside. All the spindly wattles had to be cut down, and the neighbours obligingly hacked out their hedge of golden privet. She hated the fetid smell of the garden centre, the sight of sparse rose bushes sitting in their black plastic sacks, withering in the sun. She hated the suffocating heat of the garden, the manic devotion with which her parents mutilated it every weekend, the drone of mowers every night after dinner. In a movie, she saw a woman sitting on her fire escape one summer's evening in New York, playing a guitar.

'I'm never having a garden,' said her sister. 'I'm going to have an apartment in the city with an answering machine and a big-screen TV.'

When she closed her eyes, they lived in a place beyond telephone calls and brown envelopes. She remembered resting her forearms on his shoulders and kissing him on the lips. She remembered holding his hand to her mouth and tasting the saltiness of his skin, tracing her tongue over the tips of his fingers. She remembered smoothing his shirt, feeling a whisper of soft breath, gently lifting the hair away from her face.

The baby had come early.

'Is he OK?' she asked.

'Everyone's fine,' he said. He sounded tired and relieved.

She left the seeds in their envelope on her desk; it was too soon to plant them. Snow lay piled in neat lines on the fire escape at her apartment building. When the weather turned, she would plant the seeds there in small plastic pots. She could watch them growing, through her open window, all summer long.

That weekend, he would drive the baby and his wife home from the hospital. The nursery would be ready, painted blue and yellow like an Easter egg. Spring came early where he lived, and he had planned out his garden all winter. Already bulbs would be nudging through the earth. His front lawn ran flat to the sidewalk, open like the palm of a hand. The dog would greet the car, and neighbours would stand, watchful and smiling, at their living room windows. They would all feel happy and hopeful and satisfied because everyone was fine and the baby had arrived safely, just as the weather was turning.

Her earliest memory was of the fuchsias in her nana's garden. She'd stroke them with chubby fingers until they snapped from their stems and fell crushed onto her shoe straps. She'd press her face into the bush to feel their sweet softness against her skin. Then the doctor would arrive with his cold stethoscope, ushered into the bedroom where she lay propped like a doll against lilac cushions, surrounded by a vast sterile field of linoleum.

On her last visit home, she noticed that the pink geraniums had disappeared entirely. Her mother couldn't remember ever growing pink geraniums. Her father couldn't remember them either.

'You're thinking of Nana's,' he told her, and took her for a guided tour of the bougainvillaea, now twinned with clematis to disguise the breeze blocks of the new extension. But she couldn't go back to her grandmother's garden. The house had been sold and demolished years ago, replaced by a video shop. The garden had been covered with concrete, each parking space precisely outlined in custard-coloured paint.

She walked back to the office holding the baby's book in its plastic bag with one cold, bare hand. The snow had stopped falling. Grey clouds were moving on, high above the clustered towers of Midtown. Along Fifth Avenue, despite the sharp wind, people loitered outside shop windows full of pallid new clothes.

From her office window, she could glimpse a slim strand of light blue above the smokestacks across the river. She could hear someone talking to her, saying that the snow had stopped and the sun was coming out. This was probably the last of the snow, they said, telling her that winter was over and that spring would follow, as if nobody knew this, as if it were not inexorable, as if nothing ever began and nothing ever ended.

The Ballad of Questions

Whetu-Marama Pahi

'Where you been girl? I've been ringing you all day.' Roxie's mouth going hard over the speaker. 'Navey's on life-support.'

'What!'

'Yeah, he's up at Starship, he's on life support, don't know what happened, I'm sure it was that blimmin' Mark ay bro, 'member that time Sharyn told us that he threw Boy against the wall cause he wouldn't stop crying, fuckin' prick, they're over there now they are, Sharyn and Mark –'

'Whaddaya mean he's on life-support?'

'Yeah bro he's on life-support, since this morning ... ah shit, wait there's someone on the other line.'

What. He's on life-support. Oh my God. Nah. Nah. Mark couldn't have done it. They don't even have custody of Boy. Her aunty does. That bitch! I knew there was something queer 'bout her. Moll. You moll, moll, you fuckin' moll!

'You there?'

'Yeah bro.'

'That was Kara. She was talking to Sharyn on her mobile. She's nearly there in Auckland.'

'Yeah what? What did she say?'

'Apparently Navey's been suffocated.'

'Suffocated?'

'Yeah bro ... I can't believe it eh, I mean just the other day, you know ... poor Navey, poor Navey-Boy!'

'Oh don't cry Rox, don't cry, if you cry then I'll start up, don't cry Rox. Who dunnit Rox? Do they know who dunnit?'

'Nah they don't know, they don't know. Sharyn reckons it was her aunty.'

'Have the cops been round there yet? Have they arrested her?'

'They don't know who dunnit.'

'Ow man. Rox, where you?'

'At home.'

'Come over.'

'See ya soon.'

'Oh Sharyn!'

Kara embraces her best friend Sharyn.

'Are you okay? How is he?'

'Dunno.' She shrugs.

'What did the doctors say? Is he gonna be alright? Where's Mark?'

'Bathroom.'

The ballad of Mark's shoes is heard squeaking along the corridor.

'Hey Kara,' he gives her a kiss, 'you were fast getting here, how long did it take you to drive, four – five hours?'

'Yeah 'bout that, what about you guys?'

'Yeah 'bout that too eh hon?' he says calmly, including Sharyn in the conversation.

'Man, I saw your aunty out the front, the cheek of it, saw her putting on the innocent,' said Kara.

'Pah – the rotten mongrel,' spits Sharyn.

'Gee, what happened girl?' Kara asks resignedly 'What happened to Navey? Who dunnit? Did she do it?'

'They don't know yet, they're still carrying out some investigations. But they're questioning Kauri.'

'Kauri?'

'Yeah they reckon that Kauri might have had something to do with it.'

'Who told you this, the police?'

'Nah, I was talking to my aunty before.'

'Bitch. Kauri my ass. He wouldn't do something like this. He's not like that!'

'Yeah I reckon. 'Member about that time I told you I went over to visit Navey? Yeah well he was only running around in a blimmin' nappy. And that time I went to change his bum? Yeah well he didn't want me to change it. I'm sure he was being fiddled with.'

'Arseholes.'

'Yeah ay. All she blimmin' worries about is boozing. When I went over there they were hard out on the piss. And the way those blimmin' kids talk to each other, mongrel kids, some of 'em need a good slap up man, gee they're smart as.'

'Poor Navey, poor Navey-Boy!'

'How many sugars girl? One? Two?'

'Just the one. I'm on a diet.'

'Diet – *paleese*. You're skinny as a rake, girl.'

'Hah! Tell that to the prick I got with on Friday night. He called me a jelly.'

'Jelly?'

'Yeah, jelly – blimmin' prick. Weirdo.'

'He was probably referring to your stomach Rox,' Penny said laughing, 'look at all the kids you've had. Or maybe he's referring to your technique under the sheets?'

'Where's the ashtray girl?'

Penny emptied the butts out of the spaghetti tin can.

'Here girl. Mmm.' Exhale. 'Needed that.'

'So Kara's up there now, at Starship?'

'Yeah well she should be up there by now.' Inhale. 'I don't think Navey's gonna make it ay, they reckon he's brain dead now. Poor baby.'

'Oh poor Boy. Just a couple more weeks and he would've been two years old. Poor Boy. Mind you he's probably better off where he's going. Straight to heaven. Straight to heaven.' Exhale.

'Yeah that's right. He'll be safe there, no one can hurt him now.' Inhale.

'And Sharyn you know she's having another baby right?'

'Yeah she's eight months ay?'

'You know she's got the cheek to have another baby. She couldn't even look after the first one.'

'Yeah I know bro. Her boyfriend's a prick too.'

'Gee I don't know. I don't know.' Exhale.

Goodbye

Maraea Rakuraku

Dear Cuz,

Kia ora rā, how are you?? How's everything?

Me, well there is so much to tell you ...

Remember how I told you about Daniel ... well ... he asked me to marry him!!! Yeah *me*, man I freaked but you know ... he's got himself together you know and after all those men who haven't who made me cry, well it's nice – and you know I CAN get over the fact he is blond and blue eyed although I never ever thought I would marry a Pākehā. Our babies will have no choice but to follow after their mother's bushy hair and big lips!!! God when I was at home this last time all the aunties were giggling and pointing at him and you know that hāngi pants Rangimarie she had the cheek to say out loud, 'Hold onto him tight girl, I might come and steal him off you while Taane is in the bush....'

God, she has like eight kids now!! All with hūpē noses and looking hungry. Remember that time we were going past the cowshed at milking time and heard all those noises, went running in and there she was with Uncle Hemi. And how later on that night Aunty Missy was throwing Uncle's things out the door. Boy they used to have some hooleys aye. Man we must have been about twelve and she was seventeen – well cuz, she looks a hundred now!!!

So yeah Daniel met the whānau ... and you know how they are putting on their best behaviour. He thinks everyone is great ... yeah, I know!!! EVERYONE – even Nanny K. Fry, can you believe it and she looked at him with only one eye, poking and licking her lips like she was going to eat him!! I reckon she only liked him because he held the car door open for her.

Do you think he will still like the whānau when he sees Uncle Kati giving Aunty Reihana a hiding ... and a new baby; when he sees all the drinking ... when he sees whānau squabbling about who owns this piece of land, who owns this piece. It's a bit scary ay ... how do you know? I mean yeah, he says now that he will love me forever and accept all the stuff with the whānau, but will he really, or will he make me choose??? Man I wish you were here to talk to about it ...

I felt really really sad when I saw Ratima, man you know how he was my first love and boy did he look sad. He looked at me like I wasn't even there.

I wish you were here ... I really miss you and no one knows me like you do ... you know ... when all those kids used to tease me and call me 'bush, bush, city bush' because of my hair, and you used to chase them and tell them to shut up or you were going to get Tamatu to give them a hiding.

Hey remember that time we ate all those plums and Aunty had to take us to the doctor's? And everyone was teasing Nanny that we were hapū ... stink, I mean I was only sixteen, what did I know? (hey probably too much now!!!) but then that other time we laid in the wharenui and you whispered to me you had a secret and it was that you were having a baby ... and how we looked at each other with BIG, BIG eyes, scared about how to tell your dad because you were only sixteen. I was eighteen then and itching to leave the valley.

And when you told me that you loved Ratima when I got back from my first year away at university and how miserable you looked and how angry I was. I knew though, I knew I had changed and I did not want to stay in the valley and if I was with Ratima that is what I would end up doing. I looked at the way he looked at you and knew I would not be able to do that for him and so I left. It was only when you had Meretuahiahi that I knew it was time for me to come home and once I saw you all the bad feelings disappeared. How could I begrudge my cousin happiness, as we gooed and gaahed over the baby? What would she sound like? What would she do when she grew up? How would we teach her all the things we knew so she would grow up strong?

I look at her now and she is just like you, the way she smiles, everything, the way her chin sticks out when she is angry, the way she runs, even the way she looks at me sometimes waiting for an answer the way you used to.

I find myself storing all those secrets we used to share, waiting for the time when she is old enough to hear them. So I can tell her about her mother. My beautiful, funny cousin who defended me when we were young, married my first love and was my best friend.

I miss you Moana and I'll take care of her. Haere rā tōku tuahine, haere, haere. Hoki atu ki te poho a Papatūānuku

Arohanui

Mere

P.S. I said Yes.

Keke Keke

Dianne Sharma-Winter

In the forest of the endless beginning, there is the precise foundation of knowledge from which to build a mortal life in remembrance of the gods. There is the smooth brown plain of learning and the fibre of the flax weaving the tāniko of every interconnected life, there are the vines creeping and yearning and the whisper denoting increase. There are the long-standing trees and the creak, creak, creak of branches in the forest.

Except the forest has become a rafter, around which is slung a rope. Swinging there is the body of every woman who ever had her father's hand, her uncle's lips, and her brother's penis in places on her body where they shouldn't even have laid their eyes.

She is swollen with the bitterness of self-loathing and long hours of neglect. She has run through the forest of the night to escape him and found him everywhere. As often as she denies his existence, he multiplies and increases. He is like fingers of mangrove, his hands on her body, creeping over wet mud, poking up everywhere. Or vines creeping and strangling, he is sucking her life away and begging her to forgive him. She despises herself for being frozen to the earth, he creeps all over her.

She reaches into the night long past and wraps her fingers around a tuft of hair from the topknot of Hine Nui te Pō. It opens her to another level. There she is no body, no body at all. She can look down on this pitiful scene and wait like she is waiting for a bus. Hine Nui te Pō holds her there like a kite. She is floating over time and space.

She remembers when she was the light that shimmered in the first breath of day, when she was the innocence of a newborn baby and the utter miracle of birth. She remembers when she was fragile and precious and imbued with the energy of the goddess, she remembered her life from the yearning through to the desire to the conception and increase.

She was the daughter of the dawn and as beautiful as the delight of discovery. She was the shine in her father's eye. She was the only female who loved him unconditionally, and for this he made her a woman.

Shh, be still. Shh.

Hine Nui te Pō tells her secrets, she listens while she is waiting.

Women are the waka that carry men across the ocean of existence.

She goes there in her waiting dream.

It was the fierce thrusting of Tāne that rent heaven apart from earth.

His sweat is stale and it stinks. He is thrusting and fumbling, breathing in her ear.

Her eyes are squeezed shut. Her head is hitting the headboard; he turns like a rat and pulls the body further down the bed.

There is the sound of creak, creak, and creak.

In the classroom, she is the girl with her head drooping on the desk. She has already left her tired child's body.

– See Jane run. Jane runs to Dad.

Io, in the form of Tāne, claimed mana whenua over his daughter's womb.

She is not paying attention in class. She is sly and she lies and she cries. She is altogether disruptive.

Tāne knows a karakia to allow him entry to his daughter's womb.

She doesn't go to school any more.

She still is shy and sly and still lies. Never cries.

She is the girl with a plastic bag on her face, a fifteen year old in an empty playground. Swinging on a swing. Creak, creak, creak.

– See Hine run. She runs from Dad.

The karakia took him down through the centre, he didn't touch the sides.

When she is older and putting up a bit of a fight he will spread-eagle her to the four corners of the bed and tie her there. Hine Nui te Pō covers her body like a blanket. She tells her secrets again.

She comes from the centre, she gives her advice.

Hine Tītama froze the karakia in Tāne's throat to save all her daughters hence.

She is the repository for all his anger and insecurity; she is the vessel of his loathing. He stinks of booze and stale cigarettes. He spits seed into her.

Hine Nui te Pō takes the girl's hand and turns it into a patu. She moves in the unoccupied body of the girl, springing a surprise attack. One sharp blow to the tenga and his windpipe is crushed. He is gasping the way he usually does, only this time will be his last.

He is in the shadow of every man she will ever meet and greet and have to talk to for the rest of her mortal life. This puts her at a disadvantage. He is in the shadow of the judge who will hang her. He is the man who will employ her so he can rub his hand on her backside. He is the taxi driver who wants a blowjob for his fare, the punter in the parlour.

She goes for the rope by which she will descend to the realm of Hine Nui te Pō. Climbing onto a chair, she swings from the rope and leaps free.

From long practise, she is able to shed her mortal body quickly, like a coat. She moves quickly towards Reinga, diving like an arrow into the waters below. Flying over the sea towards the magical homeland of Hawai'iki, she passes the last post of her father's house where sits the taniwha Parata.

He is opening and closing his mouth on the tide of man at the place known as Te Waiora a Tāne and there is Tāne, the originator of all life, endlessly washing away the sins of man. She absorbs him and carries on.

Te Rau Oriwa

Charles Shortland

Upoko 1

'Nā wai i mea? Nē, nā wai? Nā wai i mea kia pēneitia e rātou tā tātou mokopuna? Kei te tino riri nei ahau ki tēnei tākuta!'

Nā puehu ana te marae i a Pita. E whakarongo ana hoki te iwi, me te whānau ki āna kōrero.

'Taurekareka Pākehā! Taurekareka tākuta! Nā wai i tuku, ā, nā wai i hoatu te mana ki a ia? Kia riro rawa māna e tuku tā tātou tamaiti, mokopuna kia mate? Nā wai tēnei tākuta Pākehā i whakatū hei atua? Kia riro rawa māna e mea kia tukua a Matiu kia mate?'

'E Pita! E whakaae ana ahau ki ēnā kōrero āu. Koia tonu ēnā ko ngā whakaaro kei roto i tōku nei ngākau. E Pita, mai i tōku rongona i tēnei mea e kōrerotia nei e tātou, kātahi ka koropupū ake te riri i roto i a au. Koia hoki tēnei ko te mate ki a tātou ki te Māori. Ka kite mai te tākuta Pākehā, he mangu kē te kiri o te tangata, ehara i te kiri mā, kua tukuna kia mate. Kua mutu te hoatu i ngā rongoā e ora tonu ai.'

Kātahi hoki a Karaka ka oho ake, 'E hoa mā, e ngā whanaunga, e te whānau, ahakoa te mamae o o tātou ngākau, tēnā āta tirohia e tātou te pūtake, me ngā tikanga, i pēneitia ai e te Pākehā nei, tā tātou tamaiti mokopuna a Matiu.

Nā, e kī ana te tākuta nei, he nui rawa ngā mate o tā tātou mokopuna. He nui, he kino te whara o tōna māhunga. Kua kore kē ia e mōhio ake ki te tangata. Kua kore kē e rongo ake i te reo tangata. Kua kore noa iho e korikori. Heoi e takoto kau ana. Ko te ngākau anake e panapana tonu ana. Nō reira, ahakoa pēhea te roa ōna, e hono atu ai ki te mīhini whakaora, e kore rawa ia e ora. Nō reira e te whānau, e ngā whanaunga hoki, kia –'

'E noho koe ki raro Karaka, e kore rawa ahau e whakaae. E kore hoki ahau e whakapono ki ēnā kōrero āu, ki a mātou.' Nā ko te reo tēnei o Pare. Koia tēnei ko te whaea o Matiu, arā, o te mokopuna e takāto mai rā, ā, e hono mai rā ki ngā mīhini whakaora o te hohipere.

'Nā, ko tāku tēnei. E whakapono ana tōku whatu manawa ki tēnei kōrero, nā Ihowa i homai, mā Ihowa anō e tango. E kore rawa ahau e whakaae mā te tākuta Pākehā taku tamaiti mātāmua e tango atu.'

I konei, ka tīmata te auē, me te tangi o ngā kuia ī to rātou aroha ki a Pare. E heke nei ngā roimata, mō tāna tamaiti, mō Matiu i aituātia nei i tērā atu marama. I te tūtuki o tōna waka ki te piriti, e whakawhiti mai rā i te awa. I kō tata atu o te taone nei.

Kātahi ka tū ake a Tāmati. Ko ia te koroheke o to rātou marae.

'Hutia te rito o te harakeke,
kei hea te komako e kō?
Pātai mai ki au,
he aha te mea nui o tēnei ao?
Māku e kī atu ki a koe,
he tangata, he tangata, he tangata.

'Nā e kōrero nei tātou mō te tangata. Arā mō tā tātou mokopuna mō Matiu, kua tangohia nei ōna hononga ki te mīhini e ora tonu ai ia. Kua tangohia nei ēnei e te tākuta Pākehā nei. Tēnā pea e te whānau, e ngā whanaunga hoki, ka tutuki ngā kōrero a te whaea nei a Pare i a ia e kī ake nei, nā Ihowa i homai, tukua mā Ihowa anō e tango. Tēnā pea e te iwi, kua tae tēnei ki te wā, kua karanga a Ihowa i tāna kia hoki atu ki a ia. Tēnā pea i runga i te riri o ō tātou ngākau, ko tātou kē e ārai ana i tā te Atua i hiahia ai. Kia hoki atu tā tātou mokopuna ki a ia, i runga i te rangimārie, ahakoa tātou rurerurea e te aroha mōna. Nā, ko tāku tēnei ki a tātou e hui nei, e aku whanaunga, e taku whānau, tukua ta tātou mokopuna kia riro i runga i te rangimārie. Ahakoa te nui o te aroha i roto i a tātou.'

Nā, i te ono o ngā hāora, i te ahiahi, i te torongitanga o te rā, ka tangohia e te tākuta Pākehā ngā hono o te mīhini i te mokopuna nei i a Matiu. I te waru o ngā hāora, i taua pō tonu, ka hemo ia. Ka hoki tōna wairua ki tōna Kaihanga, ki te Atua.

Ka tūturi te whānau i te taha o tōna moenga. Ka karakia a Paora, 'Whakangaro atu e moko i tēnei ao, i runga i te aroha o te Atua, nāna nei koe i hanga, i runga i te mana o Ihu Karaiti. I mate nei ia mōu, i runga i te atawhaitanga a te Wairua Tapu. Whakangaro atu e te wairua ki te whānau e hui mai rā i Paerau, okioki mai, e hoki e te wairua, e hoki ki te kāinga.'

Kātahi ka whakahokia mai te tinana o te mokopuna nei o Matiu, e te whānau, ki tō rātou marae takoto ai. Nā, i reira te iwi e tangi ana, e auē ana, e hotu ana. To rātou riri tonu, i roto i o rātou ngākau ki te tākuta Pākehā rā.

I te toru o ngā rā, ka mutu te karakia i roto i to rātou tūpuna whare. Ka mauria ia, ka tanumia ki waenganui i ngā rua koiwi o ōna mātua tūpuna. I mua tonu i te tanumanga, ko te kōrero whakamutunga iho a tōna matua, a Puru ki a ia.

'Haere, haere, e taku tamaiti. Haere ki te wahangūtanga o te tangata. Haere e tama, nā Pākehā tēnei mahi ki a koe. Mehemea taua tākuta Pākehā nei i pūmau ki te oati, i oatitia e ia, i te rā i tū ai ia hei tākuta, ki te whakaora i te tangata i te wā e panapana tonu ana tōna ngākau. E tama! E kore kē koe e takoto mai i konā. Haere e tama, whakangaro atu i te tirohanga a te kanohi.'

Upoko 2

Nā, kua pau te toru tekau tau, mai i te matenga o Matiu. Kua pau haere ngā kaumātua me ngā kuia o te marae. Kua matemate kē te nuinga o rātou. E hia anō rānei, e toru pea, e whā rānei ngā mea o rātou e ora tonu ana. Ko ngā mātua o Matiu, kua mate kē a Puru, engari ko tōna whaea ko Pare, kei te ora tonu. Engari kua tino kuiatia ia.

Nā, ko ngā teina o Matiu, ko Piripi rāua ko Hera. Ko Hera, e whā tekau mā ono tau tōna pakeke. Nā ko tōna hoa tāne, ko Piwara, no Te Arawa, e rima rāua tamariki. Nā ko Piripi, e whā tekau mā waru tōna pakeke. I moe hoki ia i a Riripeti, nō Tainui, nā, e toru a rāua tamariki. I tēnei wā tonu anō, kua hoki mai a Piripi ki te wā kāinga. Kei te tāone tōna kāinga, kāhore noa i tawhiti atu i te marae.

Nā, e toru tekau tau e ngaro ana i te wā kāinga. I tēnei wā, kua hoki mai ia hei tākuta mātāmua mō te hohipere nei. Kei raro i tāna whakahaere ngā hau ora katoa o te rohe o te wā kāinga, me ngā kaimahi katoa o te hohipere nei.

'Tākuta Piripi, Tākuta Piripi! E karanga ana i a koe. Haere tonu mai ki te wāhi mō ngā aituā. Tākuta Piripi, Tākuta Piripi, kia tere mai, e karanga ana i a koe.'

Kātahi a Tākuta Piripi ka tae atu ki te wāhi mō ngā aituā. E takoto mai ana te tamaiti Pākehā nei. Kotahi tekau mā rima pea tōna pakeke. I taka i te hoiho. I te taunga iho ki te whenua, kātahi ka whanaia te mātenga. Nā, heoi anō, e takoto nei.

Ka mutu te titiro a Piripi, ka kite iho ia, kotahi anō te huarahi mōna. Me poka e te tākuta, ā, ka hono atu ai ki te mīhini whakaora o te hohipere.

E waru ngā rā i inuni mai, kātahi a Piripi ka titiro iho ki te tamaiti rā. Kātahi ia ka kite iho, kāhore kē he pai. Ka nui tōna māuiui, me te ngoikore hoki. E kore rawa ia e ora tonu. Ko te mīhini kē rā e mahi ana kia panapana tonu tōna ngākau.

I konei tonu, ka huri a Piripi ki te tākuta Pākehā, ki tōna kaiawhina i te hohipere. Ka pātai atu ki a ia, 'Tākuta Hēnare, pēhea tōu nei whakaaro ki tēnei o ā tāua tūroro?'

Ka rūrū te māhunga o Hēnare, ka kī ake, 'Kāhore rawa ahau i kite i te ora, mai i te rā i tae mai ai te tamaiti nei. Tae mai ki nāianei, e ngoikore kē atu ana, ahakoa ngā rongoā e hoatu nei e tātou ki a ia. E Piripi, ko te mīhini anake e whakaora tonu nei i a ia. Kāhore atu.'

Kātahi a Piripi ka tū ake, ka huri atu ki a Hēnare, 'Āe rā! He tika tēnā, ki tāku titiro. Ki tōku whakaaro anō hoki, me tango mai te tūroro nei i te mīhini nei. Tukua ia kia moe i runga i te rangimārie. E Hēnare, māu e kōrero atu tēnei ki te whānau, ki ngā mātua hoki o te tamaiti nei. Ko tā tāua whakaaro tēnei, ā, koia tēnei ko tā te Hohipere i whiriwhiri ai.'

Nā, i te rua karaka i te ahiahi, ka rongo a Piripi i te pātōtō i tana kuaha.

Kātahi ka tomo mai he kaumātua Pākehā. Ka tū mai ki mua i a Piripi. E waru tekau tau pea, ā kō atu rānei tōna pakeke. Kātahi te kaumātua nei ka noho ki raro, ka tīmata ki te korero. 'E tama, e Tākuta Piripi. I haere mai ahau ki te inoi ki a koe, kaua e tangohia te mīhini whakaora e hono atu nei ki taku mokopuna. Kia aroha mai koe ki au, ki taku whānau, ā, ki aku mokopuna anō hoki. E Tākuta Piripi kaua e tangohia te mīhini e whakaora tonu nei i a ia.

'Tākuta Piripi, e hoki ana ōku whakaaro ki ngā tau kua pahure ki muri. I tū rangatira ai ahau i konei, nō te mea ko ahau te tākuta rangatira o te hohipere nei i ngā tau ki muri. Nō reira, he tākuta ki te tākuta. E tama, kaua e tangohia te mīhini nei, nō te mea kei te panapana tonu te ngākau o taku mokopuna.'

Kātahi a Piripi ka tū tonu ake ki runga, ka titiro tonu atu ki te koroheke e noho mai nei i mua i a ia. E tūturu mai ana ngā roimata i āna kamo. Katahi a Piripi ka kōrero atu. 'Koroheke, ko koe! Ko koe! Aū, ko koe taua tākuta rā! E toru tekau ngā tau kua pahure! Nāu! Nāu i kōhuru tōku tuakana a Matiu! Nāu i mea kia tangohia te mīhini i a ia, i te wā e panapana tonu ana tōna ngākau!'

Kātahi ka tūturu ngā roimata i ngā kanohi o te koroheke rā. E tangi hotu ana te manawa, 'E Tākuta Piripi, kia aroha mai ki au. Kaua e tukua tōu ngākau kia taimaha. Ahakoa koe karanga i au he kōhuru; e Piripi i pēnei anō ahau i a koe nei. I titiro iho ahau ki tō tuakana, pēnei tonu anō i a koe e titiro iho nei ki taku mokopuna. Nā, ki tā te tākuta titiro, e kore rawa e ora, ahakoa kei te panapana tonu te ngākau. Ahakoa rānei te maha o ngā rongoā, e kore rawa e ora. Engari i tēnei wā e Piripi, e inoi ana ahau ki a koe, kaua e tangohia te mīhini nei i taku mokopuna.'

Nā i te putanga atu o te koroheke rā ki waho, kātahi a Piripi, ka noho ki raro. Ka whakaaro pēnei i roto i a ia nei anō, Nā te koroheke nei i mate ai tāku tuakana. Kāhore rawa ia i whakarongo ki te tangi, ki ngā inoi a tōku whānau, a tōku iwi, a tōku whaea, me tōku matua. Pakaru ana o rātou ngākau i taua Pākehā nei. Nā, i tēnei rā kua haere mai ia ki au, kia whakaorangia e ahau tana mokopuna. He kanohi mō te kanohi! He tangata mō te tangata! Nā, kei roto ia i ōku ringa i tēnei rā. Kei ahau te mana. Inanahi i roto i ōna ringa te mana. Nā, mate ana, tōku tuakana.

Nā, i te toru karaka i te ahiahi ka hemo te mokopuna a te koroheke rā, ā, e hono tonu ana ki te mīhini rā.

I taua pō tonu anō, ka hoki ake ngā kupu a tōna matua ki a ia. 'E Piripi, kaua e utua te kino ki te kino. Engari utua te kino ki te pai. Ko te rākau pai, he reka ōna hua. Mā te pono o āu mahi ka kitea ai koe he tangata.'

I te ohonga ake o Piripi i te moe, tatū ana tōna ngākau, i tōna mōhio, ehara kē nā te ngākau riri, ngākau kino rānei i roto i a ia, ki te koroheke rā, engari nā te ringa kaha kē o aituā, i tango atu te mokopuna rā.

The Coat in the Window

Lavinia de Silva

'Tell me a story, Nanny.'

Every night for the last eight years I have heard those words, and I probably will for the next four years ahead as my second granddaughter reaches the age of eight.

Like any other nanny blessed with raising grandchildren, those words are very precious. As is customary in our house, the youngest gets to pick the topic of each story, stories that have been about every conceivable kind of animal; about fairies and dragons; about Santa to something as simple as a present. There is no other feeling on earth that can compare with the satisfaction a nanny gets when she hears the oohs and aahs, the sighs, knowing that at certain times their eyes light up, even though you can't see their faces because the lights are out. It's a truly wonderful experience, one you can only get by doing it. One story stands out in my mind. Let me tell you, the reader, about it. My granddaughter asked me for a story about a coat.

Let me begin as I always begin my stories to my grandchildren:

'Once upon a time....'

They would always respond with 'Yes?' then they would snuggle down in bed to listen and dream. So:

Once upon a time there lived a little girl who would walk past the most amazing little shop every day as she went to school.

This shop had everything you could imagine, toys that moved every which way, lollies all colours of the rainbow, and clothes that would fit every child regardless of age; a truly amazing shop. It was the kind of shop that little Sarah Miles could only look through the window at, never to go inside.

'Don't ever go into O'Mally's shop, Sarah, there's nothing in there for the likes of us,' said Mrs Miles.

Sarah (who was ten years old, the middle child in a family of five), did as she was told. She just looked and never went in.

Julia Sycamore, who worked in the shop, would see Sarah pause outside the shop window every day on her way to and from school, and it was always at this point that Sarah's twelve-year-old sister and eight-year-old brother would always leave her. Her younger siblings were still at home, and her fourteen-year-old brother was working in the mill.

Sarah would lovingly gaze at one piece only. Julia couldn't quite figure out what she always looked at. From were she stood it looked like she was looking at a brown coat, but it surely couldn't be that, not a dowdy brown coat, not with all the other things displayed in the window. Julia could set her timepiece by Sarah's appearance outside the shop. In time she got to smile and give Sarah a cheery wave, all the time wondering what Sarah was looking at.

'I must find out,' Julia said to herself one day. She was waiting by the shop window when Sarah arrived.

'Good morning little girl, how are you today?' asked Julia.

Sarah smiled as she said, 'I'm good.'

'My name is Julia, I thought I'd say hello. I seem to see you everyday from inside the shop.'

'Hello,' replied Sarah.

'What is your name?' Julia asked.

Sarah thought for a moment. She remembered her mother saying not to talk to strangers, but this young lady didn't seem like a stranger. 'Sarah' she said, 'Sarah Miles.'

'Well, Sarah, it's lovely to meet you. Would you like to come inside and have a look?'

Sarah looked around. She could still see her brother and sister a wee way ahead. 'No thank you,' she replied, somewhat cautiously.

'Oh, are you sure? You know, you don't have to buy anything,' Julia said. 'People are most welcome to come in and have a look around – lots of people do.' She held out her hand invitingly.

'No thank you,' responded Sarah. 'I have to go now. Bye!' And she was off down the road, skipping as she went.

Julia could only look in wonder. How odd, she thought. Well, maybe not so odd: it had been six months since she first noticed Sarah looking in the shop window, and she had never seen Sarah in the shop. I wonder why? she thought. She had realized by the way Sarah was dressed that she come from a poorer family, but being poor didn't stop other families from coming into the shop to look around.... This made Julia more determined than ever to find out what Sarah liked in the window. She decided then and there that the next time Sarah stopped, which would be after school that day, she would ask straight out what she liked to look at. The day seemed to drag, just because she was waiting; the time seemed to slow right down.

As the bell rang at school Sarah was joined by her friend Rachel, who asked, 'Did you remember to tell your mum that you would be late home today?'

'Yes I reminded her about your birthday party last night and this morning.'

Quarter past three, thought Julia. Thank goodness there's no one at my counter, I can watch for Sarah. Then she saw Sarah's brother and sister coming, but no Sarah. They went past, round the corner and away, but still no Sarah. That's very odd, thought Julia. She felt somewhat disappointed and just a wee bit worried.

'Miss Sycamore! You have a customer waiting if you don't mind,' said Perkins.

'Oh, I am sorry to keep you waiting Madam, how can I help you?' she asked.

'That brown coat in the window, I'd like to have a look at it,' said the customer. 'Now! If you don't mind, I haven't got all day girl.'

Julia hesitated for a moment. Not the brown coat, she thought, she can't want that coat. She looked around to see if Perkins had gone, she had to think quickly. 'Do you mean that old brown coat that's been in the window for months and months, Madam? Or can I show you something in brown but much more modern and more suited to your excellent taste?' Julia said hoping Perkins couldn't hear.

'What do you mean in the window for months girl? I haven't noticed it before,' the woman retorted.

'Well yes Madam, it's been there for many months. In fact I was just going to take it down and replace it with something much more fashionable, something more in keeping with what your family would wear. Are you looking for something for a daughter perhaps?' she asked with forced politeness.

'For my elderly mother actually, something serviceable and respectable. That coat seems to me to be just right.'

'I'm sure from here it looks fine, but,' Julia moved up close to the woman as if to whisper, 'it's awfully faded. Please let me show you this one. What size are you looking for?' Julia thrust the coat in the woman's hand, which distracted her enough to take her mind off the coat in the window.

'Size ten,' she replied.

'That's just what this is, very serviceable, lovely shade of brown. Earth brown is the name of this fashion colour,' said Julia.

'Looks the same colour as the one in the window,' said the woman.

'Oh, that used to be chocolate brown when it was first put up, but anyway I know it's a size eight, so we'd better check some of these out for you, Madam,' said Julia, feeling a little sweaty by now. Wish the bossy woman would make up her mind and go, thought Julia.

Later, as Julia was closing up her section of the shop, she thought about her actions, still surprised at herself for doing everything she could not to sell the coat in the window. She wasn't even sure if it was that coat Sarah would look lovingly at and could only assume that it was. In fact she stood at the exact same spot as Sarah always did and at the same angle as Sarah did and all she could see was this brown, serviceable coat. Right at this moment she hoped that it wasn't that coat, because try as she did, the bossy woman had insisted on buying it simply because it was cheaper than the others and 'it was only for my mother anyway,' she'd said.

I wonder if I should put another brown coat in its place. Sarah might not notice that it was a different one, though she didn't have one exactly the same shade of brown. Julia got another coat, and looked at the time. 'My goodness, it's nearly closing time, I'll have to hurry, don't want Mr O'Mally to see me – or Perkins too, for that matter,' she said to herself. Mr O'Mally, he was very old-fashioned, didn't like to much change, that's why the window display never really changed over the years, only when something was sold from it did it change slightly. Julia, in somewhat of a hurry, was trying to move around an old wooden rocker displayed in front of the mannequin that the coat was on. The rocker had scarves draped over it, a shawl, some gloves, colourful crochet cushions, some of which moved when Julia accidentally leaned on the back of the chair. 'Bother!' she exclaimed as one of the cushions fell off and a scarf or two shifted positions. The gloves, well they seemed to get lost altogether. 'Oh well, it's too late to do anything now,' Julia muttered. Mr O'Mally was due to come and lock the doors. He did not like anyone to leave one minute early and most definitely not one minute late. The extra minutes added up over time he always said, time he could not afford to waste, so the doors were shut at 5 p.m. sharp. Once outside Julia had a quick look in the window at Sarah's usual spot. Looks pretty much the same as before, she thought.

At the birthday party, Sarah was enjoying herself. However she had a feeling she had forgotten something. She shrugged the feeling off and continued to chatter with her friends. They all sat down in a circle.

'OK,' said Rachel, 'let's all tell what we would wish for if we had one wish granted to us. Oh! and let's make a rule that we can't wish for the same thing that someone else has. Mandy, you start.'

'Well I would wish for all the money that I would ever need.'

'Your turn Elizabeth.'

'Um. Let me think ... I would wish for the goose that laid golden eggs.'

'Yay, that's a good one!' someone said.

'My turn,' said Rachel. 'I wish for Aladdin's cave.'

'I wish that I could be a princess,' said Kate.

'Your turn Sarah,' they all said together.

Sarah though for a moment. 'I wish that my nanny was still alive.'

'Aw, come on Sarah, you can do better than that,' said Mandy. Then, realizing what she said, quickly added, 'I don't mean that it's not good to wish that your nan was still here, I mean that this is a time to dream and make believe and think of one amazing wish to be granted.'

Sarah thought about what Mandy had said. She knew what she meant by it, but she wasn't going to back down. 'No,' she said. 'That's my wish and I am going to stick with it.'

'Old stick-in-the-mud, you mean,' said Mandy. 'Oh well, it's your wish. I think Elizabeth's wish is the best. Imagine having golden eggs.'

'Hey I have an idea,' said Rachel. 'I'll ask Mum if we can have an egg each and we can decorate it with gold paints and stuff.'

'Do you think she will?' asked Kate. 'You know how scarce eggs are right now.'

'I'll ask anyway,' said Rachel. Rachel's mum obliged, but only after making a small hole in the end a draining out the inside.

'Can't afford to waste,' she said. 'I can use this for an omelet.'

The day drew to a close, and it was time to go home.

'Better leave now,' Rachel's mum said, 'before it gets too late. The shops are shut. Go straight home all of you, OK?'

'Yes, Mrs Honeywell,' they all replied together. 'Thanks for a lovely party.' Each took a golden egg.

'Careful now,' said Rachel, 'they're not quite dry yet. Bye!'

As Sarah walked home, she thought about her nanny. Little did her friends know that today was her nanny's birthday as well. She had been gone two and a half years now, and it seemed like yesterday. For all of those eight years of her life Sarah had felt closer to her nanny than anyone else, even closer than her parents who always seemed to be too busy to pay attention to any one child. Sarah supposed that that was what family life was about, busy trying to put food on the table, putting the children through school, making ends meet. Not that she didn't love her family – she did – but nanny, well, she was special and she treated her grandchildren special, and deep down Sarah felt that she was just a tad more special because they shared the same love for books and would spend many hours reading together. They would have a special remembrance for nanny when she got home. It seemed strange to have spent part of the day in happy mode celebrating her friend's birthday, and then remembering that sad day when nanny was taken suddenly, and then memories of her birthday – what a contrast. Nanny always said, 'never mourn the loss of a loved one, celebrate the life that they lived for when they depart this world they will have achieved what God intended them to achieve.' Sarah could not quite appreciate those words of her nanny, but she would never forget them, because nanny said to remember them and one day she would understand.

Sarah was on familiar ground now as she approached O'Mally's store. She giggled out loud. 'That's what the feeling was at Rachel's, I missed passing the store window after school. Well, I'll make it up now.' When she got to her usual spot she looked up and gasped. 'No,' she said, 'not today, please not today,' she cried. Just then her older brother John arrived. He had been sent by their mother to meet Sarah and escort her home.

'What on earth is the matter?' John asked. 'What are you crying for?'

'It's Nanny,' Sarah said. 'She's gone.'

'Of course she's gone you ninny.' Then he remembered how close Sarah was to their nanny. 'Look it will be alright,' putting his arm around her to comfort her. 'Come on home, you'll feel better there. It's starting to get dark.'

'You don't understand. Nanny was there every day for me, now she's gone.'

'I know she's gone, Sarah.' John was a bit perplexed by her outburst.

'She was here this morning, now she's gone. I can't see her anymore.'

'Sarah, please, let's go, you are making people look at us,' John pleaded.

There was really only one person showing an interest. It was Julia, who had returned along the street on her way to the town launderette. 'Sarah,' she said, 'what's the matter?'

'That was my nanny's rocking chair in the window. She used to sit on it with me on her knee and read stories to me,' explained Sarah.

Julia looked at John.

'Yeah that would be right,' John said. 'Our mum sold it to Mr O'Mally after nanny died, and he used it to display stuff.'

'All I had to do was look in the window, close my eyes, and I would see Nanny. Now I can't, she's left. Look – the cushion is on the floor, the chair has even shifted a little bit. I really needed to see her today, it's her birthday,' Sarah sobbed.

Julia finally understood. It wasn't the coat at all, it was the rocker, Sarah's nanny's rocker. Poor little girl, how sad she was right now. 'Come and sit down here on the bench Sarah. You know your nanny will never leave you. She will always be here in your heart and maybe on this her birthday she wanted you to remember her in your heart and not in the rocking chair, because your heart goes everywhere with you, but the chair can't.'

Sarah looked at Julia. She nodded and sighed, then her eyes brightened up. She understood! She understood what Nanny had asked her to remember, thanks to Miss Sycamore, and in her heart her wish had come true. She looked at the golden egg in her hand and said to Julia, 'Please take this egg Miss, I would like you to have it.'

'Oh are you sure?' Julia said. 'It's such a beautiful egg.'

'Yes I'm sure. Maybe I'll see you tomorrow. I might come in for a look in your store – I'm sure you have nicer stuff than that old brown coat in the window.' Sarah waved goodbye and ran off with John, leaving Julia speechless.

Of course, reader, I would end our stories with, 'and they lived happily ever after. The end.'

The Elements of Drowning

Margaret Smith

The white paper-faced woman had a name once, and she lived in the same colour as everyone else. Transparent, a delicate veil of a person, she blew down the street, floating above the ground, like the leaves. Because she could not hold the weight of words, she spoke with her hands.

She wove lines in the dreaming part of children, light on the air, as clear as flowers. Her hands said the sound of the sea, and the water spilling and the washing of the moon. She caught the sun in her hands, and wore it shining under her skin, and the light flew straight through their ears and folded itself inside them.

One single night, as she was drifting towards sleep, her thoughts stretched into bubbles, and melted away into the corners of her mind. In the space behind her eyes, the night was blurred, and jumping. There was an echoing, a sound of earth and ocean leaps, and in the pounding of the moon, she held her breath. The walls closed in, and she could not breathe.

Her thoughts flew away in lost pieces. She could not remember who people were, or the colours of the flowers, or the way they smelt. She could not hear children laughing. She could not warm the air around her, not even by walking through it. There was a space between her face and the world. The sky was cold and bruised. Sometimes the world reeled sideways, and the ground under her feet lurched, so that she had to place her feet carefully one after another.

She did not have any words to speak to the white world of doctors, who, in any case, could not measure what they could not see. They sighed, and said they did not have any answers. Recovery would be slow, they said, for the lack of anything measurable to say. She did not know how long slow would be. She could not remember.

There was a wall of glass between her and the rest of the world. She swam under the surface of the water and they were all far above in the air and the sunlight. She swam and moved against it. Her mouth came open and bubbles slipped up the side of the glass. People looked at each other and talked and laughed and they didn't know about the water, or that someone was under it. If it had been winter, she would have frozen under the ice, still looking up to where the stars lived in a parallel universe.

She did not know what had happened, or how to survive. She taught herself to be calm, and to hold on, like the trees hold on in a storm, or a drought. She did not know if she could come back.

She was the colour of sludge, of dark and wet places. The children could see the lines where she used to be, but they could barely make her out. They could not take any light from her, or tell what colour she was. She wore her white paper face but they did not see the birds fluttering in her black eyes, beating against the windows.

Her face was frozen, and her hands lifted and fluttered against her chest, beating back the words. Her hands wanted to be a window, a plane of glass. They moved against the glass. I'm here behind the glass, they said. You can't hear me cry. I'm swimming just below the surface and I can't get out. The water is closing in.

But her hands couldn't say it. She could not hold even the shifting holes in the air. She was mud coloured, and her hands were only weeds that dangled in the water.

Sakura

Ngahuia Wade

'Ohaiyogozaimasu,' he called to the neighbour across the street, as he prepared to trudge the snow-laden streets of Wakamatsu. Gumboots, long johns, tracksuit, thick feather-down jacket which he'd borrowed from his daughter, hat with Māori koru design and gloves – warm bulky ones, the kind the local skiers wore. That had been his attire since he arrived here six weeks ago. Yesterday was a complete blizzard. Everyone had commented about how it was the worst snowstorm they'd ever seen. Well, at least that's what he thought they'd been saying:

'Yuki ippai desu ne! Fubuki sugoi desu ne!'

It certainly was different. Quite enjoying it too, he thought as he chuckled to himself and started the forty minute walk to the Sakaemachi church. Ten years ago, who would have thought he'd be doing what he was doing now? Who would've thought he'd be doing this one year ago? Gosh, he hadn't been back to Aotearoa for nearly six months now. He hoped his family was OK. They seemed to be, from all the correspondence. Numerous letters and a few emails, that's how he kept in touch with his whānau back home. He couldn't waste money on frivolous things like phone calls. That's why he'd left home in the first place: to make money. It was far too expensive to call, especially from Japan. They charged him per minute just to ring his daughter who lived thirty minutes' drive away. She was choice. She was the one who'd scored him the job. She hadn't even asked him, she'd just told him. 'C'mon Dad,' she'd said. 'I'm in the middle of negotiating you a contract to teach English at a local church – get ready to come to Japan.'

That was two months ago, while he'd been doing the odd job in

Sydney. She worked fast that one. As for his other children, four by his first wife, one by his second wife, two whāngai, and his wife's two kids ... that made yes, nine kids he'd raised, not to mention the numerous mokopuna which were popping out now. Wonder how all my mokos are? he thought affectionately, longing to hold them again – Hohia, Ngati Rangi, Tohungarau, Huriana, Hinekohu, Rongokarae, Aonini, Nikora – he couldn't remember the name of one of them. She'd been a whāngai to his daughter-in-law's whānau so he'd never met her. And then his latest moko, Rakei – now she had the biggest photo on his wall. He loved their names, and he was glad they had Māori names, tūpuna names. He thought of the wharenui then – how was it that his wife had described it in her last letter? That's right, 'silent and alone' – ka aroha hoki! Couldn't think about that now.

The snow was getting thicker, falling in great big clumps. He pulled his hat tighter around his head. He didn't mind the snow, however he did look forward to the sakura, the cherry blossom season. That would be here soon. He'd read so much about the cherry blossoms of Japan. Tongariro and Pihanga came to mind then. His maunga. He'd been bought up under those majestic tūpuna. In winter, they'd always been clothed in snow, beautiful too. But never as much snow as what he'd seen here in the streets. Heaps of the stuff. Today the snow wasn't too bad though. At least it wasn't icy, that's when it was terribly dangerous. He'd already taken a bad fall the other night. He'd stepped out of the car and bang – he'd ended up on his back. Better be more careful with these old bones, he thought. Mind you, he'd lost a bit of weight since he'd left home. He'd been so overweight. That's what had caused the heart attack in the first place, obesity and of course – stress. He sighed as he thought of that period in his life. The doctor had given him ten different pills after that, some for the heart, some for kidneys, some for the high blood pressure – te hōhā hoki! He only took a few these days and was really looking forward to going home later this year during his holiday time, just to show that doctor how fit and healthy he was.

God he felt good! The feelings he'd felt after things hadn't gone according to plan were in the past, back where they should be. At least he knew he'd tried, it just hadn't worked out. Seemed as if everyone wanted a piece of the action, but didn't want to put any work in. And as for whānau and hapū support – oh well, he'd learnt the lesson and that was the main thing. Now he was here. Funny how life goes sometimes. The heart attack was where he'd woken up. It had given him the big, rude awakening. He'd decided to get more work then. Anything would do, as long as it was work. After working for thirty-five years, then all of a sudden not working – played a bit of havoc with the old soul. That was when he went to Sydney. That was so much fun! Lost a bit of weight there, made some new friends, travelled around as if he was a young man, and enjoyed himself immensely. Sydney was definitely a young person's world, but he'd survived. Now, here he was in Japan teaching English. He didn't even have a degree, just a Certificate of Māori Studies he'd done while he'd been working. He chuckled again to himself – those ones at home would be cracking up to themselves:

'Get that one – in Japan eh? They'll be feeding him up on sushi over there.'

He could just imagine his nanny Paihoro and her husband Uncle Jack:

'Ka kino kē koe boy, don't you fall for one of those nip girls boy.'

You'd think he was still a teenager, the way they used to treat him. His wife had already told him how the whānau had reacted. His closest mates had cried, happy to hear the news. Others reckoned, 'Gosh if he can do it, so can I.'

That's how desperate it was back home. Unemployment was rampant – people needed a good pick-me-up. It was good to know that he was giving people back there a booster. You never know, could be just the encouragement people back home needed. They were never very far from his thoughts.

His daughter was OK, she had all the degrees. Educated up to her eyeballs. He'd encouraged her since she was five. 'You're going to university my girl,' he'd say. That was something he'd never had and had always wanted. Well, he'd finished high school, but university was just a dream back then. He'd had to go and work anyway – support the family and all. He'd really wanted to go too. He could still go. Well, she reckons that he could still go and do a degree, and even a masters if he wanted. She also said something about being a doctor, but he didn't want to do medicine. Might just try university after Japan, he thought to himself, sidestepping an old Japanese woman shovelling snow into the snow-drains. Man these old kuia work hard, shovelling all the time. Seems a waste of time, since it's only gonna snow again tomorrow. Oh well, I suppose they have their reasons, he thought. That's the Japanese, no wonder they live so long. He'd noticed that here, all the old people walked and bicycled around the place. Every day he saw the old ones trudging the streets, cycling through the snow. Wouldn't see that back home. They were all too spoilt and got driven around. Ah well, lucky for them eh?

He'd go to university when he eventually went home. If she thinks he can do it, then why not – he'd do it. God, he'd come to Japan and taught English, without any teaching experience and without a degree, what a laugh eh? He'd made it this far. He must admit too, he's a pretty good teacher. His students seemed to like him. They always commented on how interesting the classes were. He was teaching them the tititorea at the moment. They loved it. Even the Japanese teacher he taught with loved doing the tititorea. She enjoyed it more than the kids. The kids were hard-case. They got so frustrated at not being able to do it perfectly, a stick out here, a stick out there. And they wouldn't give up and would get really pissed off with themselves. He'd sit there and crack up laughing. The Japanese were a strange breed though, just different I suppose, he thought. Especially the adults. They didn't seem to have very happy lives, very serious people. He really tried to make his classes funny so they could have a good laugh. As for the kiddies, they were so cute – he loved teaching them. Natural and no holds barred, that's what the kids were like. One of them had yelled out to him the other day in the street:

'Raymond! Sensei Raymond! Sensei – genki desuka? Ima nan desuka?'

He didn't have a clue what she was saying and just nodded a polite hello.

Maybe some day soon he'd start learning the language. It was so difficult though. They didn't use the alphabet at all, only symbols – every time he thought about it, it made his head hurt. She was always hassling him about it too. 'Have you started studying yet Dad. You have to, Dad. At least learn how to count and ask for directions.'

She'd even enrolled him in a Japanese class for beginners, which started in April. He'd better get it together and start studying something soon, he didn't want to be the only kūare in the class. She was hassling him even more now that he'd gone and gotten himself lost the other night, while they'd been out a karaoke bar. He'd thought it was the door to the wharepaku – bloody small these bars in Japan – but it had been the way out. He'd wandered outside and they'd taken three hours to find him. He'd been OK, just sitting in another bar, waiting to be found. She was so angry.

'See Dad, that's why you need to learn how to speak a little Japanese. How would you have gotten home? Do you know how to say left and right in Japanese to direct a taxi?'

Boy she was angry. I could have found my way home you know, he thought. She'd forgotten what he was like. She doesn't realise that he can look after himself, even if he can't speak the language. She hadn't spoken Japanese when she'd arrived, and she'd survived – why did she think he couldn't as well? Oh well, she'd been away from home for a while now, nearly fifteen years, they all had. Kids always leave home, that's the way the cookie crumbles. He had too.

The other day he'd been asked to give a seminar to some church group about Māori religion. Just as well he had his colours from the Rātana Church. They were really interested, and when he sang a Rātana hymn they sang along easily because they knew the tune and could pronounce the Māori words. He'd learnt then just how very similar Māori and Japanese were. They had the same alphabet, but a few more sounds ... a ha ka ma na nga pa etc. They had them all and pronounced exactly the same way. But still a very different language.

His job was really easy. For one of his classes he just sat there for one hour and spoke to a koro about any topic he wanted – who's complaining about that, getting paid to sit there and yarn to someone? Some of the people he taught had been going to these English classes for twenty years, and their English was still hard to understand – their speaking was terrible. He was slowly getting his ears in tune with the way they pronounced words. Oh well, he'd do his best for as long as he was here.

Just last week he'd received the official letter for a working visa. He'd been really worried about that. Especially since he didn't really have a degree. It was his daughter that did it. The way she talked about his Certificate of Māori Studies was as if it was a masters or something. So now he needed to visit a Japanese embassy outside Japan. They were both gonna go to Taiwan. He dreaded coming back here alone though. He'd have to make his way back from Tokyo all by himself. His daughter and her mate were carrying on to Vietnam for a few days. Get them eh? Travelling around Asia as if they were just going down to Wellington. He'd been to a few places but nowhere near as much as this lot. They travelled everywhere and weren't even scared about it. They were all like that too. Nearly every gaijin you came across was on a mission to travel around the world. All educated of course, that's how they got here.

He'd nearly reached the church now. He could see it in the distance, covered in snow, just one more block to go. It was a dilapidated old thing, not very well looked after by Māori standards. The best-kept buildings in Māori communities were the churches. He remembered as a boy being dragged by his nanny into the church. It was always so clean and well groomed; everything sparkled – not like this church. It looked forlorn and sad. It had people in it every day though. They had the English classes in a room to the side, on Mondays they had gospel singing, and every other day there was a band practice and church groups had their gatherings there.

The first and only time he'd been to a Sunday service was a laugh. He'd been asked to attend as they were doing a special karakia for him. Everything was in Japanese: prayers, singing and sermons. He had to stop himself from bubbling over with laughter. It was just a crack-up to hear the Lord's Prayer in Japanese.

As he approached the church, for the first time in the past six weeks he felt a feeling of familiarity washing over him. The church WAS dilapidated, AND in Japan, but it definitely had an essence. And in many ways it was giving him sustenance too. It provided shelter for the English school where he worked, and once the heaters were turned on it was warm and cosy. And for now, it was a temporary solace and a nice, warm, well-paid, safe place to be.

For the first time he noticed a tiny pink bud on a tree by the church – his first sakura. Ka pai hoki! He took his shoes off and put on his 'inside' slippers.

Thirty minutes later he was ready for class. He looked around and greeted his first group of students.

'Kia ora everyone.'

'Kia ora Raymond Sensei,' replied the smiling Japanese faces. It felt good to be here.

Glossary

Sakura	Cherry Blossom
Ohaiyogozaimasu	Good morning
Wakamatsu	A city in the Aizu district, Fukushima Prefecture, Japan.
Yuki ippaf desu ne!	Such a lot of snow!
Fubuki sugoi desu ne!	The ferocious blizzard!
Gaijin	Foreigner
Sensei	Teacher
Ima nan desuka?	What are you doing now?

Kōtiro

Okeroa Waitai

Me tīmata pēwheai te kōrero nei? Me tīmata pēneki.

I te rā ngahuru-mā-tahi, te wā e whakaaro nui ana te tangata mō te ao me ōna tini āhuatanga katoa, i te tau 1960, tērā tētehi tokorua e noho āhuru mōwai ana, e tatari ana mō te whānautanga mai o tā rāua mokopuna tuatahi.

Kāore he kupu e whakaatu nei i te harikoa, i te aroha nui e pupū ake i roto i te whatumanawa o te tokorua nei. Kua roa rāua e tiaki ana mō tēnei wā. Ko te tino tūmanako o te kuia kia whānau mai te pēpi hou i tō rāua ake kāinga, i ngahere kē. Mā rāua ko tōna rangatira e whakawhānau, e maioha te mokopuna ki te aotūroa. Engari kāore te hoa o tā rāua tamāhine i whakaae.

'Kua mate kē ngērā āhuatanga o nehe rā. Kei ngā whare tūroro, kei te mātauranga o te Pākehā te tino oranga mō tātou nāianei. Waiho ngērā whakaaro ki te taha o te moa,' tana kī.

Kia ei kore rātou e taupatupatu ka tautokongia e te kuia.

I te ohonga ake o te rā, ka whakaaengia e te moko he wā tika tēnei mōna hei puta ki te ao. I rongo ngā tūpuna mātua i tōna hōē e ahu mai ana i te whare whakawhānau pēpi. Maringi noa ngā roimata o te kuia. Ka pupuri ringa, ka awhi rāua i a rāua. Ka tū anipā kia pōwhiri atu tā rāua hunaonga ki a rāua kia tomo ki te rūma ki te tūtaki ki tā rāua moko hou.

Tōna ātaahua, tōna roa, tōna kaha ki te hāparangi kia kīkī ōna pūkahukahu i te hau. Auē te aroha e!

Ahakoa popoki tonu tōna tinana i te korowai āhuru, koirā anō te kahukahu e ai ki ngā tūpuna, hei ārai, hei kaupare atu i ngā tūkinotanga e whakararu nei i te tinana. Heoi anō, te wairua hoki o te kōngahungahu, ka kite tonu i tōna ātaahuatanga.

Ka kōhimuhimu atu te tupuna matua ki a ia, 'Nau mai e hine e ... nau ake rā ki te aotūroa. He mokopuna koe nāku, otirā, nā Hine-tītama. Waiwai ana aku karu i te tirohanga atu.'

Ka tūpou ki raro ki te hongi i te ihu o tana moko hou.

He rā mārire tēnei, he rā mīharo, he rā rangatira i runga i te whakatapunga o te whānautanga mai o te pēpi.

Ko ōna Rā Kōhungahunga

Tōna waimārie i a ia e kōhungahunga ana. I noho tata ōna tūpuna ki a rātou. Nō reira, i riro mā ōna tūpuna ngā taonga tuku iho e whakatō ki roto i tōna ngākau. I ngā rā kāore ia i te taha o ōna tūpuna he kōtiro raweke, he kōtiro whātoro ki ngā mea katoa. He maha tonu ngā tohenga i waenga i ōna mātua. Ko te tino pū o ā rāua tautohetohe, ko te pūhaehae o te pāpā ki ōna hungawai me tōna whakaaro heahea he uruhi ngā tokorua rā.

'Kua hōhā pai au ki ō mātua. He ruarua ngā wā ka kite au i te kōtiro rā. Ka haere au ki te mahi, puku mahi au, heke te werawera, whati rawa taku tuarā, hoki mai ki te kāinga kia whiwhi kaha anō mai i a kōrua, engari kāore te kōtiro i konei. Kei te taha kē o ō *pārāri* mātua kē. Tino kino rawa atu taku hōhā ki a rāua. Me haere tātou ki te tāone noho ai!' tāna kī.

'Kaua e pēraka e te tau. He maha ngā painga o ōku mātua. I ngā wā ka hiahia haere tāua ki te karapu whutupōro, he kaitiaki rāua mō te kōtiro. Ka whakapaungia ō moni, kāore he kai i roto i te kāpata, kei reira rāua ki te āwhina,' te kōrero a te whaea.

He tere rawa te whakautu a te pāpā, 'Māu anō e whakaaro he aha te mea nui ki a koe, ko au, ko ō mātua rānei?'

Ka roa te whaea e whakaaro nui ana. I ngā pō, i te wā e moe ana te whānau, ka noho ia i te pōuri, ā, ka tangi. Rere kau ana ōna roimata. Nā wai rā ka tautokongia te wero o tōna hoa rangatira, ka nuku rātou ki te tāone nunui noho ai.

Ko ōna Rā Kōpuapua

He rerekē te noho i te tāone nunui ki a Kōtiro. He maha ngā āhuatanga hou i akongia. Ētehi he pai, ētehi atu kāore he pai. Tētehi pō nā ngā pirihimana a ia i whakahoki ki te kāinga. I mau ia me tōna hoa i tētehi kaihokohoko. Ko tā rāua mahi he tāhae. Pukuriri ana te pāpā. Nā, ka tautohetohe ōna mātua. Ka kanga atu, ka kanga mai, kanga atu, auē, auē!

Pēneki te mahi ia rā, ia pō. I te mutunga ka oma atu a kōtiro ki tōna moemanga tangi ai. Ka oma atu a Pāpā ki te pāpara haumaruru ai. Ka noho taikaha a Mama ki te kāuta. Inā he taupatupatu tino kino rawa atu ka rere atu a kōtiro ki wahi kē. Koirā ngā wā ka ako ia i ngā mahi kino.

Ko ōna Rā Taiohi

Nā te kaha o te taupatupatu i waenganui i ōna mātua ka whakataungia e rāua kia noho wehe. Ka nuku atu te pāpā ki tētehi atu whare noho ai. Ka noho mai a Māmā rāua ko kōtiro ki tō rāua whare. Mō te nuinga o te wā he pai te noho pērā. Na wai rā, ka hoki mai te āhua raweke ki a kōtiro engari ka rawekengia e ia ngā mahi kāore e pai.

Kua tino rerekē tōna hanganga. Kua pakeke a ia. He wahine pūhihi, he wahine ātaahua hoki. Engari, ko ōna ātaahuatanga o roto, i whakapupuningia.

He maha āna mahi tūkino. Ko ōna hoa tata he hunga kaha ki te inu waipiro, momi tarukino, hongi kāpia, tāhae, patu tangata, whawhai i waenga tonu i a rātou. Auē! Auē!

Tino mātau ana a ia ki ngā mahi katoa. He maha ngā wā ka ngaro ia ā-tinana, ā-wairua hoki. He maha hoki ngā pō ka noho mānukanuka a Māmā ki te whare. He tatari kia rongo kōrero e pā ana ki te kōtiro, kia hoki mai rānei te kōtiro ki te kāinga. Nā ēnei tūāhuatanga i waenganui i a rāua ka puta mai te riri, ka puta ngā kupu whakamamae i te whatumanawa, patu i te wairua. He pai a kōtiro ki te whakaiti tangata ahakoa ko wai.

Tētehi rā ka hoki haurangi a Kōtiro ki te kāinga. E toru rā ia e ngaro ana. I reira a Māmā e tatari ana.

'I whea koe? Mōhio koe kua noho āwangawanga au i koneki? He aha te take kāore koe i waea mai? Pōhēhē au e takoto mate ana koe i tētehi ara tuarongo!' te tangi auē a Māmā.

'Turituri tō waha. Koira tō mahi ki ahau i ngā wā katoa, he kōhetehete mai! Koira te take i nuku whare ai a Pāpā!' te kī whakahīhī a Kōtiro.

'Kaua koe e kōrero pēnaka mai ki ahau! Ko tō whaea ahau! Ehara au i tētehi o ō hoa!'

Kāore i mutu te kōrero a Māmā ka tū ake a Kōtiro. Ko tōna ringa mauī i mamau i te hāte o Māmā, ko tōna ringa katau ka meke i te ihu o Māmā, kātahi ki tōna poho, kātahi ka hoki ki te kanohi anō o Māmā.

Ko te tino kaha o te riri e nohopuku ana i roto i a kōtiro kātahi anō ka puta mai. Ahakoa te auē mai a Māmā ka patu tonu, ka patu tonu, ka patu tonu kia pau rānō tōna hau, kātahi ka mutu.

Kura katoa tō Māmā kanohi nā te rere ō te toto. Hurirapa ngā taputapu o te whare. I te kokonga o te kāuta ka noho a Māmā me tana tangi mamae. Ka noho porowhakawai a Kōtiro. He aha hoki taku mate? He aha kē taku raru? Ka whakatata mai a ia ki tōna māmā. Ka awhi rāua i a rāua, kātahi ka tino tangi a kōtiro. Rere kau ana ōna roimata. Ka awhi tonu a Māmā i a ia. Mō te wā roa ka noho pēraka te tokorua. Kāore he kupu i puta. Ko te tangi auē o kōtiro e kō ana i te whare.

Ka mutu tā rāua mahi ka huri a Māmā ki tōna kōtiro ka kī atu, 'Kua tae ki te wā kia hoki atu tāua ki te taha o ō tūpuna mātua. Kua roa tāua e ngaro ana. Kei reira pea te rongoā, te oranga hoki mō tāua.'

Ka whakaae a Kōtiro. Nō reira ka whawhaongia ko ō rāua kākahu anahe ki roto i ngā pēke, ka raua ki roto i te motokā. Ka pātai atu a kōtiro ki a ia, 'Pēwhea ngā taputapu o te whare Mā?'

Ko tana whakautu, 'Waiho ngā mahara ki koneki takoto ai. Me hoki atu tāua ki ngā mahara o mua whakaoho ai.'

Tino kino rawa atu te harikoa o ngā tūpuna ki te kite i a rāua. Anō ka heke, rere kau ngā roimata. Engari, ko ngā roimata e rere ana he roimata harikoa, he roimata mārire. I a Kōtiro rāua ko Koro e awhi ana ka kōhimuhimu atu a Koro ki a ia. 'Kōtiro, he mokopuna koe nāku, otirā, nā Hine-tītama. Waiwai tonu ana aku karu i te tirohanga atu.'

Ka menemene mai a kōtiro. Ka mōhio ia, ā, kua tau ia ki tōna kāinga tūturu, otirā, ki tōna āhuru mōwai.

Ngā Kupu Whakamārama

āhuru mōwai	*safe, peaceful environment*
anipā	*anxious with excitement*
ara tuarongo	*alley*
hāparangi	*bawl, cry out*
haumaruru	*moan, sulk*
heahea	*silly, stupid*
hōē	*cry*
kō	*echo, fill the air*
kōhetehete	*go on at, lecture, nag*
kōhimuhimu	*whisper*
kōhungahunga	*baby, infant (0-5 years)*
kōngahungahu	*foetus*
korowai āhuru	*membrane enveloping baby in the womb*
maioha	*welcome*
mamau	*grab*
ngahuru-mā-tahi	*11 (th)*
pāpara	
popoki	*covered over*
porowhakawai	*out of it, spaced out*
pūhihi	*slender*
raweke	*mischievous, naughty*
taupatupatu	*argue, quarrel, argument*
uruhi	*busybody, meddler*
whakapupuningia	*(lay) hidden, concealed*
whakatapunga	*sacredness*
whātoro	*explore, tutu*
whawhaongia	*pack (a bag)*

The Authors

Te Awhina Arahanga (Waitaha, Ngāti Mamoe, Ngāi Tahu, Ngati Tūwharetoa, Te Āti Haunui-a-Paparangi) is looking forward to the day when the only problem in life is working out which wine to drink.

Kerrie Blackmoore AhKiau: 'I am a descendant of Netana Patuawa of the Ngāti Whātua tribe.

Tutamoe me Whariki ngā maunga,
Kiahu te awa,
Mahuhu o Te Rangi te waka,
Taita te marae,
Kia Mahara Koutou te wharenui,
Taoho te tangata.'

Kerrie is the mother of three angels who writes to free her spirit because she cannot sing in tune or paint. On paper she allows her soul to dip its fingers in the colour of words and express whatever she feels she needs to say. She hope you enjoy a glimpse from behind her eyes.

Lindsay Charman-Love (Te Āti Awa, Ngāti Kahungunu) lives in the Hokianga – writes for a living – lives very modestly and eats fish. Has recently written poetry for environmental interpretation panels at Waitangi Treaty Grounds, Trounson Kauri Park, AH Reed Memorial Kauri Park, and Limestone Island, Northland. His short-story collection *Top Hat and Taiaha* was published by Huia in 2001, with the *Herald* noting that '... these short stories have the quality of great yarns ... Charman-Love is a writer to watch'.

Gerry Te Kapa Coates (Ngāi Tahu) is better known as a poet, and this is his first published fiction. His writing skills have been honed by years of writing reports, and four years editing and publishing an industry newsletter about aviation. Wellington-based, he still goes home to Te Wai Pounamu, especially Waihao Marae, as often as he can.

Caroline Adair Down (Ngāti Tūwharetoa, Ngāti Kahungunu, Ngāti Raukawa) is a Wellington illustrator, writer and passionate supporter of the arts. Her writing has appeared previously in *Huia Short Stories 1997* and on National Radio. In 2000 she was placed in the top three of the City Voice Short Short Story Competition.

A graduate of Fiona Kidman's 2000 Autumn Writing School and a participant on the 2000 Huia/Te Waka Toi writing hui, Caroline is taking both her writing skills and love of writing to new heights.

An avid reader of any great literature ('It may be historical, dated, contemporary or whatever, but it has to leave me changed in some way') Caroline admits to a deliberate tendency to seek out really bad, and even atrocious writing in order to keep her head wrapped firmly around what is good.

Above all she loves what she does and enjoys bringing it to others with a whole lot of heart.

'Mediocrity is the enemy! I take the cup and shake it up… however the words land, I work with them and polish them until they shine.'

David Down (Ngāti Kahungunu, Ngāti Raukawa, Ngāti Tūwharetoa) enjoys the creative challenge of writing something a little out of the ordinary. He lives on the Kapiti Coast, spends the weekends with his children Alexandra, Joshua and Stephanie and has worked at the local council for far too long.

Trish Fong (Te Aitanga a Māhaki, Ngāti Porou) lives in West Auckland and is happily married to Danny. They are expecting their first child. Both her stories in this anthology are parts of longer works currently in progress. She also writes poetry and loves the sea, rain and nature.

James George (Ngā Puhi) began writing in 1995 after his mother's death made him 'seek to define who I was and wanted to become'. His first novel, *Wooden Horses*, was published in 2000. The three stories in this collection are adapted from his second novel 'Hummingbird', currently in progress.

Wiremu Grace (Ngāti Porou, Ngāti Toa, Te Āti Awa, Ngāti Raukawa, Irish, French, Pom) was born in Te Tai Tokerau and brought up in Porirua. Enjoys: health, kids, beaches 'n' surf, whānau, music, food, reading, mates, writing, film, reo, jokes, stories, clothes, wine, and spa baths.

Aroha Harris (Ngā Puhi, Te Rarawa) is currently completing her PhD in history at the University of Auckland, where she also lectures in New Zealand history. Currently her research interests are focussed on Māori in the twentieth century, especially since the end of World War Two. She is also keenly committed to developing Māori research, a commitment she expresses through her involvement with Te Pouhere Kōrero, an organisation of Māori people interested in history.

Aroha says, 'I am a product of my people, shaped by history, held together with whakapapa – and it's that sense of connectedness that I try to bring to my work.'

K. T. Harrison (Ngāti Pāoa) writes: 'My marae is Waiti. I grew up in Tokoroa and I lived and worked in South Auckland (Mangere) for twenty years. I have five children and, at present, four grandchildren. I am a registered nurse and I work for a Māori mental health services group. My main interests are reading and writing.

Eru Hart is a 21-year-old student at Victoria University, Wellington. He is currently working on a collection of short stories and hopes to one day have several works published. He acknowledges both his Māori and European ancestry. Eru hopes to finish his degree and teach Māori and English Literature.

Vicki-Anne Heikell (Te Whānau a Apanui) was born and grew up in Gisborne. She left there to attend Victoria University where she attained a BA in Sociology. She also has a Bachelor App Sci in Conservation of Cultural Materials from the University of Canberra and is currently self-employed. Her role involves assisting iwi and hapu in the conservation and preservation of their paper-based taonga. Creative writing is a secret pastime (and passion) that most of her friends and family do not know about.

Darryn Joseph: Son of Jenny and Jim Joseph, brother of Kelly, Stefan, Jody, Shane, Janice, Tracey, Wendy, and Donna, Darryn was born and raised up the coast – the Taranaki coast. 'On the Sarten side we claim the first Pākehā settler to step foot in Taranaki – she was seasick and very pregnant. On the Hōhepa side, as our tribal maxim states, 'Ka whawhai tonu mātou, ake, ake, ake' – ahakoa kāore tētehi o mātou i te noho ki te rohe pōtae. Being feisty and creative on both sides lends itself to a harmonious blending of dual heritages. Kind of.'

Phil Kawana (Ngāruahinerangi, Ngāti Kahungunu ki Wairarapa) poses as a writer, broadcaster and musician, but is really just a tutu artist. He lives in Wellington, thinks Taranaki is the Promised Land, and would sell his own mother for a steady supply of good pāua.

Zion Komene (Ngā Puhi Nui Tonu) was born in Tai Tokerau and raised in Auckland. He was educated at the University of Auckland. Telling stories, rather then creative writing, has always been a passion for him. He is now discovering that writing is a disciplined skill in itself, worthy of pursuing, if for nothing else other than sheer enjoyment. Zion was first published in 2000, with short stories appearing in an anthology of men's fiction, and an anthology of indigenous fiction by writers from Australia, Aotearoa, Canada and the United States. Zion currently lives in Te Tai Tokerau and is working on his first novel.

Mahinaarangi Leong (Te Whānau a Apanui, Whakatōhea and iwi Irish!) was born in Taita, lives in New Plymouth and works in education. Mahina has family and friends whom she adores, and equally adored are life's little ironies – she comments: 'I love sun and light yet write *darkly*; I think circuitously yet relish simplicity; am concerned about excellence but don't believe in perfection.' Mahina still dreams dream of 'being a writer's writer, a great mum, competing across several codes in the NZ Masters Games, and doing a PhD.' She also dreams of 'one day wandering through fields of dead trees and flowers and whispering to each, "be beautiful and prosper" knowing that they will.'

Pierre Lyndon is from Ngā Puhi (Ngāti Hine), Ngāti Whātua, and Tainui (Ngāti Toa). A native speaker, Pierre is qualified in media and education. He has written a masters thesis on Hongi Hika, and he has also written a first-draft PhD thesis on Ngā Puhi karakia. A former English teacher, the short story is Pierre's favourite genre:

'Māori like short stories and magazine stories because we don't have the time or inclination to wade through lengthy writing. Like a good whaikōrero or a good song, a great short story creates an atmosphere and takes us away from our problems for five minutes.'

Michelle Manning (Ngāti Kahungunu ki Wairoa): I live in Taradale, Napier with my husband Kevin. We have three children. I am a teacher at Taradale High School and teach te reo Māori and science. I have two main interests – horse riding and writing – both I need a lot of practice at!

Dale Moffatt (Ngāi Tahu, Ngāti Mamoe) is a Southlander born and bred. She left home to work and travel the world, and now lives in Waipatu, Hastings, with whānau whanui of husband Paul. 'I have six beautiful children, work as te kaiurungi waka for Heretaunga taiwhenua, and would love more time to write, paint and shoot the breeze.'

Kellyana Morey (Ngāti Kurī) is a freelance writer with a couple of degrees in art history and English literature. Her writing can be found in *100 New Zealand Short Short Stories 4*, the *Listener*, *100 New Zealand Short Short Stories 1*, the *Herald*, and *Huia Short Stories 1997*. She was a Huia Award finalist for 'Tangiweto' in 1997.

Paula Morris (Ngāti Wai) was born in Auckland in 1965. She has spent the past fifteen years living in England and the US, working in the record business and, most recently, as a branding consultant. She has a BA in English from the University of Auckland, a D.Phil from the University of York, England, and is currently an MA student in creative writing at Victoria University, Wellington. She's at work on a novel called 'Queen of Beauty'.

Whetu-Marama Pahi: I am of Ngāti Kahungunu and Ngāi Tahu descent. 'The Ballad of Questions' is purely fictional.

Maraea Rakuraku (Ngāti Kahungunu ki Wairoa, Tūhoe): I have been writing since I was nine years old and I have been fortunate to have rich colourful characters and experiences joyful and heart-wrenchingly sad touch my life.

This story, while largely fictional, is inspired by my cousin, Moana Kym Turuwhenua, who died in 2000 aged twenty-nine of a heart condition that she had no knowledge about; and her father, Rakuraku Graham Turuwhenua, who died in 1993 aged forty-five, again of a heart condition that he had no knowledge of. Previous to Moana's birth in 1970, he had been exposed to Agent Orange while serving in the army in Vietnam from 1967 to 1969. Moana left four children behind. The untimely deaths of Moana and Rakuraku have been devastating to the whānau and while no connection has been proven (legally), we have our thoughts on this.

Dianne Sharma-Winter is a wanderer from the homeland of Ngāti Awa and the heartland of Ngāti Hokopu. She has the habits of a strange migratory bird, being sometimes here and sometimes far away. 'Life is a journey of observation,' she says. 'I am only following clues but always circling and returning.'

Charles Shortland: Nō Ngā Puhi ahau. I whānau ahau ki Motatau. I tīmata taku kura ki Matawaia, ka haere ki Tīpene.I muri i tērā ka haere ahau ki te Kura Minita (College House) i Te Waipounamu. I tīmata ake taku ako mahi minita i te rohe o Waikato. Mai i reira, ki Wanganui, ki Rangiātea, ki te Wairarapa, ki te Whare Herehere hoki o Waikeria. Ināianei kei Whangarei ahau e whakatā ana, nā, kua watea ki te tuhituhi. He kaumātua ahau i te Tai Tokerau Wānanga.

Margaret Smith (Taranaki) writes: 'There is nothing better than the feeling you have when you are writing and it's going well. It's a kind of joy and there's nothing else like it.'

Ngahuia Wade (Ngāti Tūwharetoa, Tūhoe, Ngāti Porou) writes from Fukushima Ken, Japan: '"Sakura" is Japanese for cherry blossom and they are in full bloom at time of writing this letter. It is a very special time of year for Japanese people. After long winters, which in my region last about six months, everyone comes out of their homes and heralds the arrival of spring. It really is a beautiful time of year.'

Lavinia Walker (Te Aupouri, Ngā Puhi) lives and works in Invercargill. She is nanny to three beautiful mokopuna who have inspired her to write one of their stories and she is a strong believer in the philosophy of Te Aho Mātua: 'He kākano koe i ruia i Rangiātea. E kore koe e ngaro.' The child (the seed) dispersed from Rangiātea will never be lost.

Okeroa Waitai (Ngāti Maniapoto, Waikato) has contributed work to various Taura Whiri i te Reo Māori publications. She works at Waikato Polytechnic, Hamilton, where she teaches Māori language.